S0-CEW-125

Alex Charles:

The Evening Oak

Donation Information:

A portion of the proceeds from this book are being donated to the following lung cancer organization:

Addi's Cure
19520 W Catawba Ave
Suite 200
Cornelius, NC 28031

If you'd like to support this cause and make a contribution, please use the address above. You can mail a check directly to Addi's Cure; please write "Alex Charles" in the memo section of your check. Your donations are greatly appreciated. Please see www.addiscure.org for more information about this charitable organization.

Alex Charles:

The Evening Oak

By
Kim Reynolds

Plymouth, MI, U.S.A.
www.PublishHMSI.com

Alex Charles: The Evening Oak

The Alex Charles Chronicles
Book One

Published by HMSI Publishing L.L.C., a division of HMSI, inc.
www.PublishHMSI.com

By
Kim Reynolds

Copy Editing by
Monica Tombers
Kay LeMon
Amanda Clark

Cover Design by
Elena Covalciuc

Publishing Coordination by
Jennelle G. Jones

Published by
David R. Haslam

Permissions,
HMSI Publishing L.L.C.
Suite 3b,
50768 Van Buren Drive,
Plymouth, MI 48170, U.S.A.

ISBN – 13: 978-0-9826945-1-0
LOC: 2010927061

0071-0001a

Printed in the United States of America

TKR 10 9 8 7 6 5 4 3 2 1
MK 31527-23898
40300 12:05

To Bo Johnson

If we only had more time with you

Prologue

Thanksgiving 1865

As I looked out the window on that dark evening, I saw the man who I loved fading out of my life forever. I couldn't stop the tears that poured freely down my cheeks. I knew this day would come, although I wasn't prepared for the piercing pain in my heart.

The man of my dreams was walking out of my life as easily as he had come into it. The last few unforgettable months had come to a close. Why did he have to go? How could I change this outcome, even now, as I watch him walking down the road of life without me?

My heart was pounding uncontrollably and I knew I had to go to him. I couldn't let him leave without feeling him in my arms...even if it was only for once. Surely no harm could come from that?

I got up from my perch at the window and Lucas called out to me, "Laura, where are you going? Let him go. That's his wish."

Without looking behind me, I reached for the front door. "I can't," I whispered.

Gathering the heavy folds of my black dress, I scurried down the stairs of our front porch, where only months earlier, ranks of men laid awaiting death. I could feel my pulse raging as I ran closer and closer to him.

Having almost reached his strong silhouette, I called out his name. My arms opened up and I finally met his body in one fulfilled

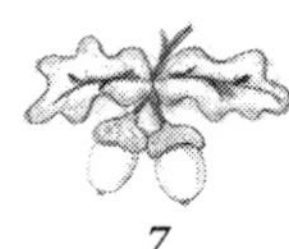

embrace. His arms locked over me and I was finally aware of what it felt like to be in the arms of the man I loved.

We kissed for what seemed like mere seconds, with me never wanting it to end. Too soon, Joseph put his hands on my face, gently pushing mine away from his. I couldn't help the liquid emotion that cascaded over my cheeks. I wanted to tell him to stay, not to leave me, to make it work. Yet I couldn't bear the guilt, the guilt which I would impose on him.

"I do love you. You must know that. I do love you," he said to me in a low strangled tone, as he delivered kisses that had been held hostage for so long. Somehow, in the way I looked at him that night, I would have to convince him to stay.

Our time together had been too short. He had been there through the worst time in my life and now things were coming back to sanity. My world was beginning to heal and resume the normal pulse of life.

From the bottom of my soul, my eyes begged him to stay, and I could see the struggle within him to continue with his plan. He comforted me again, admitted his love for me, swore that he would never forget me, and that he would never love another.

My thoughts echoed his as he continued to explain to me that we were not destined to be together. I believed to my very core that no matter what happened, he would be my only true love. Explanations did not make any sense to me.

After convincing him to stay just a few minutes more, he escorted me to the place of our first meeting. He sweetly agreed to share a few last moments in solitude.

Though our lives will take another course temporarily, somewhere in time, I believe that we will meet again.

Chapter One

July 1989

I finally made the decision. Could there even have been another choice? After all, I had no direction in my life, no more family, no dreams. In truth, the decision had been made long before the day Joe told me who I really was. I just did not know who Alexandra Charles was destined to become.

To make sense of it all, I have to back up and remember how it all started. It was that summer, the summer that began with the twins' graduation party. From that day, nothing could have prepared me for what was about to unfold.

June 2, 1989

"This evening is going to be a night to remember!" I prophesized, as we raced to pick up Claire. My other best friend, Tabs or Tabatha to her parents, glanced over at me with her exquisite Italian brown eyes and demanded of me, "Check and see for sure if you have it!"

"Since when do you care about pictures anyway?" I laughed as I looked over at Tabs. She was wearing a purple, ruffled top and white shorts. She is not the kind of girl who really gives too much thought to the way she dresses; however, tonight she looked stunning.

"Yeah, but don't you think this night is different? We are officially free!" Tabs, who rarely allowed her true feelings to show, seemed wild with enthusiasm about this party tonight.

"Yes, tonight is going to be different." I thought about our new freedom as I slid the passenger-side mirror down to check my look. Hazel eyes stared back at me under blond bangs. The lipstick was fine. Tonight was the official end of high school and I was insecure about the next step in my life. If I could just stop time and not have to think about my future that would be a perfect scenario.

"I'm going in to get Claire," Tabs said as we parked in our friend's driveway.

"Claire is probably not going to be ready," I kidded, while I dug through my small brown hand bag and spotted my camera in the bottom. Now all I have to do is remember *to take* pictures tonight, I reminded myself.

As I waited, my mind fell easily to thoughts of Claire. I knew she had been preparing for this day for months. Being best friends, I knew her all too well. She most likely changed her clothes at least a dozen times, redid her hair until the hair spray weighed ten pounds, and then finally determined that she hated how she looked in the end.

On that hot summer day in my hometown of Raleigh, North Carolina, while I waited in the car, I tried to focus on the fact that this party would be the beginning of summer. Maybe even the beginning of a new life. I needed to keep my thoughts on that and not on what happened to me a year-and-a- half ago. *They can't come back; I know they aren't coming back. I miss them so much.*

After several minutes, Claire and Tabs jumped into the car.

"Sorry about that!" Claire slid in the back seat and folded her legs up to her chest. "I was ready like an hour ago, but then I changed my mind on my shoes and you know when you change shoes, then you wonder if what you are wearing even matches. You know what I mean?"

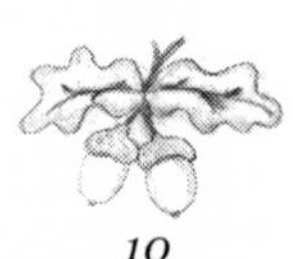

"You are making too much of this, girl!" Tabs yelled out as her brown hair flew about her face and she put the convertible into fourth gear. "Who cares anyway? We are finally out of school and can relax and enjoy tonight!"

"I knew I should have brought something to cover my hair! It is going to be a mess by the time we get there," Claire cried, as she tried to cover her head and moved down towards the floorboard.

"Oh come on, it isn't that bad. Loosen up, enjoy yourself tonight." I flung my hands up into the air and took in the warm summer air. "Besides, what can go wrong? You are with your two best friends!"

As we pulled up into our friends' yard, we could see the twins, Hayden and Jake, standing there in plastic sumo wrestling outfits. Their black wigs were poorly fitted and Hayden had already torn a hole in the leg of his costume. Time to pull out that camera!

"Double points, bro! I won!" Jake gloated.

"No, no, you did not win the last match," Hayden argued with his brother as he took the wig off his head and tossed it to the ground. "I got distracted by Gabby and her friend. Those babes would distract anyone. I can't help it that you weren't looking at them too. You can't count that one."

"Dude, I beat you. I don't care that they distracted you. Be a man and suck it up!" Jake looked over at us walking across the lawn and waddled over.

"Ladies, ladies, you are all looking lovely tonight." Jake looked directly at me. "Alex, I believe you are the Belle of the Ball." He stopped, looked at Tabs, and quipped, "Well, well, Tabs, this isn't a Halloween party. You can take your mask off anytime." Jake flipped my blonde hair as I passed by him.

Tabs and the twins argue about almost everything, and it creates this spontaneous comedy show for the rest of us. However, behind their devilish words, they are true friends to the end.

"Well at least I'm not wearing a plastic suit that has a banana hammock holding my family jewels up!" Tabs continued, flouncing past the boys and into their house.

"She never gives a man a minute of dignity!" Jake shook his head as he looked to me and then Claire for support.

"Well, don't you think you sort of asked for that one? It was a little brutal," Claire added, trying to put the whole thing into perspective.

"What's this all about?" I asked, motioning to their sumo outfits. Personally, I thought it was hysterical to see the twins sumo wrestling in their front yard. They were always up to something, whether it was trying to invent some new sport or perfecting one that already existed.

The best way I'd found to describe the twins was that they reminded me of two German Olympic gold medalists. Blonde, blue eyes, chiseled bodies; in other words, teenaged manly perfection.

"We thought we'd clown around, you know," Hayden commented slyly. "Got to unwind from a brutal senior year somehow! We figured no one would miss the party if we were standing in the yard like this." Hayden smacked into his unsuspecting brother from the backside, and they continued to wrestle while drawing a crowd from the cars passing by.

The house was a large red-brick structure, accented with black shutters. It was in a very upscale subdivision and was one of the oldest houses on the street. The heavy oak trees in the front yard did not give the house much of a chance to breathe, but the back yard was open with at least an acre of thick, lush, green grass that was kept immaculately manicured.

"They come up with the most ridiculous things to do. Who would think of sumo wrestling, really?" Claire asked rhetorically as we continued into the house and immediately saw Tabs pouring three cups of punch.

"Do you think their parents are here? It is so weird that they always attend these things, don't you think?" Tabs asked as she passed the drinks to us.

"Yeah, they're here and I bet Robert is going to be here too," I said looking at Claire. "I heard Jake mention something about it at school last week. You would think they'd have considered your feelings about him though."

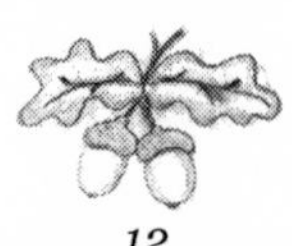

I knew she would be sensitive about him being here tonight. Claire recently broke up with Robert, the captain of the football team. She was the homecoming queen and he had been the king. They looked like a match made in heaven, except he didn't understand the concept of having only one girl-friend. Yes, we have a cheater in our midst. Somehow, he thought Claire wouldn't mind one bit.

On the other hand, Claire is such a hopeless romantic that she didn't see it coming from a mile away. Boys have certainly taken advantage of her through the years and despite my best efforts, she continues to believe the best of the male portion of the population.

"I'm going to the bathroom. I know my hair is a mess," Claire declared and disappeared behind the stairwell to the powder room.

"I have to admit, that was messed up for the boys to invite him. I guess they practically invited the entire senior class," Tabs said, taking a sip of the punch.

"Let's check out the food. I'm starving," I suggested, hoping to get Robert off our main topic of conversation. As we both moved into the kitchen, I immediately spotted the twins' parents scrambling to get all the munchies out. They were placing large bowls of food, buffet style, on their breakfast bar.

"Tabs! Alex! So glad you ladies could make it. Did you see the boys in the yard, in those ridiculous costumes?" Dr. Barry asked. She and her husband were both pediatricians. Because they were workaholics, they were, unfortunately, absentee parents. They let the twins get away with whatever they pleased, perhaps in an effort to make up for all the time they missed out of the boy's lives.

However, they did manage to surface, with bells on, anytime there was a special occasion. There was never a shortage of food, decorations or excess at their events, either. Once at a party, when the twins turned sixteen, they hired a rock band to play for the day. It was ridiculous how much money they spent, but they seemed happy to do it. After all, the boys wanted it and the boys had to keep up their reputations as the most popular boys in school. I think that's called living vicariously.

"Yeah, we saw them," I said as I grabbed a cheesy puff. "I think it is so funny. Only Hayden and Jake would come up with something like that."

"Well, congratulations on graduating!" the other Dr. Barry said. He handed two plastic graduation cap pins to Tabs and me. "And here is a little something to help you get going on the summer festivities." He passed us both a small envelope, which we knew contained some cash, as a graduation gift. Who can ever know what to buy a teenager? So they keep it simple and give us money for every occasion.

Claire, obviously very upset, entered the room wiping her nose and eyes. "He *is* here! I just saw him," she hissed. "How could they be so insensitive and invite him? He brought Gretchen Ryan too! I can't believe he is such a jerk."

Claire disappeared out the back door and into the yard. "Excuse me. We have a bit of an emergency," I said to the twins' parents. I followed her, grabbing some tissue off the kitchen counter.

"Is something wrong?" the twins' mom asked.

"No, no, be back in a few." I didn't want their parents involved, which would make Claire feel worse. Besides, I planned to get her mind off things; I wanted her to have a great night.

After sliding the glass doors closed and spotting Claire on the cast iron patio set, I walked over to her and said sympathetically, "You know, you have comforted me more times than I can remember. I guess pain is pain no matter what caused it. But you can't let him ruin your night. He has obviously moved on. I know it is hard to do, but you have to move on too."

I passed her a tissue and looked back at the house where Tabs stood at the sliding glass door watching us. She turned around and went back into the house. I immediately wondered what she was up to, knowing full well that Tabs was not the forgiving type.

"Come, on, let's go back inside and you can keep Tabs and me company. It wouldn't be the same party without you." I watched Claire, who was quietly crying. I knew she was hurting, and probably couldn't care less about the party at this point.

"Could you give me a minute? I'll come back inside soon, okay? Maybe I'll just go watch the boys make fools of themselves for a minute, to get my mind off *him*." Claire wiped her nose again, then looking at me helplessly. "Alex?"

"Yes."

"I am a stupid fool, aren't I? I need to be more like you and not fall in love in the first place."

"No, you should fall in love. Isn't there a saying, better to have loved and lost than never to have loved at all? Besides, by the time we hit the boat tomorrow, and you disappear into your romance novel, you'll be in love all over again."

"I hope you're right." She paused for a minute while she blew her nose. "He's such a jerk! He didn't mean any of those things that he said to me. And I believed it all. He said he couldn't live without me. I really thought he was *the one*. How could I be so brainless to believe him?"

"Well, I know it doesn't feel like it right now, but you really are better off without him. Who wants to be with someone who thinks cheating on you is okay? Don't you want a guy who thinks the universe revolves around you and only you?" I paused and almost whispered, "I guess that's what I would want."

I stopped to think about it and found that those really were my true feelings. When I fall in love, it will be with someone who truly thinks I hang the moon. I knew I had never been in love, so I had to admit I didn't know exactly what Claire was going through. To me, this guy was the ultimate creep, and I wanted so much to be able to give him a piece of my mind.

Claire looked over at me again and said, "You're right, that's what I do want. I wish I wasn't so hurt, though. I hope that Gretchen chick chokes on a peanut. Did you see how skinny she is?" Claire began again in a pouty voice, "I can see why he picked her over me."

"Who cares how skinny she is? She isn't you, Claire. Seriously, there isn't a girl in school prettier than you. And he didn't pick her *over* you. He's greedy and wanted you both. He had his chance and he blew it. You have to stop beating yourself up and get over him." I became aggravated with the thought that Claire would even second guess the caliber girl *she* really was.

What I said was true; Claire was the most beautiful girl in school. Gorgeous, in fact, especially with her strawberry blonde hair that always lay immaculately on her shoulders. Her eyes were this pale blue/green, clear, almost like glass. It was really her personality that trumped her milky complexion, though. And she was incredibly kind. She was wonderful inside and out. Girls all over our school wished they were her.

"I'll be there in a few. Thanks, Alex. I'm glad to have a friend like you, you know?" Claire whispered, with tears in her eyes.

"That's what best friends are for, right?"

"Right," she quickly fired back as she tried to pull herself together. I have to admit, if it had been me, I would have walked right up and slapped the dork. They've only been broken up for a week, but who pulls something like this right before graduation, anyway?

I returned to the house to find Tabs and quickly spotted her in the living room, standing right beside Gretchen. At that same moment, she winked at me, turned to Gretchen, and emptied the contents of her drink on Gretchen's pale pink shirt.

"Oh, my God, you did not just do that!" Gretchen howled as she flung the punch off her clothes.

"What's your problem, Tabatha Sebastian?" Robert yelled.

"Ooops," Tabs sheepishly replied as she smiled at Gretchen.

"Hold on just a minute," Hayden said as he came barreling in the room, two people wide in his sumo costume. "What just happened?"

"One guess?" Gretchen asked sarcastically while pointing at the recent addition to her shirt.

"Ew, I'd hate to be you," Hayden turned and headed for the kitchen. He was a typical guy, and he really didn't care about what happened to her clothes.

"Look, maybe you should go, now that you are such a mess." Tabs looked down at Gretchen and batted her eyes.

"Let's go, Robert! I didn't want to come to this uncool party anyway!" Gretchen stomped off and Robert threw his paper napkin on the floor. He followed her like a lost puppy.

"What a weak, uninteresting, boring, blob of a guy that Robert is." Tabs laughed as she picked up the napkin from the floor. "I mean, do you really think I would let him do that to Claire without any consequence? Uh, no. Not going to happen. Come on, Alex Charles, tonight is going to be our night to howl... now that we have that clown Robert out of the way!" Tabs hooked her arm around me and we walked back into the kitchen to continue our earlier project of finding some snacks.

The party flew by. One hour dissolved into the next until Hayden and Jake's parents announced that they had a graduation gift for the boys. We were all instructed to meet in the front yard, and the boys' father pulled up in a large blue Toyota truck, with huge knobby wheels the size of Texas. The spotlights on the top of the truck were covered in yellow smiley faces, which instantly made me laugh. The driver's side had a monster bar to help you jump into your seat. It was the perfect gift for the twins.

"Hot dog!" Hayden crowed as he and his brother took off across the thick grass and jumped onto the running board. "Those are some nice meats!" Jake added, almost stroking the huge tires.

"Blue bro! We are definitely Heels on wheels now!" Jake, the ultimate UNC fan, climbed up the passenger side of the truck and began popping up and down in his seat. You could hear their howls two blocks away! "Jacked and custom...totally rad!"

Guests quickly inspected the new ride, and Hayden blew out, "Get on! Jump in the back, ladies, and let's take it for a spin!" Tabs, Claire, and I climbed over the tailgate and jumped into the truck bed. Hayden peeled down the street within seconds, smoking the tires on the black asphalt. We tried to find something to hang on to, as the truck bounced all over the road.

"Can you believe it, Dudes?" Jake yelled back at the three of us as we held on in the back of the truck, each of us trying to keep our balance as Hayden sped up and wildly maneuvered the truck. "There's no stopping us now! Can you believe our parents gave us this?"

"Uh, yeah, we know who your parents are!" Claire yelled back sarcastically, as she tried to tie her hair in a twist.

"Just shut up and tell your brother to quit driving like a maniac! He's going to get us all killed!" Tabs shouted, as we took the corner on what seemed to be only two wheels. I was a thrill maniac like other teenagers, but Hayden was going life-threateningly fast.

As we were thrown all over the back of the truck, Jake pulled half of his body out of the truck and did his best to perch on the window sill. His "Warriors, Class of '89" t-shirt got stuck on the door lock and as soon as he reached around to unhook himself, the car swerved.

I looked into the cab of the truck and saw Hayden moving across the seat to help his brother. Instantly, we almost collided head on with oncoming traffic and Hayden grabbed the steering wheel to jerk back. It was an overcorrection that caused the truck to flip up on two wheels and seconds later, it was heading for the median.

Chapter Two

Evening, June 2, 1989

In what seemed like an instant later, my body was lifted out of an ambulance and I tried to jerk to a sitting position, feeling disoriented and scared. I was strapped down and obviously couldn't get very far. I couldn't tell if I was injured, where I was or who I was with. All I could see was a large man in a blue shirt pushing me along as white ceiling tiles flashed intermittently.

"Where am I?" I felt a dull ache in my side.

"Lay back, Miss. We'll get you taken care of," another man, with an oversized stomach, requested. I could see his large sausage-like fingers holding the silver rim of the stretcher.

"What happened? Did we wreck? Where are my friends?" I couldn't understand what was going on, even though I distinctly remember seeing us flipping over and within seconds feeling airborne from the truck.

"You are going to be okay, Miss. Please give us a chance to see what is going on," the first man urged me with his words and a heavy hand, to lie back on the stretcher.

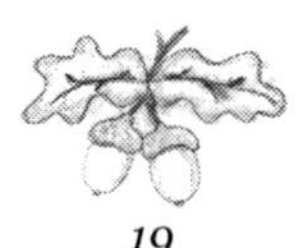

My mind was running wild. I didn't feel injured, but my heart was racing like a rabbit's and a horrible dread was coming over me. Was everyone okay? It was all I could think about as we slammed through the emergency room doors and two doctors moved quickly to work on me.

Before I could think, two nurses were cutting my clothes off and a white light was flashed over my eyes. "Who is this?" the older doctor asked.

The first man in blue answered crisply, "We don't know. Just picked her up from that accident on Briar Street. Overturned vehicle. She and some other kids were riding in the back of a pickup."

"Miss, can you hear me?" the soft-spoken doctor asked urgently.

"Yes, I can. What's going on? What happened to my friends?" I pushed my elbows under my body and tried to sit up again.

"Lay back, at least until we have assessed your injuries. Are you in any pain right now?" a female doctor asked me. Her short brown hair draped her face and she stooped over to talk to me. Her soft perfume helped distract me from the sharp medicinal smell of the hospital.

"I...I don't know. My head hurts. I feel sick to my stomach. I don't know. I feel bad, but I can't exactly explain it." I didn't care what my injuries were. I wanted to know how *everyone else* was. I can't believe how stupid we acted. How could the twins be that reckless! Were they alive?

"Try to relax. I'll see what I can find out about your friends," the soft-spoken doctor reassured me. He immediately began working on me as a team of nurses moved in and out of the small emergency area. A thin woman stepped over and started writing on her clipboard as she quizzed, "Your name, dear?"

"Excuse me?" I wasn't prepared for answering any questions. I wanted answers!

"What's your name, dear? Do you remember?" she tried again.

"Yes, sorry. I'm not really myself right now. Uh. Alex. I'm Alexandra Charles."

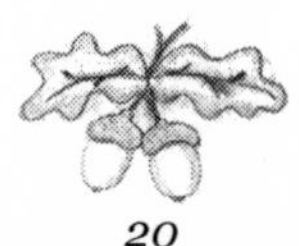

"Okay then, dear, do you think you could give me your phone number? We'll call your parents to come to the hospital." She looked down on her clipboard again, ready to continue filling in her form.

How do you tell someone who is obviously trying to take care of you that there isn't anyone at home to call?

"Are you with me, dear?" She looked down at me as two slow tears rolled down my cheeks, without any additional emotion on my face. Not only was I scared and worried from the accident, now I was reminded of the painful tragedy of my parents. "Alex?" the nurse queried.

"Yes. I'm okay. You'll need to call Lilly, my guardian, at..." I continued giving her the information and thankfully she didn't ask any questions about where my parents were. As my bones were checked, wounds cleaned and bandaged, the pain started to really hit me as my adrenaline was wearing out.

In what seemed like an eternity, Lilly finally arrived at my side, looking frightened half to death. She relayed to me that I had a concussion, several large cuts on my legs and a bruise the size of a frying pan on my left side. Other than that, I was relatively unharmed from what turned out to be a bad car accident, totaling the twins' graduation gift.

"Where are Tabs and everyone else? What happened to them?" I surveyed the bandages on my legs and instantly wondered how far I flew out of the truck. I couldn't seem to remember anything much past seeing Hayden pull the wheel over and the truck tipping.

"They are all here and they are all doing okay," Lilly told me as she patted my hand and took a deep breath. "I think Jake got the worst of it, as his back was sandpapered by the asphalt. They are wrapping him up as we speak."

"Thank you for coming. I'm sorry. Everything was going so great, and then, I guess, not so great. We just took the new truck for a spin." I shook my head trying to remember back to what seemed like a single second in my life.

"It could have been a lot worse, Alex. We're all lucky. I hope to take you home tomorrow and this whole ordeal will be behind you. Accidents happen. You know this could have been a lot worse. I'm just thankful you're alright, the others are alright, and new trucks can be purchased." Her speech was growing rather faint.

Lilly, my neighbor, my friend, my guardian. She had been there for every year I'd been alive. Though she had no children of her own, almost from the day I was born, she took me under her wing and didn't miss a moment of anything that happened in my life. More than next-door neighbor/babysitter, she was a beloved "Aunt Emeritus." She jumped in when my parents passed away and respected my strong will, always loving me for who I was. Lucky for me, her husband traveled on business eighty percent of the year. That left her with plenty of time to devote to me.

I sincerely felt awful that I'd worried her. I wanted to go back in time and tell myself not to be so careless. Not to get into the back of that truck. It didn't seem like any harm would come from test driving their graduation gift.

But now I know how lucky we really were. It could have been so much worse.

Chapter Three

June 10, 1989

A week passed before any of us were able to resume our normal summer activities. The twins were ready to meet us at the lake with their parents' boat and we all agreed to be there early Saturday morning. Hayden called first thing.

"Alex, hey, it's me." He sounded low, not at all the happy twin who I was used to hearing.

"I know who you are, Hayden. Your voice stopped changing years ago. What's up?" I was glad to hear him since it was the first time since the accident.

"Well, I just wanted to tell you..." his voice trailed off.

"Spit it out! What's wrong? If this is about the accident..." I began when Hayden quickly interrupted.

"It *is* about the accident. I'm sorry, Alex. I mean, really sorry about what happened. I hope you aren't too banged up? Are you?" Hayden, a usually hyper male, was calm and somber.

"I'm fine. A little bruised up but I'm okay. It's alright, you know. We all learned a lot and in the end, we're fine." I really wanted to tell him that in my mind the whole thing was life changing. During

the week that we were apart, I realized that somehow I had been given a second chance at life. God was allowing me a "do-over". Whatever lost path I was on, it was my wake-up call to get in gear and figure out what I wanted to be in life.

"Good. I..." he hesitated again. "This was no little thing..." Hayden paused and then slowly began again, "Losing the truck is nothing compared to the possibility of having lost you... or any of the others. I just don't want to dwell on it. Can we just get back to the way we used to be? I'd really like for us to head out on the boat today, if you think you're up for it."

"That sounds great."

Hayden, who usually drives, allowed Jake to pick me up; I didn't ask questions. Once we were on the boat, Claire immediately began reading her latest romance novel. I could tell something was on her mind, but I hoped that she stayed buried in her book. Being a hopeless romantic meant that Claire enjoyed a good love story with a little bonus. She actually believed that there were men out there like the ones who she reads about in her novels. Maybe that was her first mistake with Robert; he was no Fabio.

Laying on the swim platform for several hours, with my blonde hair dancing over my eyes, I could see nothing but sparkles bouncing off the water from the luscious sun shining down. My body soaked up the warm rays and I welcomed the flicker of wind that ran across my body every few minutes.

Under the southern summer sun, my skin toasts from living outside every waking moment. I know I'll regret being a sun goddess some day, but not right now. Focusing on your looks was typical high school stuff, even though I despised that about being a teenager. Who said I had to be logical?

I tried not to make any purposeful notice of the stitches and bruises that plagued everyone on the boat. I wanted to ask everyone how they felt, but things seemed to be right back to normal. Why ruin a perfect summer day?

With a deep breath, I sat up, Indian style, on the back of the boat. I brushed my blonde bangs out of my eyes and began braiding my long, straight hair that hung just past my shoulders. I examined green bruises on my legs and dreaded the stitches being taken out next week. They looked monstrous. There were sure to be strange tan lines.

Tabs' cheek was still bruised and she had a long scar on her arm. Claire, the fairest of us all, looked like she had been beaten with a baseball bat. I knew she didn't want to be out on the boat looking like that, but we all understood why we looked the way we looked. It was weird, but no one seemed to want to talk about it. We stuck to our usual dialogue.

"*Jaaakieee*, how long are we staying out today? I'm *staaarving* to death," I yelled. "I haven't eaten since last night and my stomach is making a meal off my back bone!"

Hayden made a wave of water splash up on the deck of the boat. "Alright, you know I hate to get wet when I am tanning. Cut it out! Seriously, what's the deal on lunch?" I whined as I grabbed one of the red towels that were neatly stacked in the boat.

Claire closed her book and stood up. "I made sandwiches. They're in the cooler. Why didn't you tell me you wanted one? I should have asked you about it, but it honestly slipped my mind. I get so involved in my books; you know I can't resist a stud with a hidden agenda!"

"Sandwiches? What? Nobody tells me anything!" Tabs pretended to be mad. "Move over, and let me get on the darn boat already." She pushed Hayden off the ladder and popped him on the top of his head.

"If I could hit a girl, you would be toast right now," Hayden threatened. "If you smacked my guns, you would get a boomerang smack back. Nothing can hurt these giant Smith and Wesson's! You know I've already proven that I am invincible." By her expression, it was obvious that Tabs was not impressed with Hayden's body.

Tabs snapped back, "I think you owe me one. You deserved that if for no other reason than you totally messed up my arm forever. Look at this scar."

I was relieved that the topic was finally out there about the accident.

"Look, I told you that I was sorry. It was dumb, I know. But can't we just get back to the way things were? You hating me for no good reason, and me hating you for..."

Claire burst out and interrupted his thought, "I made one for everyone. I just didn't know how you all liked them, so they're all the same with lettuce, tomato, mayo, and turkey." Claire quickly reached for the cooler and pulled out a large plastic bag with the squished sandwiches.

"Please tell me you are joking. You know I hate may-o-naise. Who would like that slimy mess?" Jake grabbed his sandwich and used his towel to wipe the mayo off, ignoring the earlier exchange from Tabs and Hayden. I couldn't help but notice his back, which was one big scab. I wanted to reach out and touch it, but it kind of gave me the willies.

"Now that's a slimy mess! Really, mayo on your towel? It's going to get all over the place. That's totally disgusting!" Tabs grabbed his towel and threw it into the lake.

"You'll pay for that one...go get it!" With that loud proclamation, Jake tried to push Tabs into the water. She slapped him on his chest.

After things calmed and lunch was well underway, Tabs threw a piece of her sandwich bread over the other side of the boat at a mallard duck cruising by. Irritated with the duck's surprise, she shouted, "I threw you food. Get it!"

"Please, Tabs, like the duck knows you threw food and not a rock at him? I mean, have some patience with the little guy!" Hayden looked over the side of the boat. This was certainly a sympathetic approach that I had not seen from Hayden. He seemed puzzled about where the duck had swum off to. The mere fact that Hayden was not usually so compassionate made us all turn and look back at him, puzzled at his comment. Maybe the accident really did change his perspective on things too.

As this day was unfolding, like many of our summer days did, things were quickly getting out of hand. I don't think that there was one single day on the lake that didn't end with one of us getting unexpectedly doused with water. At a much slower rate, we were all still clowning around and having fun.

When the day came to a close, I dreaded going home to my empty house. The summer would either prove to be a long agony of worry before dragging off to a college life that I wasn't looking forward to, or an enlightening process of discovery. How could I tell them, the friends who have been with me through thick and thin, that I didn't want to go to college? I didn't know what I wanted to do with my life. But that accident was definitely my wake-up call. I did not have a plan, a dream, a direction. Until this month, my only goal was to graduate from high school.

Truthfully, I just wanted to read the last few pages of the novel about my own life, and then I would know how it all turned out.

Would I be a chemist? No. I would blow something up for sure; too much math anyway. Would I be a track star? No. I learned that I enjoyed being an athlete during high school, but did not want to make a career out of it. Would I be a nurse? Blood and needles? Uh, no thanks. Even the high school counselor's career test had not helped me. My academic mentor told me, "You're smart, you can be anything you really want." Like that clearly gave me a direction.

I knew I was confused, worried, and, maybe most of all, alone in my decision over where my life would go next. Simply nothing felt right. It was like my intuition was trying to tell me something, but I couldn't decipher the message. I needed my parents to be there and help me make up my mind. But they were not there and they never would be again.

I was left alone at the awkward age of 16. My parents passed away in a car accident, in the middle of my junior year of high school. Obviously, it was a tragedy of immense proportion in my life. My parents and Lilly were all the family I'd really knew about. The few other family members I had even heard about were dead, I guess. I thought it was sort of odd that I was pretty much all alone, but I was used to the concept by now.

My Dad, Bruce, was an engineer. He was an orphan. Mom said she "adopted" him when they fell in love. I never thought I favored either my Mom or my Dad. My Dad was a tall, handsome man, about

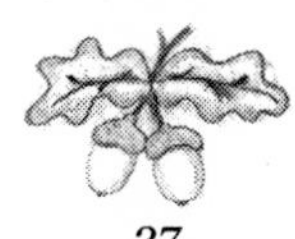

6'2" and in great shape. His hair, soft and brown, remained only two weeks long, as he had a standing appointment with the barber shop that he never missed. He had hazel eyes that were kind and loving. His temperament was gentle and understanding. Above all, he loved having a daughter. I thought I was the luckiest kid in the world.

Dad spent all of his free time with his family. We were the Three Musketeers. Two vacations a year fit in like clockwork. During our required family meetings, we decided when and where we would go. It never failed that I would slip "Disney World" on my little handwritten vote, no matter what age I was. Those trips were a guaranteed mix of heavenly food, fun and adventure.

My Mom, on the other hand, was focused on not only our family but every other cause and humanitarian effort in the world. She constantly volunteered for public service groups and non-profit agencies.

This 5'7" brunette was diligent and committed to every possible way to help the world. Her eyes, clear and blue, could pierce right through you. She was so passionate about so many things, her eyes always conveying the whole story.

It was as if she was trying to compress ten life stories into one. There was never a moment to lose and she had a strong conviction to meet the needs of others. Even to this day, I can't imagine how she got it all done. And then she was suddenly gone.

It did not seem to make sense that I had no family left in the world. How could everyone be gone? But that was the truth for me. I was literally alone and now that I have finally graduated, I felt alone with no direction.

Little did I know that my life was about to change...and change into a direction that I could never have imagined.

Chapter Four

June 11, 1989

Our neighbor, Lilly, was the kindest person I had ever known; she gave herself selflessly in every situation. She has been a lifeline for me. When my parents were alive, she helped my Mom with everything, whether it was an event or organizing our garage. My Mom could not have made it without her. Thinking back, neither could I.

Lilly was with me on the night when I was told my parents had died. She held things together while my world fell apart. Her constant attention and love helped me to make the right decisions. Once my parents died, I needed her help with everything. I was in the middle of a tragedy; I knew I wasn't thinking clearly.

Lilly and I agreed early on, that the least disruptive thing to do was to allow me to continue living in my home. I didn't want to move, even if it was next door. Then again, sixteen going on seventeen, I had no clue about how to run a household. I didn't know how to pay bills or what to do when the ice maker would stop working. I leaned on Lilly to make decisions and send me in the right direction. She knew what to do.

The next morning began as it typically did, with a call from dear Lilly to check on me. "Alex, I left a tray of baked ziti in the refrigerator. I hope you'll have your friends over for some homemade Italian. I know you love that large ziti, so I made it just the way you like," her sweet voice chimed over the phone.

"Thanks. I really can't tell you how much I enjoy your meals. I don't need to eat out as much." I laughed, simply thinking about how off course a teenager's diet can become. I have never been much of a cook. Cooking was not something I enjoyed, so I really appreciated Lilly's meals.

"Well, you have handled a lot more than any kid your age should. Especially now, after the accident. Don't you think you deserve a break? Aren't you glad school is over and you can spend the summer with your friends?"

I stopped for a minute and sighed, "Yes, it's a relief to have made it through high school in one piece."

"Well, you did, and with flying colors! Everything is going to work out just fine this summer and then you'll be off to college." I could hear Lilly pause as if she wanted to say something else. "Could I drop by tomorrow? Are you going to be around?" She knew I didn't mind when she came over; I was always happy to see her.

"Anytime. Believe me, my calendar is wide open. Come on by whenever." Was there something about Lilly's tone of voice that sounded as if something was up? I tried to analyze our conversation after we disconnected but soon I started thinking about that baked ziti. It was my favorite. She layered it with sweet, fresh basil and ricotta cheese. It was a masterpiece that melted in my mouth every time I indulged.

The next day Claire called around noon and asked if I wanted to meet at the deli for lunch. I told her that I was waiting on Lilly to come over and I honestly thought she would have been by earlier. I knew she would be there before too long.

Claire rambled on about this cute guy who worked at the deli, Dirk. No good would come from any guy named Dirk, I thought. She was heading over there to see if he was working today. Something about selling subs just makes a guy more appealing, I guess. If it were me, I would not be interested in a guy wearing a cheesy paper hat and ringing people up while picking up chicks.

She couldn't help herself. She was *the* most hopeless romantic in the world. I was very relieved that she was getting over Robert. At least she was moving on, even though Dirk could be another possible disaster.

I wish I could save her from all the pain she seems to have with the male persuasion. These relationships were hard to watch. It is like the being on the Titanic and you are the guy in the crow's nest who could have called down and yelled, "Iceberg, dead ahead."

I cuddled up on the couch to finish the latest edition of my favorite magazine. Luckily, I wasn't having as much trouble sitting comfortably anymore. I tended to sit Indian style, and the stitches on my leg bothered me from time to time. Thankfully, the doctor would be removing them soon.

Just as I began to read the last article, the door bell rang. I slipped my flip flops on and walked to the door. Lilly stood there, looking like she had seen a ghost; her face was white and strained. "Hey, I wanted to talk to you in person about something. I meant to come over earlier, but my day just got out of control, I guess. No time like the present." She spit the whole thing out in one long sentence.

"Slow down, what's wrong?" I pulled back a few steps to look behind her to make sure there wasn't someone standing in the bushes with a weapon or something. I instantly remembered that she had been hesitant on the phone yesterday.

"Come inside and sit down. Tell me what's going on." I had to admit, I was curious.

She took a few steps and exhaled deeply. She stood in front of me scratching her head as if she was trying to determine how to get the next sentence out.

I raised my eyebrows and looked over at her, finally asking, "Are you coming all the way in?"

"Yes, yes, I know this seems a little odd. I guess I just need to say it. Believe me, Alex, I am not trying to add any more stress to your life. I know that you have a lot on your plate right now. Things are moving fast and you are trying to make the right decisions. You have so many choices to consider. You certainly don't need another complication..." she quickly rambled and then paused for a moment.

"Lilly, whatever it is, I'll deal with it. Unless it's about your health, I really can't think of anything worse than what I've already dealt with. Right?" I was surprised to find that I was the one comforting her for once.

"I guess I just need to spit it out. Well, it seems that you have a new addition in your family. I guess, new in the sense that we didn't know about him before today," Lilly said as she took another deep breath and stared at my face, as if she was waiting for my response.

My mind went blank. What in the world was she talking about? Maybe my lost twin who had been separated from me at birth? In the years that I have known Lilly, she had always been so calm and focused. It was weird to see her struggling.

Lilly sat down on the couch. She grabbed both of my hands, pulled me down beside her, and then patted them gently. She was hesitating greatly over what to say. "Alex, I think you know me well enough to know that I care about you and your happiness. It was a difficult time with the passing of your parents. You and I believed, at the time, that you had no other family ties."

She looked away and scratched her forehead nervously. Her smooth brown hair was tucked behind both ears. Her tense face muscles made her wrinkles appear more pronounced. "But it seems that there is someone, a family member who we didn't know about." Lilly looked at me and slowly said the words, "You have an Uncle."

It was one of those times in life when you hear someone talking but the words are floating out of their mouth and appearing in a great big bubble over their head. What she said hung there in mid-air.

An Uncle? "What in the world are you talking about?" I asked, surprised and impatient.

"Well, I got a call yesterday from a man who asked if I knew an Alexandra Charles." She paused and got up off the couch. She started to pace back and forth in the living room. Finally, she sat back down while twisting her pearl necklace nervously between her fingers.

"I'm certainly not the nosey type, but had no idea why someone would call my house looking for you. So I asked him what this was regarding. He said that he knew Bruce and Beth, your parents of course, and that Beth was his sister. He said he had been away for a while, had just heard about their accident, and didn't want to shock you with the news of his existence. He wanted my help to figure out how to introduce him to you. He said he knew it would be a lot for you to absorb, but he thought that you would want to know he was around and that he very much wanted to meet you." This time her speech was almost rehearsed, slow and deliberate.

I was silent; I didn't know what to say.

She continued, "I was hesitant to provide any information to him and I told him that I would pass along his number to you, giving you the decision on whether or not to return his call." She stopped again and darted her eyes at me as if to see whether or not I was still following her. "It sounds like you might have an Uncle, Alex. He could be your Mom's brother." Lilly's voice finally raised and got more excited. "He knew how close your Mom and I had been."

At first, I just sat there. I was not really sure if I was in a dream or if this was really happening. An Uncle? A blood relation? A tie to Mom?

It was overwhelming to believe that there could be someone else out there who belonged to my family...who could be someone of my own flesh and blood...who knew Mom and Dad...who I didn't know about. I can't put into words how happy this thought made me initially.

As I continued silently to think it through, I found that I felt more skeptical. My Mom had never mentioned any brother at all. She told me she was an only child. Why would she not tell me that there was someone else who we could have been close to? Why wouldn't she mention a brother, someone who could have been there for me through my suffering when they died?

I couldn't figure out how to answer Lilly. I mean, could this be some weird estate scheme to claim my parent's inheritance or something? Why reach out to me now? What could he want? Why would he want to be a part of my life when he had been absent before now? Those were all questions that I didn't know the answers to, and now they were falling on me like a ton of bricks.

"Could you just give me with his name and number?" I asked Lilly, in shock, waiting to see what she would do.

Reluctantly, Lilly copied the information down and left it with me. "Call me if you want to talk this through. I'm sorry for dropping this on you like this, Alex, but I'm sure I'm doing the right thing by telling you." She stepped out the door and carefully closed it behind her.

After Lilly left, the rest of the afternoon dragged by. My mind was in a total state of confusion. I didn't know what to do. I must have looked at the name and number a hundred times.

"Joseph Graham." Who is this person? Yes, Graham *was* Mom's maiden name. Where had he been all my life?

That night I had a horrible nightmare. I suddenly woke up in a pool of sweat. Sleeping in the house alone was not easy for me anyway. Every crick and snap of the house propelled my imagination into overdrive. Eventually I had fallen asleep that night, and just before dawn, entered a nightmare.

My parents were alive. Life was normal and I remember feeling so happy. I felt like a normal teenager. The nest was intact. My life was whole.

But then the dream turned ugly. My parents died all over again, except this time I watched as it happened. I was standing on the side of the road as their Benz came around the corner. I ran out and screamed, "NO!" as they swerved to miss me. They ran directly into the large elm that sat on the side of the road. All I could do was drop in the middle of the road and scream over and over, as the rain pounded on my back.

I woke up that morning, so abruptly; I was shaking. I was unable to stop crying. It was so fresh in my mind, as if I could feel the pain they felt when they slammed into the trunk of that tree. As if I had been responsible. As if there had been something I could have done to prevent it!

I knew right then and there that I *had* to call Joseph Graham. If there was someone in this world who could help me feel closer to my parents, I needed to know that person. I couldn't miss this chance to have some small part of Mom and Dad back. I was hoping against hope that he would bring the word *"family"* back into my life. The dream helped to put things into perspective. I was missing so much without my parents in my life.

After I calmed down, I wondered what I'd done with that piece of paper I found it on the nightstand next to my bed and examined it, remembering all the scenarios I had come up with last night before finally falling asleep. There had to be a plausible reason for my Uncle to be completely absent from my life until now.

As I looked at the paper again, I was firm in my decision. My hand flew to the phone that was sitting on the nightstand and I hurriedly dialed the number. I wasn't going to over think this; I was just going to do it. Who cared what time it was?

Even after several rings, there was no answer. Not even an answering machine. I hung up the phone, no closer to solving the mystery. Getting out of bed, frustrated, I decided to move on with my day and try calling him again later. After a few pain killers, a bowl of horribly sweet cereal and a bunch of chores I had been avoiding, I called Hayden and Jake.

"Hey! Are you guys picking me up today?" I asked.

"Dude, we have been trying to get you all morning," Hayden quipped as Jake hollered in the background. "Was your phone off the hook? We've been ready to roll for hours! Get on your swim stuff on and we will be there in five!"

"Alright, see you in five." As I hung up the phone, I wondered if I should ask the group about my Uncle. What would they say? I would have to discuss it with Claire for sure. She was the most level headed one of the bunch and would think rationally. It was only when it came to her own romances that she was not a clear thinker.

Jake arrived with everyone else in tow and once we were finally out on the lake, I tried to relax but Claire was obviously annoyed about something. She finally groused, "I'm so sick of these pimples! I mean, what is the deal? I'm about to scream here. Can you see what I'm talking about? How attractive is this?" Truthfully, those bumps were nothing compared to all the bruises on her body that none of us, including Claire, mentioned.

Literally, there were two tiny white dots on her chin. She is one of those girls who has perfect skin. You don't become the Homecoming Queen with a crater face. I laughed, thinking about how now suddenly she is beginning to feel every teenager's pain of embarrassing pimples.

"Claire, I don't see anything. You are still gorgeous no matter what." I was trying to comfort her but I knew that skin imperfections seem bigger than life when they are on your own face.

As the afternoon unfolded, I felt like I was spiraling into mindless confusion, unable to do anything at all, or even to think clearly. This situation with my Uncle seemed like one more thing to worry about. I couldn't figure out his angle. What would he want with me now anyway?

I slipped off my t-shirt to reveal my pink bikini, and threw the anchor overboard. We stopped in our usual spot, and everyone except for Claire and me jumped off the boat. Claire settled into her usual seat on the front of the boat and opened her newest romance novel. She was practically drooling by the time she turned the first page.

Sitting down across from her, I pulled my legs up to my chest. Claire stopped and marked the page she was on in her book. "You okay? You seem a little down. Still worried about college? Or thinking about the..." Claire stopped. I don't think either of us wanted to be reminded about the car accident. But I wasn't thinking about that.

I chewed on my lip, still not sure if I wanted to involve anyone with what was really on my mind, the news about Joseph Graham. But Claire would be the right one to give me advice, I knew.

Finally I started, "Actually, I do have something on my mind. I had an unusual visit from Lilly yesterday. I'm not quite sure how to react to what she said." I looked into the water at Tabs, who was doing the most perfect breast stroke I had ever seen.

"Wait, let me guess, she wanted to know what shade of green paint would go best in her living room?" Claire laughed as she pulled a hat out of her bag and shoved it tightly on her head.

"No, she told me that a man called her house, looking for me. Says he's my Uncle." I found myself twisting my hair as I spoke.

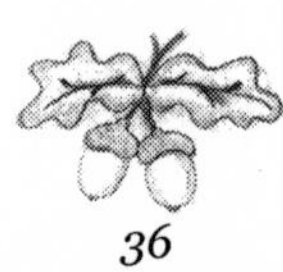

"Huh?" Claire seemed more engaged now that I explained why I was so heavily in thought today.

"I guess he wanted to contact Lilly so she could break the news to me. He told her that he's my Uncle, my Mom's brother," I answered.

Claire's mouth dropped open; I knew she was shocked too, seemingly at a loss for words. Thankfully, my news seemed to negate her earlier issues with her face. "Well, I don't understand. Where's he been all this time?" Claire was thinking exactly what I was thinking.

"I don't know," I murmured, trying to be as quiet as possible so that the others didn't hear us and want to join in the conversation. Neither of us knew the answer and we sat in silence for a moment.

Claire shook her head. "Alex, this could be really great news. I mean a relative? You are like the only person on the planet who has no family. Finding another family member is a Godsend! This is like an answer to *my* prayers and I am sure yours too! And he just popped right out of nowhere?" Claire's body became much more animated and her whole face lit up with excitement.

"I did try to call him once this morning already but I didn't get an answer. I didn't have time to try again before the twins picked me up. I guess the only hesitation I'm having is that I don't want to run the risk of losing another person in my life again. What if I get my hopes up and it turns sour? You know what I mean?" I was slightly nervous about the whole thing, but after my dream, it still seemed like the right thing to do.

Claire confirmed for me what I was already thinking: having an Uncle would be a good thing to welcome into my life. "Yeah, and you will be able to scope him out right away and figure out what's going on. No matter what, he is worth looking into," Claire added as she opened the cooler and passed me a cold drink.

"It's kind of weird, though. He just makes a decision to call my neighbor one day, out of the blue. I'm sure there is a logical explanation to all of this though." I grabbed the top of the soda can and popped it. I drank, slowly, deliberately, as the cool refreshment slid down.

"Alex, I've been your friend a long time and I really think you should call him again," Claire urged. "Seriously, I don't think that you have anything to lose."

"Oh, I know, I'll call him again. Thanks for making me feel better about it though." We left things there; I would try him again.

There was still no answer to my call that evening. After exhausting myself on the lake, sunning and swimming, I fell asleep on the couch.

Chapter Five

June 13, 1989

The next morning I had to get up early to get my hair cut. I dropped into my Dad's old beauty, a red 1965 Ford Mustang. Getting behind the wheel, I once again felt in control, as if I had some power to make decisions that affected my life. Over the past year, this car provided me with a quiet place to go think and make decisions. Nothing was too difficult for me to handle when I gripped the leather steering wheel in my hands.

Yes, this had been my Dad's car. It had been his baby. He had meticulously restored it and allowed me to help every step of the way. I had learned everything I knew about cars from him, as he had been a great teacher.

Sometimes, when I had things to work through in my head, I would sit in the car, imagining him sitting there next to me. Sad but true, I would talk things out as if he were sitting right there helping me think through the problem. As I broke away from my thoughts of Dad, I still knew I had to sort some things out about my future, still feeling unsure about college. I peeled down the street, having faith that my imaginary Dad and I would work it all out.

After I got my hair cut, I decided to meet Claire and Tabs for ice cream. I skipped lunch and opted for a sweeter option.

"I can't believe that the woman standing over there by the cash register is wearing tights with that dress," Tabs joked. "Is it not summer? Uh, hello?" She was too smart for her own good and often gave snobby comments. Being part of the popular crowd in high school gave Tabs an often superior way of looking at things.

"Well, we can't all be perfect, can we?" Claire retorted.

"I think she looks just fine," I empathized. "She's with her little girl. She probably couldn't care less about what she looks like when she is busy taking care of her child."

Claire changed the subject, "Hey, whatever happened last night with your phone call? Did you call him?" She scraped the bottom of her ice cream cup.

"Who?" Tabs asked. She licked the sides of her waffle cone as the mint chocolate ice cream was beginning to slide down. She looked thoroughly confused as to what we were talking about.

"It's a long story." I was not willing to say much more as I didn't really want my totally logical-thinking friend to tell me all of the possible reasons why my Uncle had never called before.

"Seriously, who are you talking about? Did you find a dreamy Dirk at the deli too?" Tabs joked.

I thought about it for a second more but felt it only fair to go ahead and answer Tabs. "No. Apparently, I have a long lost Uncle, of all things. My Mom has a brother who I have never met or even heard of until two days ago."

"Wow. An Uncle! How did you find out about him?" Tabs stopped eating to inquire. She grabbed a napkin and quickly cleaned her shirt. The chocolate had finally made it past the waffle cone and onto her green polo.

"I have a wet wipe, here," Claire announced as she grabbed the pack out of her bag and gave it to Tabs.

"He called Lilly and told her that he wanted to get in touch with me. He asked me to call him back. It's weird, though. I'm curious and a little excited at this point, although I had kind of gotten used to being the only one left. Two might be too crowded in my family." I grinned, not meaning a word that I was saying.

"Too crowded? Alex, listen, call him. Find out what he wants. I mean, what else *could* he want other than to get to know you? You're no multi-millionaire! Where has he been all your life? Did he say?" Tabs was demonstrating a quality I had never seen in her: blind faith.

"He didn't say. But I'll find out. After I get home today, I'm calling him again." I got up and dropped my ice cream wrapper in the waste basket and stood at the door. I found I had goose bumps all over my arms. This was really going to happen; I was going to talk to my Mom's brother today. I felt sure that this time he would answer.

"Alex, how about we go back to your house and add some support while you call him?" Claire suggested. We all agreed.

When I got home, Lilly was in her front yard and bounded over to me as I pulled up in the driveway. "Alex, oh thank goodness you are finally home." Lilly met me at my car door.

"What is it? Everything okay?" I opened the door and stepped out. Lilly looked like she did the day she told me about my Uncle, white faced and confused.

"Yes, yes, but I did think of one other little thing that Joseph mentioned on the phone the other day. Have you talked to him yet?"

"I haven't, but I was going to try him again. The first two times, I couldn't reach him."

"Oh good, I'm glad you're trying to contact him. I just wanted to be sure to tell you this before you called him," Lilly said, exhaling with relief.

"What?" I asked, intrigued by the urgency Lilly exhibited.

"Well, I didn't think too much of it at first, but then I remembered something that he said," Lilly noted. "I thought I would tell you in case it made any difference. Joseph told me on the phone that he needed to talk to you as soon as possible."

"Wonder why that would matter? Sooner, later, what difference did it make? After all, he did *wait* almost eighteen years to reach out to me." I shook my head and walked towards the house. Tabs and Claire pulled into the driveway behind my car.

"No, I'm missing something," Lilly recalled as she nervously plastered her hair behind her ear. "Let me say it correctly. He said he was *running out of time*."

We all stopped and looked at each other. What could that mean? I instantly wondered if he was dying and needed a kidney transplant to live.

"Well, you know what? I am going to call him right now, so we can get to the bottom of what is going on." Now everyone seemed curious about the new fact.

I tried his number once we got inside, and once again, there was no answer. There was nothing left to do about the call at this point, so we continued on with our planned evening. The girls and I enjoyed a relaxing evening of fun and food. There was plenty of leftover ziti. All the while, my mind was wondering about why he wanted me to call him but had not been around to answer. It did afford me some time to develop questions. What should I ask him, what would he say?

We all giggled about the possibilities of where Joseph Graham had been all my life. Tabs suggested that he had been on a submarine that sailed from port to port, never allowing him to be in any particular place for any length of time. Claire thought he was a top executive from Switzerland who didn't have time to be bothered with family, until one day he learned that he was dying and had to leave his fortune to the only living relative, me.

We enjoyed boasting about what he would be like and I contemplated how lucky I had been, despite the problems of the past year-and-a-half. Having this new family member would surely turn out to be a wonderful thing, right? After all, I did I have my best friends and Lilly, no matter what. What could go wrong?

My friends, Tabs and Claire, were two very different friends, yet neither one more valuable than the other. Both there for me, no matter what was going on in my life. And I was glad that I could be there for them too.

Claire, the optimist, was always the one happily whipping up s'mores when everyone else was crying over the bug bites during a camping adventure. She holds it all together when the world falls apart. She is the catcher's mitt in the game of baseball.

Claire has comforted me more times than I care to admit, when I couldn't help but cry. There'd been moments when I was an emotional wreck and she had willingly taken me on as her project. She was so understanding about what happened to me; it seemed like she was going through all the same emotions that I was going through, at the very same time.

And then there is my dear friend Tabs, who has a chronically dry sense of humor which only adds to her intense intelligent personality. Because she is so mysterious, beautiful and smart, many people don't know how to approach or befriend her.

I think she believes that because everything is so scientific and so logical, she gives off an aura of unwillingness to warm up to people. She sticks to what she knows is true. If someone seems outwardly unkind, she takes it as who they truly are. I always reminded her that a first impression is not always a true reflection of who someone is. But she has trusted Claire and me to the ends of the earth.

Looking at both of them sitting on the couch, I realized that I couldn't live without them. They had been there for me through thick and thin.

And Joseph Graham, who would he turn out to be? A Swiss banker? An incredible, but very private, artist? A CIA covert agent? 007? What part would he play in my life?

After everyone left my house that night, I again had trouble falling asleep. Thinking about this Uncle of mine, sadly, made me think of my parents. I wished they were here so that I could ask them about him. I wished I could ask the questions that I needed answers to. Despite our silly guesses about who he might be, I did feel sure he would have a good explanation as to where he had been all my life.

I missed my parents terribly and thought of them constantly. While laying awake, tossing and turning, my mind wandered to that terrible night when I found out my parents were never coming home.

Chapter Six

December 1987

The night they died, I had gone to bed early because I had a chemistry exam first thing in the morning. My junior year of high school was critical. This was the year to prove my strengths. College deans would be trolling through my high school records and would decide whether or not I was a fit for them.

I quickly fell into a deep sleep that night and awoke abruptly. It was storming and the elm outside my window scratched the screen in a very irritating way. Dad can fix that tomorrow, I thought; I can't live with that noise. I laid there, rehearsing my chemistry formulas, trying to keep everything in some logical, memorable order. Trying to get back to sleep.

The doorbell rang. I froze. Why is the doorbell ringing? And who would be ringing the bell at this time of night? Midnight? Maybe something happened to Lilly? I'm sure my parents will answer and deal with the problem. Dad will report on what happened in the morning. I tried to fall back asleep, only mildly curious about the door bell.

The bell rang again and again. I was frozen in my bed, absolutely terrified to move, almost like I was paralyzed more and more with each ring. The bell has never rung in the middle of the night. Who could it be? Won't they just go away? Why aren't my parents answering it?

Once again, the bell rang. This had to be about the tenth time. I looked around, into the darkness of the room, and a wave of sick fear came over me. *Where are Mom and Dad?* I know Mom isn't a heavy sleeper, so surely she would have heard it by now.

My internal dialogue continued; maybe it's Lilly. She might need help. She might be standing outside in the rain wondering why no one will answer the door. Maybe Mom and Dad are not back from their dinner yet. I need to get up and check this out.

I slowly got up and put on my pink housecoat, leaving my baby blue pajama bottoms to hang out of the bottom. I stood at the top of the stairwell and looked down to the front door. The large white frame held the door and two side windows. I could see that there was definitely someone there as the shadows were moving back and forth. Yes, two bodies moving back and forth. The rain came down harder now.

It was such a stormy night. The thunder and lightning were pounding into the melody of the doorbell's song. Whatever was out there was certainly getting soaked. I could hear the rain blowing on the side of the house.

I walked into Mom and Dad's room and quickly realized that they were not there. They were not back from the church dinner. They must have locked themselves out. That's what this is! Relief washed over me! I began down the stairs, yelling, "I'm coming, hold on!" I laughed thinking of what a hard time I would give Dad about forgetting his house keys. He wouldn't live this one down. I smiled.

Just before I opened the door, I began formulating the words to tease my parents and suddenly there were two people standing in front of me *who were not my parents*. Two police officers were staring me in the face. They were both wet, tall, and had very grim looks on their faces.

"Miss, sorry to bother you at this late hour, but is this the home of Mr. and Mrs. Bruce Charles?" the first officer asked.

"What is this about? What's going on? Are my parents okay?" I pleaded, having no clue as to why in the world they were standing on my porch at midnight.

"Well, Miss, we need to know who we are speaking with here," the taller of the two officers asked.

"I'm Alex Charles, the daughter of Bruce and Beth Charles. What's happened?" I was beginning to panic. My heart was literally stuck in my throat. I wanted to stop time and go back to rehearsing chemistry in my bed.

"Miss, could we step inside?" The officers showed their badges and then continued, "We have some news that we would like to talk over with you." The taller officer had very sweet eyes and seemed to understand that he was talking to a teenage girl in the middle of the night.

"Yes, sorry. I'm half asleep." I was honestly trying to lighten the mood, hoping if I stayed cheerful, this whole situation would go away. Maybe they are here because a neighbor was complaining about too much noise and had gotten the address wrong. Or maybe Mom and Dad had won the raffle, the fundraiser for the police-sponsored youth group. Something totally logical and understandable had to be the reason for this intrusion.

"We understand, Miss," the shorter officer said. "Take a minute. We're in no rush," The one with the badge name *Owens* carefully wiped his shoes off before coming in.

"Well, what is this about, exactly?" I finally asked, not wanting to hear the answer. I was scared to death.

"Miss, we're sorry to be the bearers of some tragic news, but it seems that your parents were in a car accident this evening, as they were coming down Highway 64." Again, the taller officer with the understanding eyes spoke.

"They are okay, aren't they? Are they recovering at the hospital? Will you take me there?" I started to run up the stairs and Owens called out to me.

"Miss, please stop! We need to tell you more. They're not at the hospital." He had a slightly sterner tone and spoke loudly to get his point across. I stopped suddenly and felt a lightness in my head that I had never experienced before.

"They didn't survive the crash."

Thunder cracked loudly and made me jump suddenly. My mind was racing. They didn't survive the car accident? No! It can't be!

Immediately my body felt sweaty, cold and clammy all at once. A horrible sick wave came over me. No, that can't be true. I didn't want to hear it. No, they went to dinner and they would be home soon. That is all. They have the wrong couple, that is all there is to it. I clutched the stair rail.

"Sir, I am sure you are wrong about who you have. That's what this is. My parents will be home soon and we can straighten this whole thing out," I begged. *There is no way this can be true,* I thought to myself. *I can't believe it. Maybe if I don't open my mind to the possibility, I will just wake up from this horrible nightmare.*

"Miss, if you would just stop and listen, I believe that we can explain what is going on here," Owens continued.

"NO!" I yelled. "They are not dead! You're wrong! I will not listen! No! I don't want to hear anymore! They are all I have in this world! They are the only family I have!" I yelled at the officers as I froze at the bottom of the stairs. I would not listen anymore.

Owens looked at his partner and sighed. I leaned against the wall, allowing it to support me. Slowly, I let my body collapse to the step, sliding along the banister. I kept my hands holding onto the banister above me. I wanted that wood beam to stabilize me as if it were a lifeline and it would keep me from drowning from the weight of the news.

"No, just don't say it. No, please don't say it," I whispered as I began to cry uncontrollably. This wave of pain and despair overwhelmed me. There is no pain comparable to the pain of losing someone you love. It hits you so intensely that you feel like your heart will literally burst into flames.

"Miss, is there someone who we can call to come over and be with you at this time?" Owens inquired. "We will stay with you as long as you like, but it might be best to have someone you know here to assist you through this."

I was animated again, "Who cares! I want my Dad! Where are they? Can I go to them?" Now the rage was boiling up in me; I sat on the step, fuming. I wanted to see this couple who the police *thought* was my parents. They were not my parents. They had to be someone else. Not my Mom and Dad.

"Miss, I believe it best that you not see them. You being young and all, it could be a little too traumatic," Owens stated as if he was reading from a piece of paper, so matter of fact, so cold. He didn't love my parents like I did. He wasn't feeling like his heart had been thrown in the incinerator. "We have identified your parents by automobile and their drivers' licenses that they both had with them at the scene of the accident. We could certainly confirm that with a relative or close friend when the time is right."

"Didn't you hear me? They are all I have! No family left. They can't be gone!" I was howling at them, as if they had the power to change what had happened. Then, slowly, I just sat there, dazed.

After talking among themselves, the taller officer walked out the front door and went to Lilly's house. Shortly afterwards, she arrived, soaking wet and white as a ghost. "Alex! My God! Are you alright?" Lilly cried out.

I was not able to answer. This can't be happening. This is not supposed to happen to me! My parents would never do this to me. They would not leave me like this, all alone. No, they must be wrong, I can't be an orphan!

"Lilly, tell them!" I grabbed her and pulled her body down to the steps with me. "Tell them that they have the wrong people! They can't be talking about *my* parents!" I was sobbing with tears dropping like large diamonds off my chin.

"Honey, calm down, I'm here now," Lilly said as she wrapped her arms around my body. "I'm here. We will get this all sorted out," She looked up at Owens and asked, "Mr. and Mrs. Bruce Charles were involved in an accident this evening, is that what you said?" she asked, speaking calmly and slowly.

"Yes, Ma'am. They were coming down Highway 64 and with the rain and all, I am afraid that it was pretty slick on the road. They may have been trying to avoid a deer. Their car hit a tree. And, well, they did not make it," Owens looked at his partner to see if he had anything to add.

Lilly's eyes quickly filled with tears. She believed what the officers were telling her. "If it is alright, I'll take it from here. If I could get your contact information, I will be in touch with you in the morning for some details on what needs to happen next," Lilly requested.

"Of course," Owens passed her his business card and said that they would be on duty all night. He asked Lilly to escort him to the door. Lilly looked at me and quietly whispered, "Just a moment, dear. I will be right back. Right back." She then stood up and walked over to the officers. They talked for a few minutes and then Lilly closed the door behind them.

Lilly came back to me and asked, "Can you stand up, sweetie? Let's get to the couch." Lilly pulled my body up and we slowly walked to the living room.

"This can't be true, Lilly. Please tell me this is not true! Please tell me," I continued to sob and beg for this to just be a nightmare. Lilly held me and slowly rocked. She softly cried and patted me on the back.

After what seemed like forever, I fell asleep in Lilly's arms and woke hours later. As I opened my eyes, Lilly was still holding me, herself wide awake. The horrible truth washed over my mind like a giant tidal wave. It was not a dream. That rainy, horrible evening had *really* happened. What now?

"Lilly, where are my parents?" I asked her in barely a whisper.

She looked patiently at me and slowly said, "Alex, your parents passed away last night, very unexpectedly."

"That's what I was afraid of. It wasn't a nightmare. Are they sure? What am I going to do? What will happen to me?" I pleaded; the tears so readily available again.

"Your parents did leave specific instructions in case something should happen to them. They planned ahead, of course not realizing... And I want you to know that everything will be okay. You are going to be okay. I know it does not feel like it right now, as you have a grieving process to go through, but you will make it through this. They need you to go on and be strong." Lilly's eyes filled with tears again.

"I don't want to believe that they are gone! I don't want to be strong. They were just coming home from church! How could this happen?" I could not stop the tears I felt hollow and cold. I felt sick and frustrated. I felt mad and disbelieving. Honestly, I did not want to feel anything.

"Alex, I hope you will agree with your parents' wishes. They requested that you remain with me until you turn eighteen. I can help you until you are on your own. And even then, I will not leave your side. I will always be with you. I'm right here and this is where I will stay."

Now I was to meet my Uncle. I awoke in the morning with all of this fresh in my mind, my heart aching as much as it had that night. Just like the reality of the accident had occurred again.

I stared at the ceiling and my thoughts drifted back to Joseph Graham. Who was he and how did he fit in with everything that had happened? I picked up the phone again and dialed a number that I had memorized by now.

Again, nothing but endless ringing.

I frowned and felt increasingly frustrated about this situation. How could I figure out where "my Uncle" fit into this puzzle if I couldn't reach him on the phone?

Chapter Seven

June 14, 1989

After I collected myself from my nightmare, I dressed and ate a quick breakfast. I had no plans that day, so I thought I would escape into one of the books that Claire recommended. After a moment or two of comfortable reading on the couch, the doorbell rang.

Good grief, what now? I looked out the living room side window, at the front door, and didn't know who was standing there.

The man was medium height with thick, short, wavy blonde hair. He had a five o'clock shadow and a kind, cheerful face that seemed so full of life. He was bouncing around outside so much so that he reminded me of someone who you would meet when you went to the zoo; one of those happy animal-lover types who conducted the tours. He looked adventuresome and excited.

The doorbell rang again and I realized that I had been standing there, staring out the living room window at the man, without moving. My mind was apparently lost in the details of his face.

The man turned away and walked to his car. He got into his blue VW Bug and backed out of my driveway. Was he a salesman? Someone lost? I never opened the door to a stranger but I was curious

as to what he might have been. Some minutes later, the phone rang and I let my answering machine pick it up, as I was quickly engrossed in my novel again.

My answering machine beeped and a man's voice quickly said, "Alexandra, uh, hi. I know that this is a little bit of a surprise, but it's me, your Uncle Joe. I hope Lilly told you that I called. I would really like to talk with you face to face. It might make this whole thing a little easier. I don't know if you have tried to reach me over the past couple of days, but I'm in town now and I would really like to meet you. I'm going to come by one more time before I head back. I was there just a few minutes ago. Uh, I guess I'll maybe see you soon?"

As I listened to his call, my stomach dropped and I felt sick. That was my Uncle. That funny, kind-looking man was my Uncle. I'd finally heard his voice for the first time. He was on his way back to my house? I wasn't expecting it to happen this way at all.

I hopped up and anxiously looked out the window for the blue Bug to return. As I stood there, those few minutes seemed like an hour. All the things I rehearsed in my mind to ask him left my thoughts completely. I was standing there trying to make up my mind about what to do.

Finally, I decided to run back to the phone and call Lilly. I told her about the message and asked her to come over. I thought I would feel more comfortable if she was there with me. Moments later, I saw the Bug pull back into my driveway.

It was finally time for me to meet my Mom's brother. As I stood at the door, my adrenaline began to pump, giving me more strength to move forward and open the door when the bell rang. I turned the doorknob, thinking that I needed to appear calm.

"Yes, uh, hello?" I asked as if I had no idea who was standing in front of me. The man, with the kind eyes blinked in surprise.

"Alexandra Charles? Are you, Alexandra Charles?" he asked so cheerfully.

"Yes, I am, and are you… Joseph Graham?" I said hesitantly.

"Yes I am!" He smacked his hands together. "I *am* Joseph Graham. Well, actually, I go by Joe. I am your Uncle, your Mom's brother," he quickly introduced himself.

I didn't know if I should step out onto the sun-lit porch or just stand there in my doorway. What is the proper etiquette for meeting your long-lost Uncle for the first time? The funny thing was I felt like I had known him my whole life. Strangely, there was no doubt in my mind that he was who he said he was. I felt calmer with each second passing second.

He was my Mom's brother. By the look of things, there was no doubt about that. My mother and I have heavy dimples, and I could see from the smile on his face, he had them too. He was wearing a white t-shirt and a pair of cargo shorts loaded with pockets. He was about 6' with his brown deck shoes. His body was built and tan, again, reminding me of someone who takes you out to see the giraffes. I don't know what it was; he just had a kind nature about himself that instantly made me feel comfortable and completely at ease with the situation.

"Welcome, come in. I wasn't expecting you to show up on my doorstep today." I was trying to keep myself poised. This was his first impression of me, so I wanted to seem mature and educated.

I opened the door wider to allow him to step inside. He immediately took a long, deep breath, as if he just walked into a bakery and smelled something delicious, something that he wanted to stay inside his lungs forever. His hands were firmly on his hips as he quickly looked around at all the photos on the nearby wall.

I was waiting for Lilly to come bounding through the doorway, so I stood there a moment while he reviewed the pictures on the wall. I think we were both nervous about getting the conversation going. He finally broke the ice.

"I realize that I am just showing up today without invitation. And I know this is all a shock for you, but I'm ready to answer any questions that you might have. I hope that this is okay?" He smiled as he asked me the rhetorical question. What could I say? No, it isn't alright?

"Lilly is on her way over. She is anxious to meet you too." I noticed that he was meticulously scanning the family photos again.

He turned back to me. "Oh good! I'm looking forward to meeting her too. Gosh, it's sure nice to finally meet you in person, Miss Alexandra Charles. You're all grown up. It's hard to believe."

Before I could respond, Lilly greeted us from the front door, cheerfully exclaiming, "Well, Mr. Graham, it's nice to meet you. What a surprise it is to see you here today." She reached out and shook his hand. They looked at each other as if they were old friends.

"You must be Lilly! Please call me Joe. Yes, well, I realize that I sort of jumped the gun a little with my unannounced visit today. But as I mentioned to you on the phone, I certainly did not want to waste any time in meeting Alexandra." He was grinning from ear the ear, looking over at me as if to gain my approval of his unexpected arrival. "I'm just so darn excited to meet you both. This is better than Christmas!"

"Come on in and let's all sit down. It's not like every day that you have a long lost relative show up on your doorstep." I didn't know what else to say. It was awkward with the three of us standing in the hallway by the door.

We all sat on the couch, Lilly beside Joe and me on the other side. Our couch was beige, leather, wraparound with a large coffee table situated in the middle. Although it was the most comfortable piece of furniture we had in the house, I felt like I was sitting on a board. I was feeling excited and nervous at the same time. I didn't know what to expect, though his pleasant demeanor did put me quickly at ease.

"I believe that I have a lot of explaining to do here. I want everyone to feel comfortable. I'm more than happy to answer any questions that you both may have," he continued, speaking as if he had rehearsed this a hundred times in his head.

I sat observing his strong arms, the gentle waves in his hair, the face which seemed so familiar. His facial features were much like my Mom's. I couldn't help but review everything about him physically as he spoke, as if he was a long lost friend who I was seeing again after so much time.

He continued, "Well, where to begin? I reckon I should go first and explain a thing or two. I'm sure you are curious about why you have never heard about me." Lilly and I both nodded. That was the main question that I had. He started again, "Your Mom, Beth, and I are brother and sister, obviously. I'm the older brother, the big brother." You could tell how nervous he was trying to get started in the explanation of things. He looked back and forth at Lilly and me. Lilly sat motionless; it was strange to see her look so engrossed when she is usually the one doing all the talking.

"Alexandra, I'd like you to know that I wanted to contact you much sooner than today. You'll just have to believe that I wanted to be part of your life since you were born. I wanted nothing more than to be here with you, to watch you grow up. It's not that your Mom and I weren't close, we just went our separate ways early in life." He massaged his hands together as he spoke. For the first time, he looked sad, sorry almost, instead of nervous.

"Your Mom and I grew up in a small town, on a farm, as I'm sure you have heard a few tales about, right?" He stopped to hear my response, and to finally focus on me.

"Yes, I did know that. And then she met Dad at college and they moved here and got married," I finished. Nodding as I looked over at Lilly, she nodded her head in agreement too.

"Right!" His demeanor began to change and he became more animated. "Well, your Mom and I grew up as normal kids do, and then she eventually left home and married your Dad. I decided to follow in our family business. Unfortunately, the family business takes me away for big chunks of time. I can't seem to stay in one spot for very long. Anyway, Beth and I decided that it would be best for me to just stay in touch with her and not to introduce me into your life." Joe paused and waited for me to respond.

"Family business? Why would Mom want that?" I quietly asked, not being able to imagine why this man, a seemingly pleasant person sitting right there in front of me, should not be in my life. "Why wouldn't she want you to be a part of my life? That doesn't sound like her."

"Well, for any child, I would think that it would be hard to form an attachment to someone and then not see or hear from them for many years," my Uncle explained. "Working in our family business isn't the most accommodating profession. But I was able to call and write letters from time to time, so she and I could catch up. She kept me in the loop about what you were doing. I have always cared about you, Alexandra. I always wanted to be here with you." His voice was so calm, so kind, that I could tell he honestly regretted that he had not been a part of my life.

Joe rolled over to one side of his hip and pulled out his wallet. He had photos of me through the years. I was embarrassed that he had several photos, like the two Christmases, when I was missing either my top or bottom two teeth.

He *had been* there all along. He knew that I was, I just didn't know that he was.

"The truth is, I found out just a couple of weeks ago that my sister had passed away. I was away for some time and when I got back, my neighbor told me the sad news. Beth's passing has been a tremendous shock. Of course, I know this has been hard for you as well." Joe slowly put the photos back into his pocket.

"It has been hard for all of us," Lilly agreed.

I really didn't want to start thinking about my parents' death at that moment. I had so many questions and I wanted to learn as much as I could about *him*.

"Let me ask you something. Why did you call Lilly and not me?" I asked.

"Yes, we *were* wondering about that," Lilly chimed in, looking more intently at Joe. Her body was so hard and focused; it made me feel a little curious about what she was thinking.

"Well, as I mentioned on the phone with you, Lilly, I knew that this would be a huge surprise. What was I going to do, call out of the blue and say, 'Hi, I'm your Uncle?' That seemed a little too bold. I wanted you, to help me ease into things, Lilly. In all honesty, I didn't think I was ready to hear that Alexandra wasn't interested in hearing from me, if that was the case. But then my plans changed over the last couple of days and I was able to be in town. I got a wild hair and decided to just come on over. Whatever it was going to be, I would face it, right?" He looked at Lilly as if he was asking for affirmation of his decision.

Lilly finally shook her head in agreement and he began again. "Beth told me a lot about you, that you are a wonderful friend. I know you have been here for the family all these many years. You seemed like a logical choice to talk to Alexandra about me."

Joe rubbed his hands together again and without waiting for Lilly to respond, he started again. "Some years ago, I remember her telling me about a time when you both got lost in a rainstorm. Your car almost got washed away in a pizzeria parking lot. As Beth described it to me, I thought it was really funny but she didn't seem happy about it."

Lilly looked at me, still at a loss for words. I quickly added, "Oh yeah! And you blew a tire. I remember this trip!"

"We never let Beth navigate another trip after that episode," Lilly added slowly.

"Honestly, Alexandra, all I'm hoping for is to spend some time with you. I hope you'll allow me to be a part of your life. We have a lot of time to make up, don't you agree?" Joe stopped and waited for me to respond again.

"Well, first of all, I go by Alex. Only Dad ever called me Alexandra." I looked back at Lilly, hoping to read her mind on how to answer his question. I finally continued, "And if you really are my Uncle, I would certainly like to get to know you too. I really can't believe it. It's so weird, you know?"

"Yep, I do. Just hang in there, I've got plenty of patience and we will get through this together. The important thing is that I hope you'll give me a chance to get to know you," Joe said, his eyes pleading.

"I can't believe Mom wouldn't have told me about you. What could be the harm, you know?" I wasn't about to let this fact slip by me. I needed a more solid explanation.

"Our family business, well, she knew it was..." he paused, obviously trying to get his thoughts together, "something that was too complicated to explain to a child. I'm sure she intended to explain it to you when you were older. She never got the chance, I would imagine. I'll explain more about that later. For now, I'd really just like the opportunity to get to know you better."

I was so shocked that he was really here, that I really had an Uncle. I didn't care about where he had been all these years, just that he was here now, a part of my life that I really should have had all along. *Family.* I have family again. There were no words to say how hopeful I was at this moment. The silence stretched.

Lilly ended it. "Well, I can see you both have a lot of catching up to do. I have a pot roast in the oven, so I'm going to excuse myself. We can chat later, Alex dear. Good to have met you Joe and I hope you will join us for dinner," Lilly stated it as if he had no choice but to confirm her invitation.

"Yes, I would love to." Joe stood up and watched Lilly exit the house.

"Wow. This is kind of heavy, you know. You'll have to forgive me. I'm happy that you are here. It's just a shock. There are so many questions..." I began to formulate my next question when Joe interrupted.

"Let me just interrupt here, Alex." He smiled, I assume by the fact that he got my name correct now. "I just want to get a few things out of the way. *I don't want anything from you.* I am not here to ask you for money. I am healthy as a horse, so I don't need a body part transplant or anything. My only hope is that I can spend as much time with you as possible. I only want to build a relationship with you, nothing more. You're all the family I have left too."

He paused, rolling his eyes around apparently searching for the right things to say next. "I'm single, forty something, I hate those details. No children, just me. It's just me who is left from your Mom's family." He looked at me focusing on the "just me" so that I understood. "I'm so grateful that we are finally together." I was glad to hear Joe say these things as they greatly put my mind at ease.

And so it began. Joseph Graham, my mother's brother, entered my life. And *everything* changed. As relieved as I was, I could never have prepared myself for what he was about to tell me. No one could have.

Chapter Eight

June 18, 1989

As another week engulfed me, it seemed like time literally stopped. I couldn't say what was different from one day to the next. All I knew is that I found peace in my heart. The nest was small, but it was a nest again.

Joe was very easygoing, fun and exciting to be around. He let me pick and choose whatever I wanted to do. Dinner at the nicest restaurants? No problem, and he made for a handsome escort. A quick trip to the beach? Sure. I talked constantly about my life, trying to catch him up to everything he missed, and adding to what Mom had written to him. I was having the most wonderful time of my life since the passing of my parents. Things were coming back into focus. It was all about family.

I had Joe's complete and total attention. He wanted to know everything. I explained to Joe how much my friends meant to me, and shared all the details about how real they were.

"It's not like friends are everything to most people, but when you lose your entire family, they *are everything*," I said as I was climbing into that little Bug which suited him so well. I think it was a

'70's model, though we never discussed which year it was. I had to laugh; it had pressed plastic seats that I stuck to as the heat permeated the inside of the vehicle. I quickly learned to get in or out very slowly.

"I understand. Friends are golden. They are part of the memories of your life that are so important. I'm glad they've been there for you. How are they handling the news of me being in your life?" He looked over his sunglasses and grinned.

"Of course, they are naturally jealous that I'm spending so much time with you. I've really only talked to Tabs and Claire. I need to take a different approach with the twins, but they will understand and I know they'll be happy for me." I pulled my blonde hair out of my face and held it in a side pony tail, as we drove down the road with what Joe called "12/55 Air Conditioning." Roll down the window 12 inches and drive at 55 miles per hour.

"Something that I have wanted to ask you about, and I hope you won't mind, but I'm excited to know. Are you married?" I had to talk loudly over the wind, looking straight ahead as a garbage truck pulled into our lane and sprayed debris all over the windshield. "Oh, gross!" I yelled out.

"To answer your question, I'm pathetically still in love with the first woman I really fell for, but I was never fortunate enough to marry her. You are the only family I have now too," he quickly spit out, as he swerved to miss the garbage truck that had come to an abrupt stop in the middle of the road to pick up a trash can.

"Still in love with the same woman? For how long?" I imagined he was the type of guy who just did not want to marry, maybe dating the same woman for ten years, never able to commit.

"Well, I met her when I was young, and it just wasn't meant to be. I do still love her very much and have never really been interested in anyone since. I know it's strange, but true." Joe zipped around a long black car in front of us.

"That's really sad and kind of awful, really." I was still thinking about this woman, but he did not seem to want to tell me anymore about it. What could have happened between the two of them? I was sure the story would unfold sometime.

Changing the subject, I continued, "I'm so thankful that we met. I'm sort of dreading the end of summer. I'm already worried about going to college. It's like hovering over me right now. Lucky me!" I ended sarcastically as I blew a giant bubble with my gum while we sat at a stoplight.

"I know it. And *that*'s why I had to tell Lilly I was running out of time." Joe looked at me with a frown, as if he had something very difficult to talk about. It was a strange face for him, since he was usually so upbeat. It reminded me of that first day we met and he was trying so hard to explain things.

"I forgot you said that. I *do* want to know why you said you were running out of time. I honestly thought it was because you needed a kidney transplant. Glad we cleared the air on that point early on," I said with a laugh.

"We need to talk more when we get to the park. I think I need to be looking at you when I talk about this," Joe responded, and then stopped abruptly at the next light. I was a little shocked by his comment.

"Of course. But is this bad news? I don't know if I can handle any bad news right now," I tried to joke as I twisted the tag on my purse in a knot. The thought of something happening to our new, happy family unit was more than I could bear.

"Not *bad* news. I have no plans to leave you any time soon, but I would like to talk with you about our family business," he continued as he drove through the park entrance.

Family business? There it was again. Maybe now he would finally tell me all about it. Are we rich oil sheiks? Wild life explorers? Royalty? I know he told me on the first day we met that there was something odd about it. Who knows?

As we drove to the park, my thoughts passed easily into the reality that it was Father's Day. My Dad wasn't there to celebrate it again. This was the second time I had to endure it, in whatever small way, without him.

At the park, we laid out a little picnic lunch that Lilly packed for us. She was always so thoughtful. There were triangle chicken salad sandwiches, pickles, potato salad, lemonade and some of my favorite chips. She even decked us out with a red-and-white-checkered tablecloth.

As we sat eating our perfectly packed lunch, we watched as a cute little boy fed the ducks with his Dad. “Daddy, look, that one likes me. See, he is taking my food!” He screamed in delight as he pointed to a white duck with an orange bill. “Look Daddy, look, he wants more!”

“All right! Good job, Cal. You really are an expert at duck feeding. Just give small bits, since you want to make all the bread you have last,” the dad congratulated his son. “Animals seem to love you. You have the right touch, buddy.” The tall brown-haired man reminded me of my Dad. He was probably in his mid-twenties, but he had that boyish look about him that made him seem much younger. It was a day just with his son; I could tell he took a lot of pride in being a father. Yes, that’s what Father’s Day is all about: being with your kids.

I took a big bite of pickle and crunched a bit too loud. Observing how I was entranced with little boy, Joe commented, “I bet you miss your Dad.”

“Yes, that boy over there reminded me of when Dad used to take me here. He was such a great dad. I miss him so much. He was there for everything, every laugh, every cry. He never missed anything. I always came first in his book.” I could have said a lot more as I recalled what a good man he’d truly been. It was wrong what happened to my parents. It should *not* have happened.

“Do you hope to have your own family someday? To fall in love and have children?” Joe seemed intensely interested in my answer.

“I really don’t know what I want to do. I’m really torn. I don’t see a clear direction. I have never really been in love. I know that sounds sad, but I haven’t been interested in that sort of thing.” I stopped and looked over at Joe. He seemed concerned. “I mean, don’t get the wrong idea about me and love. I like guys; I just haven’t wanted anything serious. It seems like a painful process. I’ve watched my friend Claire go through it enough. And I get plenty of testosterone from Hayden and Jake, believe me.” We both laughed as we continued eating our lunch.

"Of course, there are not many people like you who love one person for a lifetime and don't even end up with them!" I said loudly as I wiped my mouth with the ironed napkin that Lilly had provided.

"Well, you're right. Not many people get the chances in lifetime that I have. Once I fell in love, she was it for me. No one could compare, I guess." I watched him as he drifted off in thought. "It's not all bad."

"But that brings me to what I need to talk with you about. Sorry for all the cloak and dagger, but I guess I was trying to find the right time to lay it all out." Joe chewed the last of his chips, snapping out of the earlier thoughts of this woman who had captured his devotion. "I have nothing but your best interests at heart, and I want you to be happy. But I think that you should know about your family, your special heritage."

I smiled, trying to lighten the mood. "This sounds major. Am I ready for this?" I wavered as I folded up the picnic blanket and put the remaining containers in the basket.

"Do you mind if we take a walk? Walking always helps me talk things through," Joe asked. We got up from where we were sitting and walked side by side admiring the wonderful scene the park provided. The picnic basket wavered back and forth on my clenched hand.

"I don't know if I need anything heavy right now, Joe. I mean, don't you think I have hit the limit for one lifetime?" I was a little worried; the feeling of the day had changed so drastically over the last two minutes.

"You *have* been through a lot. But it would be unfair to you to not tell you everything. You should know about your family. I want you to know what choices you have for your life. I guess there is no perfect time to tell you this," Joe said as he bent over and picked up a small round rock. He threw it across the water's edge and it skipped off the calm lake.

The sun was shining down and the wind was gently blowing through a tall weeping willow that was firmly planted near us. As the wind blew, its limbs moved closer. It was as if the tree was bending to hear what he had to say.

"Alright, I trust you. I guess I'm ready, then." I relaxed my shoulders, enough of this childish fear. How bad could it be? Of course, I'd not yet considered bank robbery or paid assassins. I smiled encouragingly. No, that just did not fit Joe!

Joe scratched the back of his neck, took a deep breath and stared straight into my eyes. "Your family comes from a long line of time travelers, Alex." He stopped, gauged my reaction and picked up another rock. I froze. "Time is like skipping this rock across the water. You can jump in and out of time." Joe picked two up this time and threw them both at a once.

I barely suppressed a smile. This was a joke, right? "Uh, huh. This is what you had to tell me? Thought we were about to have the serious conversation. Glad it was just about time travel." I laughed, pretending to wipe sweat off my forehead.

Joe stopped throwing rocks when he heard my sarcasm and placed his hands on my shoulders. He looked seriously at me now. "Listen. This is the truth. I know it's hard to hear, but you need to have an open mind. If you had been my daughter, I would have explained all this to you early in your life, like my parents did. You would have grown up with it. But your Mom did not want to involve you." Joe rubbed my shoulders as he seemed to realize that he was holding on too tightly.

Thoughts raced through my mind. Time travelers? There is no such thing. They make science fiction movies about this. I live in the real world, with real pain, and unchangeable loss. Who is he kidding? How could this be true?

"Come on, do you expect me to believe that you really travel through time?" I pulled back and shook my head. Things had been going so perfectly. I could not understand where he was going with this. "Time travel is stuff that books are made of, science fiction." I walked past him to the edge of the lake to watch more ducks enter the water.

I could hear Joe sigh. He didn't seem to know how to help me understand this other than to just tell me. "Alex. Your family is part of a long line of time travelers. *It is the truth,*" he stated firmly.

"You know, Joe, this has been a blessing, meeting you, having this time together. I just don't understand what you are trying to tell me." I felt weird; my stomach began churning my lunch around.

He came up behind me. "I have no intentions of lying to you." He continued patiently, "I'm here because I love you, because I care, because you are my family. You have got to listen to me. Just open your mind to what I am saying. You are a logical, straightforward young woman. Should I approach it in any other way?" I turned and Joe followed me down the bike path.

"Approach me about time travel? What are you saying? I don't know how I'm supposed to believe this!" I guess I *did* need another way around this information.

"Alright. Let me start from the beginning," Joe offered as we reached the park bench and he sat. I sat down too, still not sure what to make of this whole conversation.

"As far back, as recorded history, there have been time travelers. There are families of time travelers all over the world. I don't know exactly how many, but we are chosen by God. I guess sort of like angels. I mean, that's how I've looked at it." He paused and took a deep breath. "We set things right that should have been right in the first place. We can *change* things, Alex." Joe sat forward and looked at me anxiously. "Everyone who I'm aware of in our lineage has accepted the gift of time. Beth and I were raised by our parents to grow up to be time travelers. But your Mom decided... Well, something happened and your Mom decided not to." He looked even more frustrated now. "It's complicated there were reasons. It was not totally unheard of."

"She was raised to be a time traveler, but didn't?" I asked, feeling a sudden appreciation for my Mom; at least I knew *she* wasn't delusional.

"There were reasons, but that's not important now. But like I was saying, once you are eighteen, you can begin to time travel but not until then. You have to learn more about the world, be old enough to handle the challenges and understand relationships." Joe seemed aggravated, like he didn't know the right words to say or how to explain the concept to me. I sat there staring at him. I expected someone to jump out of the trees, telling me I was on a Candid Camera. This was just the sort of thing that the twins might pull.

Joe started to speak again. "Your Mom's choice not to be a time travel sort of translated into her not telling you anything about it either. I'm not sure why she chose not to tell you *anything* at all, but that was her decision. Even though I did not agree with her, I supported her."

He paused in thoughtful contemplation.

"She and I stayed in touch, but she didn't want me to be involved with your life. I think she didn't want me coming in and out of your life with no understanding of why. You would have had too many questions, too much to cover up. I tried to understand her wishes." Joe checked for any reaction from my face. Although he seemed to be dealing with the pain of my mother's decisions, I was still stuck in the fact that he said he was a time traveler.

"So what you are telling me is that *you travel through time* and that Mom didn't want me to know?"

"Yes," Joe stopped. He seemed to be waiting for an opportunity to see if I had absorbed what he just said, pleading with his eyes for understanding and acceptance.

"You can imagine that this is a little hard to believe?" I felt frustrated with his tale. "Why are you telling me now? Why did you tell me any of this? Especially if my Mom didn't chose that life for me? I mean, okay, you are a time traveler, why did I need to know?"

"Because I wanted to give *you* that same choice. After all, Alex, you are the last one in our family." Joe seemed so deliberate in answering me, almost methodical. Looking into his eyes, I could see that he truly believed what he was telling me.

"I *am* trying to follow along, just have some patience with me," I scowled as I flicked off the bug that landed on my knee. He seemed so serious about this, but how could time travel be possible?

"You can rewrite history," I stated.

"No. Not rewrite. Actually *change* what happened." He took another deep breath. "I don't have all the answers. So I'll just tell you what I know. I'll do the best I can to answer any questions you have, if you will have patience to listen and hear me through," Joe stopped again. Now there was such sympathy in his eyes. "Normally the kids in our family grow up knowing about it, just like you know that the earth is round and the sun will rise again tomorrow." I nodded my head. I wanted to hear more. I was trying to understand what was so important to him.

Joe began again, "Wait, let me start from another angle. You understand the concept of 'free will', right?"

"Yes, I think I understand it," I agreed.

"*Do you believe in God*? I know that is a blunt question, but I need to know what you believe in your heart," Joe asked as the weeping willow swayed like a mop in the wind trying to keep up with our conversation.

"Of course, yes, I do believe in God. I think my faith has certainly been tested, and there is no doubt in my mind that my parents are in heaven and looking down on me. I have to believe that God took them for a reason." I felt true conviction in my answer.

"Okay. God *is* there for us. But he created all of us to have free will. He has a plan, but things happen that are out of our control. And things happen that should not happen. That's where we come in. We set things right. I guess he selected our families to make sure that the right things happen...as they should have, to begin with." As Joe spoke, I was beginning to be more curious instead of insulted about what he was saying. But it did not make sense. God could do anything.

"Sometimes bad decisions are made." Joe continued, "And people's lives change in ways that were not meant to be. Accidents happen that were not supposed to happen. Haven't you ever heard that hindsight is twenty-twenty? Or ever heard, 'That was meant to be'? The only way to make things right is to recognize those errors and correct them." His words became more intense as he looked deep into my eyes. "We are part of God's mercy, a very human and interactive part. We are students of empathy. We see time from another dimension."

Change things? But how? How can he be a time traveler? Mild curiosity now changed into wanting to hear the mechanics of how this *could* be possible.

"Alex, if you need time to digest all of this, I can understand that. But what I'm telling you is true. We were chosen to travel through time. Remember what I was saying earlier about me running out of time?"

"Yes, I remember." Now I took a deep breath. What was this going to be about?

"Well, we are only allowed seven time travels in a lifetime. You can only jump back in time seven times. And I'll soon be leaving on my last trip back in time. Alex, I wanted you to know everything. I know the decision that your Mom made for you, yet... to be honest with you, I was hoping that you would want to be a part of this legacy. After me, you are the only one left to carry on our family's gift. There isn't anyone else to give it to." Joe's forehead beaded with sweat. He pulled out an old, yellowed handkerchief with a monogrammed letter "L" and wiped his head with it.

Reaching for something normal to say, I asked, "What does the 'L' stand for?" I was curious, but still lost in the fact that he wanted me to follow in the family business...as a time traveler?

"Do you mind if we cover that later? I think I have given you quite enough information to digest right now. Please think about it all. I can take you home when you are ready," Joe said, looking defeated and tired. Wordlessly, we got up and walked back to the car. I was carefully considering every single thing that he'd told me, even though none of it made any logical, scientific sense.

"Let's get together tomorrow." Joe seemed worried as he got ready to start the car. I don't think he expected me to easily or gladly accept what he was telling me, but I could tell that my reaction was less than he was hoping for.

"Why don't you just call me?" I answered, feeling so strange about the entire day.

We drove the whole way home in silence. I was willing to hear more, but I was confused. He was right; I needed time to digest it all. I just could not imagine that Mom would keep such a big thing from me, especially if it truly was a calling from God. She was such a spiritual woman. I had a hard time not being skeptical about all of this, but I had only seen truth in his eyes.

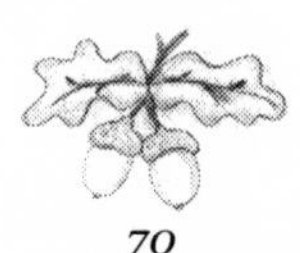

I walked to the door and let myself in. I knew Joe was standing by his car and waiting for me to turn around. But I didn't. I guess I should have asked him more questions. I needed to think about everything he said with a little quiet time at home. The thought that was currently on my mind was that either he is completely insane or I am about to learn about one of the greatest secret's that mankind has ever kept?

That night was like the first time when Lilly told me about Joe, all over again. I tossed and turned and couldn't get to sleep, no matter how hard I tried. If I believed him, did that make me crazy? Seriously, how could it *possibly* be true? Why would he tell me something that was untrue? Why tell me at all? He seemed perfectly sound to me. Maybe I should just allow him to *show* me. That's it! I needed proof. I needed to see it in order to believe it.

Chapter Nine

June 19, 1989

The next morning, I called Tabs and she confirmed that they would be by to pick me up shortly. "It's been a lifetime since we have seen you! What, your Uncle comes to town and our names are mud?" I finished dressing and pulled together my lake tote, just in time so see Tabs turning into the driveway. She quickly pushed open the door to the passenger side when she saw me coming out of the house.

"Please, no guilt trips. I did not pack *that* bag." I grinned as I got into the car. I was feeling grouchy but did not want to show it. Why spoil everyone's day with my worries about my crazy Uncle, the time traveler? Especially since our scratches and bruises were very evident reminders of how much worse things could be.

"Well, tell us everything. I want to know all about him. Skip no detail! Was he a missionary in Africa? Or, I know, a Swiss banker who could never leave work due to all the secret codes he knows?" Claire popped up from the back seat, dying for the mystery to be revealed.

"Hate to disappoint you, but neither is true," I chuckled.

"I don't know exactly where he has been. He just said that he has been away on business, that he was in constant contact with my

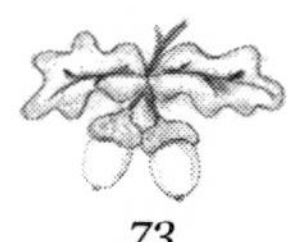

Mom and that he missed me and loved me. Isn't that all that matters at this point?" I looked around the car at the girls and they both gave disapproving looks. It was hard to be evasive, but they would think I was crazy if I explained the events of yesterday afternoon!

"Details, details Alex! Please don't keep us in suspense," Claire pushed. "What is going on? We haven't seen you in a week and now we need some details!"

"I told you what I know. All this time we have spent together has mainly been focused on me. He wanted to know about *my* life, what I have been doing. And we have really enjoyed each other's company. It's been great. It's just been family stuff the past few weeks, that's all." I paused to see if they were following.

"So, does he live in Alaska and does he have plans to take you back with him? Is that how all of this is going to end?" Tabs choked on her soda as she tried to drink, talk and drive at the same time.

"No, although I don't know exactly where he lives. I guess I haven't gotten that far. We've just been busy doing stuff. Going places. Having fun!" I agreed that was an important question that I should have asked Joe by now. Hmm, I did wonder where he lived; I was surprised I hadn't already asked him. "He's single and obviously, he doesn't have any other relatives besides me."

"Well, I think it is positively wonderful that he is in your life. I'm so happy for you, Alex. It's like a dream come true. Aren't you just so happy?" Claire, my hopeless romantic, loved that my life had something really good happening in it. "What does he look like? Michael Keaton? What?"

"I guess he is hard to describe, since he is my Uncle, but I think you would find him handsome, for an older guy. He is a little older than my Mom. He makes me feel comfortable and happy when I am around him." I smiled just imagining his fun-loving demeanor. I tried not to think of the serious conversation we had been in the day before.

"Of course, I'm starving for some time with you crazy guys! Let me hear what is going on in your lives. What have I missed?" I smiled at Tabs as she pulled up to the boat launch. We saw Hayden and Jake pushing the boat off the trailer into the water.

"Not much," Tabs laughed. "Hayden got in a fight at the last swim meet at Green Acres, watching that Logan guy. He got a good smack in the nose, but that's about it."

"Over what?" I had never heard of the twins getting into a fight.

"I'm not sure. But I think it had something to do about Logan having the hots for you. Anyway, I finished ten novels in the time that I haven't seen you," Claire woefully explained. "Seriously, isn't that what summer is all about? You just relax, enjoy it, and then get mentally prepared for college? Do not pass go, do not collect $200." She sounded sad about summer flying by.

The walking wounded all climbed on board and I draped myself over my usual spot on the back of the boat. I looked out across the water, requesting that all my questions be answered. My hair constantly tickled my cheek as the wind blew over the open water.

Some time later, a dragonfly landed on my elbow. Its opaque yellow wings flittered around as if he was trying to tell me something, as if he was a messenger for the answers I sought. He seemed so happy, so unafraid. Isn't that what I want for my life? Maybe that was what was missing, not being afraid of my future. Too bad I didn't speak dragonfly.

The twins had invented this little air-filled, raft thing that they thought could be the newest water sport fad. Hayden jumped off the boat and plowed onto the make-shift toy.

"I am telling you guys, we are going to blow this deal out of the water. They will be killing each other to grab one of these. It will take water sports to an all new level," Hayden explained as he shook the bottom of the raft and knocked Jake into the water.

"Dude, this was my idea, don't even tell the girls that it was yours. I *am* the genius behind this money maker!" Jake explained, his frustration evident, grabbing the raft and pulling it up to the boat to showcase his invention. "See, if you look at the quality of the workmanship, you will notice that it could only be 'the master' who could produce this type of detail." He proceeded to show all the areas that he'd handcrafted.

Without warning, Tabs took her car key and jabbed it right into the side of his yellow gold mine. "That's for all the times you threw me in the water. And for wrecking a truck that happened to be carrying me in the back. How do you like them apples, boys?" Tabs took a quick dive into the water and disappeared, swimming to the other side of the boat.

"That's just totally messed up. I can't believe she would do that," Jake said, incredulously, in quiet anger. The twins looked heartbroken as they stared at their raft deflating into a sinking pile of plastic.

"That is meanness to the core. I mean it takes a real animal to do something like that," Hayden sulked. "We didn't even finish the demo."

"I thought it looked really promising," I said, smiling. It really was a piece of junk, which I could see no promise in whatsoever, but I couldn't let them lose their dreams.

A few hours into the day, a thick, heavy cloud was rolling in quickly, and we decided to head back to the dock. I had been out on the lake many times when the clouds turned dark instantly. It can be hard to tell if a thunderstorm or even a tornado was coming. Once, a whole house was literally yanked up from the ground, like a loose tooth, right in front of us. It is terrifying to be on the lake in a storm.

We hit the pizza parlor after the boat that day. I was so hungry and still wanted more time with the guys before I went home and called Joe. Soon Claire was busily picking off all the pepperoni from her pizza while Tabs buried her slice in parmesan cheese.

"Are you going to ski on that slice or eat it, Tabs?" Jake couldn't help himself. There was more cheese than sauce on that slice. She continued to absentmindedly pour the cheese on.

"Real funny, real mature." Tabs gave out a fake laugh. I guessed they were over the key puncture incident.

"So, Blondie, where have you been for the last decade?" Jake joked.

"Just getting to know my Uncle," I said, as once again I began to think about what Joe told me. What if time travel is real? Who would not jump at the chance to travel through time, to do good things, to see how things really were?

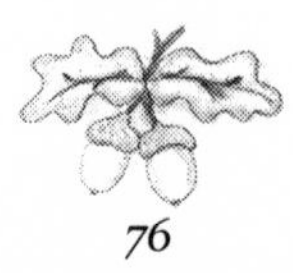

"Your Uncle! Since when do you have an Uncle?" Hayden butted in as he was spitting pizza, like a water sprinkler, on everyone at the table.

"Yes, an Uncle, you bonehead!" Tabs quipped. "Did you have water in your ears all day?"

The waiter walked up and slapped the check on the table, as he juggled a couple of empty plates. "Is that all?" he asked, relatively uninterested in our reply.

"Yep, we are good," Jake answered in a snappy tone.

"Yes, can we get back to our conversation people?" Hayden blurted.

"Yes, my Uncle. I didn't know I had an Uncle, but that is now entirely beside the point." I shoved as much pizza in my mouth as I could, so they would give me a minute to think. I had to be careful about what was said in front of the twins. They were just not as mature as Tabs and Claire. Or maybe I should say that they are not as careful, with what I would consider sensitive information.

"Oh, well, good news!" Jake changed the subject. "Speaking of bones, Alex, are you going to throw Andy one? I mean the guy has called you every single day this summer. I think it practically ridiculous that you aren't even trying to be available for him. You have to give a dude some hope," Jake said as he stared at me while I continued to stuff my face.

"Hope? Dude, why does she have to give him hope? Since when are you the ambassador of love?" Hayden snapped. It took me a minute to think about why Hayden said that.

"It isn't that I'm not interested," I gulped while thinking about my next statement. "It's just that I don't want to date anybody this summer. Andy is nice, but I'm just concentrating on you guys, my Uncle, Lilly and college. Possibly in that exact order. That's all. No room for anything else." Was that a look of relief on Hayden's face?

Tabs sucked up the last of her drink, making a loud slurpy noise with the straw. "Well, I think he is positively the stupidest person I have ever met, cute but definitely in the dumb jock category. Good thing that you are not interested, Alex."

"Who? Andy is the dumbest person you have ever met?" Jake shoved his way back into the conversation.

"Forget that, who else is in the dumb jock category?" Hayden quizzed as he elbowed his brother. "That's what we really need to know." It was laughable to think he genuinely was concerned about the answer.

"Well, there are you two, for starters," Tabs stated, her dry sense of humor evident. She did not give out even a complimentary laugh.

"Us? What, that's totally not true. We are smart, shockingly attractive, suave and tough as nails! We got it all, baby!" Hayden raised his hand and smacked Jake's hand, giving a loud high five.

"Boy, we better move out of this booth soon. The way their heads are blowing up, there won't be room for us." Tabs had to have the last word. Claire and I watched as the comedy team continued their entertainment.

It felt good to be with them. I laughed so hard, my sides hurt. Being with our group definitely was distracting me from what I had to do. I really had to make another decision.

That night, I went home, settled into bed, and called Joe at the hotel where he was staying. We had set up our daily adventures this way, me calling him the last thing before bed at night. "Hey, it's me. Did I wake you?" I *was* ready to talk to him now.

"No, no, not at all. I was just about to finish my book and call you."

"Can you come by in the morning? I'm sorry we did not see each other today. I needed to see my friends and get a break to process everything. You've laid a lot of new ideas on me, I hope you didn't mind. I know we have a lot more to talk about. I think I'm ready, and I want to know more." I waited to hear his response, while I nervously twisted my hair.

"Of course. I was planning on it. I know I shocked you with what I said but believe me, it will all make much more sense when you hear me out. Alex, it *is* all true." Joe sounded so calm, so deliberate.

"I *am ready* to hear everything," I comforted him. A lot had happened over the past few of weeks. Graduation, the accident,

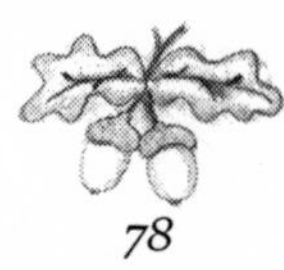

learning of Joe's existence, and now finding out about our family secret. It was so much to digest over such a short period of time. It was certainly intriguing. Joe said he was out of time. I didn't want to lose him. I wanted to ask more about everything.

My life was about to turn into a real life science fiction story. I took a deep breath and curled up in my bed. What would tomorrow bring?

Chapter Ten

June 20, 1989

When I woke up that morning, I realized I had overslept. Me oversleep? I was the girl who woke up at five in the morning like clockwork. My usual routine was simple. I jumped into my workout clothes and went downstairs to the basement, where my parents had set up a boss exercise area. I did a cardio workout for about an hour. Then a quick jump in the shower and out again. Breakfast was typically a bowl of oatmeal and a cup of coffee. Yes, at seventeen, I had to have coffee.

This morning, I slept until 8 o'clock. That was more sleep than I usually need. It was almost like I was releasing all my worries and resting at last, finally at peace with my mind. However, all of the questions that had been plaguing me about my future were now even more complicated. College, Uncle Joe, and now time travel. If Mr. Right comes along now, I'm in real big trouble.

When Joe arrived I was so happy to see him, so excited, and ready to learn. I felt like the first day in class at the beginning of the year. What would he say? We left right away and headed to a nearby little hole-in-the-wall breakfast hang out.

Joe put two packages of raw sugar into his coffee and stirred. Taking a large sip, slowly slurping up the hot java as he went, he looked straight at me. "So, how was your night?" Joe slurped again.

I laughed. Grown men just don't usually slurp like that. "I guess it was great. I literally crashed. I mean, I slept and slept. It was a strange thing for me. I'm kind of a light sleeper and I usually only sleep about six to seven hours a night. So I feel good today. I can't explain it." I took the creamer and poured it into my coffee. No sugar, but the cream makes it taste just right.

"Well, that's good. Rest is good. Calms the body and gets things in perspective. I feel like I could take on the world when I get a good night's sleep." Joe smiled at the waitress as she refilled his cup a second time.

"Can we just talk this thing out? I am *trying to believe* what you are telling me, but you have to admit, it's a little off the planet." I took a bite of my toast and waited for Joe to begin.

"Alright, I agree it is not a part of the normal human experience. But yes, let me just walk you through this whole thing. My parents told me at a young age about our family history. So I grew up knowing a lot about what our family did. The time travel, or jumps as we called it, were discussed in explicit detail. When someone returned from time travel, our whole family gathered around for days to hear all about it. As I grew up, I really looked forward to it being my turn. I had a conviction that I would serve others. To help others be on the right course." Joe's dialogue flowed along while we continued with our breakfast. A runny egg dripped down his fork and he hurriedly licked it up.

"I learned all about time travel, how it actually works, but I also learned about why we time travel. When you are young, you just think about yourself, your wants, your needs, your life. You feel like you will always make the right decision, almost as if you are invincible." Joe was using his fork in conversation, moving it around as he talked.

"But when you are trained from day one to serve others, it is pretty easy. I guess that the hardest part is deciding who gets chosen. Whose life is going to be changed? There are so many wonderful things that could be changed for the better. There are so many good things that could be done. There are so many people who deserved better than they received. Like I said the other day, we only get to travel through time seven times."

"Seven, huh?" I asked, remembering he had already told me that.

"Yep. So as I was saying, as time travelers, a lot of our lives are spent researching history. Deciding on the person or people who you will help. You get to decide on the wrong that needs to be set right." Joe thanked the waitress and she took his plate. What friendly service they had here today. Or was it Joe?

"So, do you mean that you could go back and shoot Hitler?" I wondered, as my thoughts began to digest some of what he was telling me.

"No. You can't change major historical events. Who knows what could have happened if Hitler was killed early in his life? There are too many events tied into killing Hitler that would change *all* of world history. I guess that sounds strange, but we have to be silent angels. We have to help everyday people who would never know that you saved their lives or helped them be with their true loves, that kind of a thing." Joe scanned my face for a response and then started up again.

"You have to carefully select those who you help. God won't let you create a big ripple in time. These are situations that will flow into the passage of time and not be noticed. It's a very long process, a research project that can take a while. Well, sometimes it is easy, and sometimes it isn't." Joe had the kind face that made me trust him from the day I met him. Things were definitely beginning to make more sense than the day before yesterday.

"I guess I wonder why God doesn't make sure things happen right to begin with," I asked, then swallowed a large mouthful of orange juice.

"Well, it's like I was telling you about free will. He has a plan, but if you jump in front of a bus and kill yourself, that's not what was supposed to be. That's where we come in; we are the stewards of time travel. We help humanity with setting things right." Joe was raising and lowering his eyebrows. What a clown. Even in the most serious of subjects, he could not seem to help himself and tried to make me laugh.

"Seriously, why did you decide to do this? What was the reason for you?" I wondered.

"I guess it was not a decision for me. It was continuing with the work our family was allowed to do. But really, more than that, *I want to do what I do*. If I ever had any doubts, they were immediately gone once I jumped the first time." I appreciated that he was being so understanding about my questions and concerns. The waitress stopped Joe's explanation with her presence.

"Get anything else for you today, hun?" She pushed the pencil in her hair, winking at Joe.

"No, we appreciate it. The check'll do." Joe smiled at her again, even though it took her a moment to walk away.

I sat in the booth across from Joe, finishing my banana pancakes, watching the syrup drizzle over the delicious stack. It was starting to make sense. In some ways, I was already beginning to believe him. I wanted to know so much more. I felt like a kid in a candy store. "So, I guess if I join you, we would travel through time and set things right as the dynamic duo?" I laughed.

"No, I wish we could. That's not how it works. You would have your own jumps. And then, when you get married, your husband would also become a time traveler. I mean, both of you will go on your own jumps, separately, you see?"

"Oh, really?" I quizzed, as I wiped the syrup drizzle from my chin with my napkin. I finished my last bite and moved my plate over. The waitress quickly came by and grabbed my plate, as smoothly as she possibly could, while lowering the check onto the table. It was like she was operating in slow motion deliberately, as she was decidedly fixated on Joe's face. She had been flirting with him the entire meal, but I didn't really pick up on it until just now.

"Hun, can I get you anything else? It would be my pleasure." She drew her syllables out in one easy sweet line and winked at him again. It was true southern vernacular, the way she talked.

"Nope, we are all set." Joe smiled at her and then back at me. He was oblivious to her flirtations. I never really thought of him as being that attractive, but it was clear to me that others certainly did.

Joe picked up the check and paid at the cash register, as the waitress yelled out, "Come back and see us again, won't you?"

"Wow, she was drooling on you like a hound dog on a bone!" I laughed.

"Huh? What are you talking about?" Joe was clearly embarrassed.

"As you would say, she was on you like white on rice. Are you seriously saying you didn't notice?" Of course, I had only just noticed it myself.

"How about let's just head home and I will keep answering questions. Questions about our family, not about the waitress, shall we?" Joe asked as I spotted a young boy hanging off the bubble gum machine in the doorway of the restaurant. He had his lips firmly perched on the spout so at the exact moment the gum came down, it would roll right into his mouth. Glad I was too full for gum.

"Can we keep the top up so we can continue talking?" I asked once we reached the car. We usually took the top down and enjoyed the summer sun.

"Good idea. Whatcha got for me?" Joe started the Bug.

"Do I just decide to start time traveling now, when I turn eighteen? Traveling through time by myself sounds a little scary and lonely, to tell the truth." I turned the radio down and looked over at Joe.

"It won't be scary. Lonely at first, yes, but you will learn how to make friends. It's part of what you have to do. It will seem like a mission, a safari, like an adventure. A big comfort is that you will be going back home at the end. And you can't imagine how incredibly cool it is to go to another time in history. It's just mind blowing. The details will really get to you at first. History books don't have sounds and smells. And, to answer your question, it does generally happen when you turn eighteen." Joe pulled into the flow of the traffic.

"And you are about to leave on your last mission?"

"Yes. Soon."

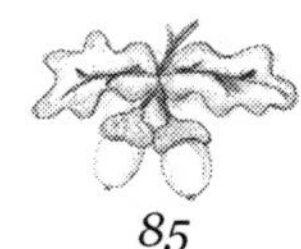

"What then? What then when you finish? Can you go on and live a normal life?"

Joe stopped the car at the red light and looked over at me. He looked as if he was trying to figure out exactly how to formulate his words.

"Actually, *I don't come back to this time*. I have stay in the time of my last trip," Joe slowly explained. "This is my seventh, and last, time travel."

"This is the reason that you are *running out of time*? Now I have to deal with you leaving me?" The banana pancake in my tummy was a little upset about this news.

"Let's not worry about that right now. We are going to have time together. Alex, this thing that we have, this gift, it is a privilege. It is the most awesome opportunity that anyone could ask for. And I would really love you to do me the favor of considering this possibility for your life. I know it is your life. It's your choice. I'm hoping that you will appreciate that I wanted you to know everything, that I'm not hiding this possible future from you." Joe paused, waiting for me to answer. I could tell he was anxious to hear what I was thinking.

I nodded my head, looking straight ahead at the traffic light as it turned green. "I actually do appreciate it all very much. I'm at a crossroad in my life. It seems so coincidental that you showed up on my door step when it was so unclear as to where my future would take me. I didn't have a direction. I felt lost. You have already given so much to me. Just knowing you over the past few days has given me hope. I *am* trying to believe you. And I *do* think you only want the best for me. You have to admit, proof does help with understanding things."

As I spoke these words, it became very clear to me that I would have to learn more. But if it was all true, if our family was what he said, I did want to be part of it. As my mind drifted into the imagery of a million different scenes in history, I wondered what it could be like if it were true.

If you stop and think how many times you have heard people say, *I wish I could go back in time and....* By my count, it was endless. And the thought that I could actually go back in time and change things for the better and experience history, up close and personal, was enticing.

Once Joe and I settled in on the couch at my house, I began the questions again. "What happened to all of our family? Why is no one left?" I cozied up with a blanket on my legs. It was a red and white knitted throw that Mom made for me several years back. I would not give it up for anything in the world.

"It's like I said, once you take that last time travel, you don't come back. So, whatever year that you take your last jump into, you stay in that time and continue your life. A quiet life, because we don't want to play with history. We just settle in, often stay to ourselves, and go with the flow. We all know it's coming, and it's hard. No one wants to lose their family, one at a time, but that is the price that you pay. By the way, did your Mom ever mention an Aunt Polly?" he quizzed.

"Vaguely, maybe. You know, I never saw any of our family through the years." I pulled the blanket up around my neck. I had a cold chill for a minute.

"Hmm... Beth didn't tell you very much. Well, Aunt Polly went back to save a man from drowning, and although she saved his life, she died of pneumonia." Joe stuck his pinky in his ear and gave it a tug as if he had water in it.

"What? Even when you are saving lives, you can end up losing yours?" I said, feeling aggravated. "You're not...protected?"

"Yes, it can happen. But in the end, she did the right thing. She knew the risks and felt it was worth it. The man she saved was able to make a lot of other lives better, without upsetting any major time currents," Joe comforted. "We go as prepared as we can and, like a soldier, we know that not everything is under our control."

"I guess that makes sense, but it is so bizarre that my parents...*Oh my God!!* I could save my parents! If it is all true, then I could go back and stop them from driving on that stormy night. I could change their history!" I jumped up off the couch and hugged Joe in total happiness.

"*Wait, wait, Alex.* I need to tell you that's not possible." And with those words, my heart sank and I let go of Joe.

"Why, why not? Why could I not save people who should not have died so tragically? I can't imagine a more perfect reason to change history. That was definitely a wrong that needs to be righted!"

Joe's smile was gone; he was calm and focused. "There are some things we just can't do. Unfortunately, you cannot personally profit from a time travel event. Believe me, I would have already saved them if I could do that." Joe sat me back down on the couch.

"I don't understand. What would happen if you did it anyway?" I scowled. For that I would risk anything!

"I'm not sure what would happen. You just never know. Some things have never been well explained. But I know we can't change our own family's destiny. A lot of this, the mechanics, is handed down verbally or in the archives of our family's library, in journals. For now, I'm sorry to say, our family can't save members of our own family."

"Well, that's simply awful," I pouted. I had to get my mind on something else quickly. I didn't want to think of their deaths at this moment. A new question popped into my mind. "I was wondering if you have already decided on your last travel. Where will you go? Do you know that already?"

I hoped to hear more about all of his travels. That surely would add some reality to this whole science fiction deal. I definitely wanted to know how he picked them and what happened during these events.

"Yes, I do. There are still a few more things to do, but I am pretty sure that I am ready. Leaving a modern age and joining one that is not as modern can be a little strange, but I will adjust. There is a lot of research, ways that you have to do things, learning about the local culture and such. You have to have an angle, a niche, and then blend in. It's harder than you think. Watching people without them noticing that you are watching is hard. Not using modern methods can be the hardest." He laughed and began again, "I'm not worried about it. But I'm sad that you and I won't be together longer. *I will miss you,* Alex. You have changed my life in so many ways. It feels so good that I might not be the last one in the family business and that the family may even grow again."

Joe looked happy at the thought of it. He pulled out his pocket knife and picked nervously at his nail. I started again, "You said earlier that when you get married, your husband can time travel. Why didn't Dad do it, then? If you knew him, you'd know he really loved an adventure."

"I think I know, but I'd better not guess at something like that. He knew about our family business, that much is for sure."

"It's just weird. I thought I knew everything about my parents. Dad said he was an orphan, which I know is true because he never knew his family, and I've seen all of the legal documents. Mom just said people died and she didn't have any living relatives left. I mean, I knew she grew up on a farm near a beach, but I guess I never thought to ask where it was or even ask to see where she grew up. She kind of avoided the subject, so I did not ask a lot of questions. Our lives were really busy with the present. I didn't take much time to think about relatives until my parents were gone. And even then, my friends pushed me along, trying not to stop and think about the loss too much."

"I can imagine that this has been hard, the last year-and-a-half. I wish I had been around. I was gone on a time travel jump that, well, let's just say, didn't go exactly as planned."

"What happened?" I was completely engrossed in what he was saying.

"I went back, I'll save the date for a later discussion, and had to set some things up for the future. It took a lot longer than I'd hoped. Someday, you'll meet her, I hope. The lady who I worked with, her name is Heidi. She is a good woman, but there was a lot going on. Honestly, the whole thing took a lot longer than planned."

"Did you save her? What happened?" My curiosity was overflowing.

"No, well, can we maybe wait on this question until later? It's complicated and won't likely make any sense. We would be kind of putting the cart before the horse."

"Well, at least tell me *how do you time travel*?"

"I'll show you. Can that question wait until I can show you?" Joe winked at me. "We're creating quite a list, aren't we?" He smiled.

"Yes, when will I see it, then?" I asked.

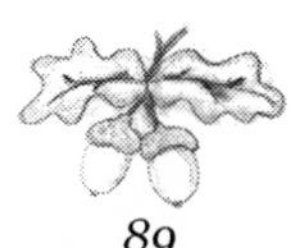

"I would like to take you to Wilmington; that's where the magic happens. It will all come together and make perfect sense. And then, well maybe then you can make a decision." Joe finished his nail job and snapped his knife back together.

"Is it possible to go soon?" I must admit, my curiosity was getting the best of me.

"Soon. Yes, I'll arrange it. We will go soon." Joe seemed so comfortable with the decision.

"You know, seeing is believing, and all that." Maybe if I could see how it happened, touch the things that make it happen, it would then all come together.

"Well, I have something for you right now that will surely be proof, if that is what you need," Joe added.

"What is it?" I sat forward and looked at Joe as he pulled his shoe and sock off.

"You and your Mom both have a birthmark, am I correct? And it looks the same?"

"Yes, how did you know?" He walked over and sat beside of me.

"Well, if I remember correctly, your birthmark is on your arm. And Beth's was on her leg. It's the shape of a heart. Very unique, wouldn't you say?"

"How did you know that? Did you see it?" I pulled my elbow up so that we could both examine my birth mark. It was a perfect pink heart.

"I knew about it because everyone in our family has one." Joe raised his ankle to the couch and we both reviewed the curious spot on his skin. "I occasionally caught a glimpse of yours in the pictures your Mom sent."

"We all have it?"

"Yes"

"Wow. I guess I did ask for proof, didn't I?"

"You did. We *are* human angels. I guess this is a way we are all marked."

"So how soon is soon?" I pressed again. Joe laughed with glee and replied, "How about tomorrow? Soon enough? Eight o'clock?" I

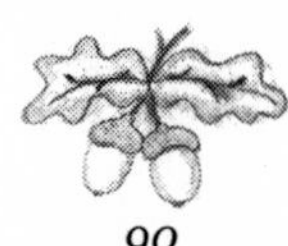

had a big smile on my own face when I gave him a hug and walked him to the door. Shortly, I could hear the "purr" of his little blue Bug go down the street.

I was alone again. I looked around the room, noticing everything. The family photo that we took when I was twelve, with a mouth full of braces was glaring back at me. The butterfly night light in the socket closest to the TV was buzzing. I even noticed every little tick Dad's pendulum clock made. And then I sat on the couch and stared at my birth mark.

Remembering another treasure, I walked over to the small cedar box on the coffee table and took out a tiny hair comb. It belonged to someone in my family tree and had been passed down to Mom. As far as I knew, it was the only thing she had from her relatives. I played with it as a child and imagined grand ladies wearing it in their hair. Maybe Joe would know. I'd ask him sometime.

Time travel? Could I really go to another time? Be part of the crowd and blend in? I've never watched people in this way. I needed an experiment, an adventure, to test my theories at this point.

Chapter Eleven

Evening, June 20, 1989

That evening, I decided to test my theory on blending in. I wanted a public place to people watch. I was going to try out my little experiment and see how it went.

Cedar Hill Mall is the biggest mall in the Raleigh Triangle area. Everyone goes there. Tabs and Claire joined me and we hit the ice cream shop first thing, as usual. Spending time with my friends I would miss for sure, if I decided to do this. And yes, if I *can* do this. But for today, I was on a simple mission and needed to focus on blending in and watching people. I needed to watch one person, to see if they noticed that I was following them.

I quickly picked out an older lady who was with her husband. They were in their late seventies, I would say. She was short, and very nicely dressed. She looked excited as if she had planned this trip to the mall for a week. Her clothes were simple, a cute flower linen top and some blue polyester elastic banded pants. Everything was carefully pressed.

Her husband, (yes, I was guessing) who held her hand, was tall and balding. Maybe that was as bald as he was ever going to get. He had numerous brown spots on his face. He was thin, with a small round belly that barely showed through his collared polo. He had on a brown pair of pants, brown socks, and brown shoes.

I kept an eye on this couple for most of the time we were there. The couple also did a lot of people watching, but I was sure to sit on a bench near to them each time they sat for a break. Boy, this was hard with friends in tow! Maybe that's why you time travel alone.

The couple looked so happy. I wish I knew what their lives were like. Did they have children? Were they retired? Had they been happy in their careers? Did they lose someone? What tragedies happened to them? What could have been *fixed*?

Towards the end of our trip, Claire asked to go to the food court for a little snack. She had to have a cookie, one of those overpriced kind with the two inch slab of filling in the middle. As we were standing there at the cookie counter, Hayden came barreling up.

"Why didn't anyone call us? We didn't know you guys were going to be here," he said, out of breath.

"Obviously, there was a reason for that," Tabs fired back.

"Oh, so you only want us for our bodies, then? Only when we are hauling you all over heaven's half acre on the water? In our swimsuits?" Jake blurted out.

"People, we are in a public place, keep your voices down," Tabs reminded them.

"Hey, Blondie, I got another one for you," Jake was infamous for coming up with new blonde jokes. He really wasn't trying to insult me; some of them were hysterical, and I got used to them through the years. After all, he was blonde too.

"Alright, whatcha got?" I smiled.

"What did the blonde say when she opened up a box of Honey O's cereal for the first time?" Hayden was already starting to laugh.

"What?"

"Oh goodie, doughnut seeds!" Hayden doubled over as Jake got the last words out.

"Another one, come on, another one!" Hayden begged.

"How do you get a one armed blonde out of a tree?" Jake raised his eyebrows and looked at me.

I jokingly answered, "I'm sure I don't know the answer to this one."

"You wave at her!" He jumped up and gave Hayden a high five in mid air.

"You guys are really mature. How'd you get so mature?" Tabs did not think the jokes were funny. She was getting irritated with how loud they were becoming. People were beginning to look over and watch us.

"Got it, let's go," Claire said as she reached to grab her cookie from the red-headed lady behind the counter.

As we walked away, Jake yelled out, "Wait up! What are you mall chicks up to tonight?"

"Alex asked for some G-I-R-L time, not some brainless wonder time," Tabs answered.

"You mean wonder-full time, like time well spent with us?" Hayden added as he slid in front of me and walked backwards.

"Guys, guys, I appreciate your interest. This is a girls' night for sure. We are going back to my house, painting our toenails, watching chick flicks, and talking about maxi-pads. Are you in?" I opened my eyes extra wide, waiting for an answer.

"No," said Jake, deflated.

"Let's go, bro. She had to go there! I mean really, all she had to do was say no." Hayden hung his head down, quietly laughing, and walked off with Jake. It wasn't like there weren't plenty of other options for the boys.

"That was rough," Claire said as she took a mouthful of chocolate double-decker-yumminess.

"I know. I just wanted to hang out with you two tonight. You never know when it could be your last day with me. I mean, with my luck, who knows?" I joked as we walked to Tabs' convertible.

"How morbid! Don't you dare say things like that, Alex! You were meant to do something important in life. There is a reason for everything that happens. Maybe you don't know it right now, but you will." Unknowingly, Claire was confirming what I was already feeling. I was beginning to see the bigger picture.

"Well, you never know when that handsome prince is going to carry me off to his romantic castle," I added to lighten the mood. Then Tabs put in her two cents. "Besides, we are not done torturing you yet, and then there is cleaning out your fridge of Lilly's leftovers." We were back in a good mood.

The parking lot was packed and it took a while to get out. We sat in silence. I guess she had a point. Claire was right. I was meant for something, some real purpose. Something that was really wonderful. I knew it now, for sure.

The next day, Joe told me all about "L" and I finally understood his sacrifice to be a time traveler and why he chose her. Anyone would be compelled to choose her after they knew the truth...

Chapter Twelve

June 21, 1989

From the moment that I met my Uncle Joe, my life changed. It was like being in a dark room, and now someone had turned the light on.

Joe was so fun, so exciting, so sure with what he wanted out of his life. It was intoxicating. It was what I craved; I needed a place to feel at home and a place that made my troubled heart feel at ease. My hopeless future now seemed hopeful.

What I had with my friends was true; it was the one real thing that kept me going along. But now I have more. I have a complexity to my future that I never dreamed possible. What did concern me was that Mom had wanted me to stay away from time travel. I worried that I would be going against her wishes that I would disappoint her. What were her reasons for not letting me know in the first place? Would she have told me when I turned 18? What if nobody told me and I accidentally jumped?! I would have to push Joe to tell me what happened.

I knew Joe would tell me everything that he could. He was literally crying out for someone to teach. He needed a perfect pupil.

And that was me. I resolved that I would absorb everything I could from him.

On the evening before I learned about “L”, I had a dream. A dream so real that for hours the next morning, I had a hard time believing that it had not happened. I hoped that it was no coincidence that I dreamt it on that night.

In my dream, Mom and Dad were still alive and it was just another normal day of school, homework and dinner. After eating our meal, my parents asked if they could talk to me for a while. This was not unusual either, since my parents were such an important part of my life. They were always involved.

What was different about this day, as it unfolded in my dream, was that my parents told me that they were going to die. They wanted me to know something tragic would happen to them. I was horrified that they thought they would die. But Dad leaned over close to me and asked me to listen, to have faith in what they were saying.

They told me that I was meant to help others. They needed me to learn a truth that they had hidden from me. Mom said not to worry, that there would be help. There would be someone to guide me along my journey after they were gone.

I felt confused and frustrated in my dream and, of course, didn’t want them to go. Dad said that they would never be totally gone. This was all part of the plan.

I woke up with such pain in my chest it felt as if my heart was literally breaking. I missed them so much! It was a horrible sick feeling realizing that they were *not alive*, although I felt I had just talked with them. They did die; it had all happened. Was this my psyche reliving what happened and trying to comfort myself with the idea that they believed in time travel?

By the time Joe picked me up, I felt more confident. I was ready for whatever lay ahead of me. Joe walked around to open my side of the Bug’s blue car door. “I am glad to see your smiling face, my dear. It looks like you had a good night and a good sleep, yes?” As usual, Joe was grinning from ear to ear. I quickly hopped into my seat.

“I did sleep well,” I happily lied. Joe walked around the car and slipped inside the plastic seat beside me.

"Alex, before we leave this driveway, I have to ask you something. I hate to put you on the spot, but are you feeling like this is the right thing for you? That you want to know all there is to know?" He asked me as if the world depended on my answer, depended on my giving the *right* answer.

"I have made a decision, and it was partially due to a 'wonderful' dream about my parents last night. I do think this is the right thing to do. I am at peace with this. Besides, I'm dying to know more, to really understand!" I smiled at him remembering what Dad said in my dream. Was Joe my guide? I now felt a crazy curiosity to open door number one.

The decision was thrilling and scary at the same time. It was the mother of all sky diving jumps. It was the worst case of goose bumps on a hot day. And at the same time, it was like holding a baby kitten. Or maybe it was simply like driving a car for the first time, sweet, wonderful and free. I was truly happy for the first time in almost two years.

At graduation, when I'd walked across the stage to pick up my diploma, there was a great sense of accomplishment. But I was so sad at the same time. Sad that there was such a great void in my life. Anyone who has lost someone close to them knows exactly how it feels. You never get over the loss. You learn to live *with* it. For a long time, you feel as though you will never be truly happy again. But I *was truly happy* this day.

"I am so relieved, you have no idea! Of course I knew that would be your decision. Never had a doubt. I was hoping that we could spend the whole day together. How would that be?" Joe asked, as he smiled knowing that there was only one answer that I could give him.

"Yep, it's a plan then!"

"Okay! I'll show you everything I can about time travel. I can't wait to see your reaction to some of it. It's incredible and beautiful. I am so happy that I can share this gift with you! Now, before I tell you about 'L'..." He asked me one more question before we backed down my driveway on that sunny day. "Alex, I know you have never been in love, but do you believe in true love? Do you believe that love can last a lifetime? Even beyond life itself?"

Joe's question gave me great pause. Did he love this "L"? Had she been *the one* and he had to let her go?

"The reason that I need to know this is because the "L" who you want to know about was my one and only true love. I have to know that you can open your heart to my story without judging me. Not everyone can accept that you can love someone so completely that no one could ever replace them. I don't expect anyone to agree with what I have done. It's a choice that I made, but one that I need you to have an open mind to."

Wow. I felt so important that he felt comfortable enough to tell me something so precious to him. That he trusted me enough to share what he held closest to his heart. To open himself up to my reaction.

"Yes, I *do* believe in true love. I just never experienced it myself. But I know it was shared between my parents. I know that they truly loved one another. I do believe that it happens, that you can love someone for a lifetime."

Joe seemed glad to hear my response. He turned the key in the ignition and celebrated, "And with that, we are off!" The little Bug hummed down the road and headed to our regular breakfast spot.

"I thought I would take you back to the park after a quick bite, does that work?" Joe asked.

"That's perfect." I dropped my head back on the headrest and soaked up the summer rays. I wish Claire was here. She loved a good love story. I wanted her to hear what Joe was going to tell me. Maybe someday, somehow, I could tell her. I wouldn't have to mention names.

We continued to talk about time travel as we finished our breakfast, and he answered another one of my big questions. "Can we go anywhere, like France, and save someone there? Of course, I don't know French, so I would have a little trouble there."

"Yeah, good question. Well, I guess so, but generally speaking, you don't want to wander off too far from where you start your time travel. If your mission was in France, it could take months, years even, with the way transportation worked in the past, to get there and then home again. I guess it is possible to do that, but with their being other time travelers, we usually stick to our own neck of the woods. Stay kind of local and help out our surrounding people." Joe shook his head as if he was agreeing with himself. "We usually don't want to take on real long projects because it becomes important to complete all seven time travels. To make the most use of the gift."

"Oh. Hmmm. Well, how far have you been?"

"No more than about one hundred miles away. I think it's really as far away as you should go from our family's home. Yet, other time travelers have gone further. Of course, the further you travel, the harder the logistics. We'll get into that."

We finally headed to the park. I was working through my mind that this love in Joe's life must have been a high school sweetheart, someone who he had to lose in order to pursue his destiny of being a time traveler. I was glad I did not have that decision to make. I would never leave Lilly or my friends forever. I would have to explain what was going on somehow. However, after all, I really didn't know at this point what impact it would have on my life.

We walked back over to our little bench, the one that sat beside the curious weeping willow. It seemed happy to see our return, and rustled from one side to the other in the summer breeze. As I sat down on the bench, I quickly closed my eyes and listened to the leaves, the branches, the sounds so calming, so relaxing. I took a deep breath and found an inner peace that told me I was *ready* to hear everything.

Turning and looking at Joe, I said, "I want to hear your story." I was comfortable and looking forward to hearing every detail about a woman who seemed to mean so much to my Uncle.

"Alright, here it goes. "L" stands for Laura. Laura was the subject of my first time travel. She was the first history, if you will, that I chose to change," Joe began. "And this is a story with a moral. A moral that I hope you will keep in your thoughts for the rest of your life, Alex. The moral is simply to always do the right thing, even at your own expense. You will find out the price that I paid." Joe relaxed and looked out at the calm, quiet waters of the lake, and began.

"I was eighteen years old when I took my first jump. I was excited and worried, all at the same time. It seems like it takes a very long time to choose exactly the right person to help, especially on your first go at it. You feel that it needs to be a strong and worthy cause. Seven is not very many choices when you realize the possibilities. When you research, you see so many events that you feel could be changed for the better. You have one end of the spectrum, with an everyday person who doesn't win a trophy and leads a depressed life after that. Or the opposite end of the spectrum, with some major historical event that impacts world history forever.

I have always felt that love and life were the only two reasons to change history. I probably got that from your great-grandfather. Saving someone's life and helping love to happen as it was meant to be. I decided that would be my focus with every time travel jump; I promised myself this from the first day I started my research.

And when you get started, you naturally gravitate to the time in history that you are most interested in. The time you want to know the most about. In school, being a history buff already, I really paid close attention to those historical events that created the most interest for me.

I liked learning more about the Civil War than any other time in history. I was a little worried about going back to those years, mainly because of health issues and the fact that there was obviously a war going on. You *do* worry about those things. If you get hurt or sick in the past, you can always come back, but sometimes you can't make it back. If you die in the past, you're dead."

"What do you mean, if you die? Like what you were saying about Aunt Polly?" I sat up a little on the bench and picked a willow leaf off the tree.

"Yes, well there is that. You could get sick in the past and then end up dying in your own time. There isn't any pain or injury sustained as you time travel. Anyway, like I was saying, the Civil War was a time of great chaos and I could have died there from any number of things." Joe plucked a leaf too and started rolling it with his fingers.

"I understand. Sorry to interrupt. I'll probably have to ask a few questions along the way," I said with a smile. A bike rider whizzed by, his new helmet bounced sunlight into our eyes with a quick blinding effect.

Joe continued, "I learned as much as I could about the Civil War, knowing full well that there would be plenty of opportunities for me to help someone. But who would I choose? When you go to another time, it can *actually take some time* to achieve your goal. You don't just pop into that moment, fix it, and jump back. Several of my jumps took longer than I expected to achieve the goal."

"Does time change in the present?" I tried to wait with more questions, but I couldn't help myself.

"Well, your life continues, no matter what. Meaning, the length of your life elapses at the same rate. If you are in the past for a year, when you jump back, you will physically be a year older and the time will be a year further along. Time passes here at the same rate."

"So if I jumped when I was eighteen from the year 1989, and went to 1930 for a year, when I got back, it would be 1990 and I would be nineteen years old?" I was drawing the paths in the air with my fingers.

"Yes, that's right."

"Alright, I'm sorry; I threw your story off track."

"Okay, so, I'm a kid trying to figure out my first jump. Then I read a story about a girl who died in the Civil War; her name was Laura. When I read about what happened to her, I could think of nothing else. Her story was so unbelievable to me, so horrific, that I knew beyond a shadow of a doubt that she was who I wanted to help first. It was so clear. Yet, she was the one who *taught me* the true meaning of selflessness.

My first jump happened to the year 1865. It was a very well-documented historical time in our nation's history. There were many history-changing events going on: brother against brother and all that jazz. I'm sure you have heard about in school." Joe looked at me. I could already see his passion for that time period by the way his speech elevated in excitement. I loved history as well, so the Civil War was a time that also intrigued me. It's still all around you in the South."

I jumped at the chance to answer him. "I do remember a lot about it. It was a very tragic war and there was a lot of suffering. It's really hard to believe that Americans even fought against each other in that way. It was a time full of hardship and loss." I was already beginning to take myself back to that time in my mind. The willow created such a peaceful movement that it truly allowed me to quiet my mind and focus only on Joe's calm voice and the place he was taking me to.

Joe continued, "There were a lot of farms back in that time. People in the South grew what they ate. In fact, most men were farmers. Crops were everywhere, on every road, at every house. Ella Laura Chestnut lived on such a farm.

Their farm was called Chestnut Grove. It was about 90 miles north of Wilmington, South Carolina, in a small town called Bentonville. It was a beautiful, calm town that captured the earth and its beauty in its purest form, perfect and simple. Yes, perfect and simple... that also describes Ella Laura Chestnut." Joe looked at me again; his eyes were so full of compassion, so centered on thoughts of her. "The town as it was then does not exist anymore; it's just a battlefield, a museum, now."

He sighed and then started again, "Like I mentioned before, you don't go back and save JFK or anything. You chose from your heart and you will *know* it is the right thing to do. Laura's plight was the one for me. She had such a kind and gentle heart, unlike anyone who I have ever known. She had a loving father and mother at the time of her birth, the third child in her family. Only her older brother, Lucas, was still alive at the time of my jump. By the time he was eleven years old, he was as much the man of the house as his father. Her father died that year, when Lucas was eleven, and then her other brother died from chicken pox and left Laura and her mother to manage the farm alone with Lucas."

I broke the story with a question. "Her father died? From what?" I wondered how traumatic this story was going to get.

"I don't know, but he was a young man. Things happened much quicker back then, marriage, children, everything. You talk about having stress to make decisions at eighteen. Imagine being married at sixteen or even fourteen!" Joe laughed. "But seriously, I don't know why her father died."

"This is already sounding like something I know about." I ached, thinking about my parents.

"Laura took on all the normal chores that children did in those days, from laundry, cooking and cleaning the house, to picking the crops and canning. She learned early in life that she had to work to survive. It was the way for most everyone in the South. In 1860, South Carolina was the first state to leave the Union. In a way, that was just politics. What does a kid care? But a depression had been growing for years. And then, the war was horrific, you know. Laura had been living with the war since April 1861, almost four years before I arrived.

By the time I jumped into Laura's life, everything was barely surviving, including the soldiers who were wearily heading back to their homes. They were filthy, tired and injured. Most of them were so starved and diseased, they would literally eat anything or do anything for food. There were stories of starved men eating bark and grass, going days without real food.

In all, about 620,000 Americans lost their lives, either in battle or afterwards from famine and disease. About 50,000 came home as amputees, and could not live normal lives after the war. When I went back in time, it was during the Battle of Bentonville, which was very close to Laura's Chestnut family home. So as you can probably imagine, it was a grisly scene for so many.

It was during this time, when Laura was seventeen years old, that this battle was fought so close to her home. By now, they had lost everything, including their Cause, their crops, their livestock and their men. It was a time of great sadness in history and in Laura's life.

Lucas had been gone for years as an enlisted soldier. There had been no word from him for some time. Early on, he had written and seemed upbeat and looking forward to coming home soon. But it had been several years and there had been no more letters.

Laura and her mother tended the farm and home as best as they could with very limited supplies. Her mother seemed to get sick a lot, and Laura tried to keep things afloat. With the livestock gone, all of the work had to be done by just the two of them. Hauling bucket after bucket of water from a well or the nearby river was a task in itself. No indoor plumbing back then, you know."

"I know. I can't imagine it. I don't think I could live without a hot shower." We laughed as Joe resumed his tale.

"Laura once told me a funny story about this time. A Northern troop invaded their property looking for food. Laura pulled all the meat out of the barn and covered it with flour, as the enemies headed up her clay road. The troops thought the flour was poison so they left the pork. It was a real good hiding-it-in-plain-sight trick. That pork and some potatoes were about all the food they had left. She told me about this when I was there, about how she outsmarted the men. She was proud of her achievement, saving what little bit she could of what they had left.

Yes, this was the period when I made my first time-travel jump. I went back to stop what I knew was going to happen to Laura and her mother. I knew what would happen because I read the diary from an injured soldier who had been to the farm, and from the letter that Lucas wrote. Those were both saved in the archives that we have stored at our family home." Joe stopped and looked at me.

"Our home? Where *do* you live? I have been wondering about that," I asked, happy to think that I had a family home.

"I hadn't told you? It's in Wilmington, North Carolina. It's a home that I will take you to. It is where all of our family has time traveled from. Yes, I will take you there as soon as we can arrange it. It's the place that you need to stay close to when you time travel. Anyway, this battle occurred not very far from our family home." Joe rubbed his feet back and forth on the gravel. I could hear the sand paper-like noise; he seemed a little nervous now.

A tall, dark-haired woman bounced along the path in front of us, with a small terrier on a leash. She took a long appreciative glance at Joe and continued on. Joe did not even notice.

"Yes, I do want to see the house!" I jumped in with hopes of getting him started again. "I would love to see where our family grew up and lived." Just the thought of being close to a history of my own, to *my family's* history, made me feel so excited. I could see where Mom had lived when she was a child. It was suddenly so important for me to know who I am and where I came from. I'd felt like a single puzzle piece for the past year-and-a-half. And now, pieces were beginning to connect to me, building a larger picture, one part at a time.

What would my great-grandmother have looked like? Would there be something with her handwriting that I could touch, and see for myself who she was? Were there any portraits? Would there be one with a lady wearing the hair comb? What brought her and my great-grandfather together? Who time traveled first? There was so much to learn, so many people to learn about.

But right now, I wanted to hear more about Laura. I ached to know how she impacted my Uncle, this man I was really beginning to love. Finally, Joe began again, "I think I am going to stop telling you about my trip to the past, here. I would like to tell you first why I picked Laura, what happened to her in history, before I went back and *changed her history*. It's a very hard story to tell and you will have to bear with me. I can't believe that anyone went through what she did, which of course, is why I did *what I did*. That is why I chose her."

"Joe, don't worry. Whatever it is, I can handle it. I'm tougher than you give me credit for." I wanted to make it clear then and there that I was a bull when it came to getting what I wanted.

"Maybe early next week," he regressed, "I would like for us to travel to Wilmington and show you something that will help you understand how I was able to help her and change her life, to put it back on the right course. Are you okay with that? I have to know that you will hear the whole story through. Will you be able to handle not knowing the whole sequence of events for a couple of days?"

"I think I can handle it. I'm sure I can keep in mind that it is not the reality of her life, that you changed the awful thing that happened." And with that comment, I pulled out a bag of apple slices I had stashed in my knap sack. Offering Joe one, we both took a mouthful and crunched, while I anxiously waited for him to begin Laura's tragic story.

"As I said, Laura and her mother were awaiting Lucas' return from the war. There was no man at their house, and the home had served as a mock hospital during the battle. I can only imagine that the cries and pleas from the soldiers were unbearable. Medical attendants did the best they could to help the victims, but countless amputations took place with no anesthesia, among other things. There was no Red Cross. Two thirds of the dead did not die in battle.

Laura and her mother baked loaves of bread and prepared soup and shared what they could with the soldiers. Only keeping the soldiers fed and clean could help the men to mend. Laura would fill up their canteens with water and feed them with what she had. By the time those horrible weeks were over, they had helped over five hundred men at their home.

I found that it was a very interesting time in history as I learned so much more, so many things that we never have to think about now. For example, today, you would go buy a loaf of bread at the grocery store. Back then, in order to have a loaf of bread, they used something called a dough trough. It was a little wooden box where you put the flour and baking soda in to allow the dough to rise." Joe raised his hands to show me how big the box was and laughed when he began his next sentence, "I guess I now know what is bigger than a bread box!"

I had to jump in. "That is neat, though, making bread for food and taking care of the sick and giving their home to help the soldiers. What a compassionate thing to do," I added as we continued to munch on our apple slices.

"I honestly think it was a matter of survival. Many of them could not go any further. I must admit I was shocked to see men like that. Times are different now. You don't see people looking like that in our time, obviously. Anyway, their home was situated close to a riverbed, Mill Creek. The location alone naturally drew in soldiers in search of water and rest, in addition to those who were sent there from the battle.

Laura must have had so much on her mind, so much to bear. I'm sure all she needed to know was that things would get better, that she would survive, and have a life and a family of her own. And then it happened. She was outside one evening, at the old tobacco barn, when a rogue soldier in blue uniform found her along his way. An unwelcomed Yankee on a Southern plantation." Joe put his hand over mine, as if to reassure me everything would be okay.

"This is when it gets rough, isn't it?" I nervously asked, swallowing my mouthful of apple in one gulp.

"Yes, this part is very hard to hear, but you must in order to understand. And remember, you won't know how things changed until we go to Wilmington. Remember that it did turn out okay." Joe was obviously still grieving over what happened, his tone more somber, even though now it had *not* happened at all.

"I can handle it. I'll remember what you told me." I smiled at Joe and focused on the swaying willow. The peaceful noise reassured me and Joe continued.

"I could not imagine anyone going through this and my heart ached for her pain. The soldier forced Laura into the tobacco barn and he...violated her in the worst way. A short and horrific experience, but nonetheless, it left her pregnant." I gasped and put my hand to my mouth. I couldn't believe it. Why would someone do that to an innocent girl?

"Let me continue on. One of the southern soldiers caught the nasty wretch and killed him. While Laura kept her little secret and continued to care for the wounded, her mother began to lose faith that Lucas would return. She lost her mind more and more with each passing day. After only a few short weeks, she was unable to continue on, to contribute to the work. She kept to herself in bed all day. Laura was in the worst possible situation. Only seventeen, no family to count on, and an unwanted child on the way.

Day in and day out, she cooked, cleaned, helped to mend the sick, and kept her mind busy. It was life, not a life worth living but she made it a matter of survival. She was just trying to survive. One of the southern soldiers in particular, who knew what happened to Laura, wrote an account of it for Lucas to find. He also wrote about her mother's ranting; she truly had lost her mind, what I can only imagine to be a nervous breakdown. And it got worse. Her mother discovered that Laura was pregnant. It is a mystery as to how this was revealed.

What happened next is just horrifying and unreal. But it happened. Laura's mother, in a state of delirious confusion, took her daughter into the woods one evening after finding out about the pregnancy. No one knows what she said or how she accomplished it, but she took her deep into the woods and tied her to a tree – and she left her," Joe almost whispered and stopped again. "The soldier's pages told us only a little of what happened. When her mother returned home that evening, all she would say was that she would not have a daughter of her flesh and blood bearing a child of a stinking Yankee."

"She left her. What do you mean?" I became suddenly sick to my stomach.

"She left her. *To die.* Tied to that tree." Joe began to softly cry, the tears dripping down his cheek. He grabbed his "L" handkerchief. "That was what happened to my 'L'. And now you know why I could not let that happen. No one should die in that way. She was a good person who did so much for so many. Her life was too precious to waste." Joe wiped his eyes again and sat up from his slouched position.

"Yes, I chose her life to save first. I think I felt love for what she sacrificed for the soldiers. She helped men continue on. Men who had been so ravaged by the war. I couldn't see why she could not go on to have a family and have a chance for a real life." Joe stopped and took a deep breath. "Do *you* see why I chose her?" He looked so innocently at me.

"I do. And I can't think of a more noble reason to change history. I understand. I can see the pain; all you wanted to do was save her."

It had been a long day already. As he talked me through what she had experienced, it was like I was back in time with Laura, feeling her pain, feeling her loss, feeling her trauma. My body was so tense with worry about what happened. I could feel that my shoulders and my chest were tight.

And then I could feel another wave of sickness in my stomach over what must have happened to her in the woods. What grief she must have experienced, knowing her mother did this to her. That the only person she had in the world right then had betrayed her. She needed help from someone, somewhere, somehow. And then I focused on Joe who must have gone to her, and surely, she never knew what almost happened.

It weighed heavy on me as we drove home. We were quiet in the car on the way back. I knew all would be revealed in Wilmington. I would find out how he helped her, and I could only imagine that it was a beautiful story.

Joe left me that night with so much to think about. In such a short time, I found out a great deal about my family's work. His story seemed so real, going back in time and saving this woman. The pain was all over his face. The potential loss so real for him, even years later.

Is it true? It's got to be true!

Chapter Thirteen

Morning, June 22, 1989

First thing the next morning I thought of Claire. I called her after my morning workout. "Hey! What the heck are you up to? Where were you yesterday?" Claire squealed over the phone.

"I know, I spent yesterday with Joe," I said as I hoped she would come over and spend some time with me, but wasn't sure what Joe was up to either. He had not called me yet and I figured if he did, he would understand Claire being there for a while.

"Well, I know it is early. I wanted to know if you and Tabs had any plans this morning?"

"No plans. We've got to get you out on the lake soon. Hayden blew up the tube on Saturday. He took it to the gas station to fill it up with air and, being the dumb butt he is, he didn't tie it on the back of his truck. And what do you think happened? Yep, once he hit forty miles an hour on the highway, it flew off the back and blew a giant hole into it. Scared cars behind him half to death, no doubt. But at least he is driving again. That much is a good sign," Claire giggled.

"Oh geez, what a mess. I would be sick. He paid a lot of money for a tube in the first place. But what a totally normal thing to expect

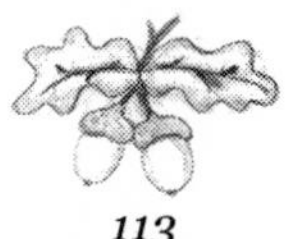

from the twins. Can you come over this morning?" I was hoping I could relax and just have some mindless gossip with a girlfriend.

"Alrighty then, I can be over in a few. Have you eaten yet? I can bring over buns and coffee." I was already getting my lips set on the deliciousness of the sweet and pungent combo.

"I'd love it! See you soon. Make that sooner! I love your culinary sources."

When Claire arrived, we talked for hours as she covered every tidbit of news that I had missed. The licking and lip smacking was out of control. Sticky buns and coffee can make quite the mess, but we managed to pretty much keep it together as we chatted away.

"So Melanie, you know that quiet girl from school, is dating this guy who that is built like a Trojan. I mean, I think he falls into the giant category. I have never seen someone with size fourteen feet, but guess what, I literally saw the shoe size myself," Claire croaked as she was tickled to death over her discovery. "Believe me, that is how bored I was when I saw him."

"Who cares what his shoe size is? Break out the sizzle, sister, and tell me how she met him!" I could not wait to hear how Melanie's famously overprotective mother allowed anyone into her life.

"Well, the 411 is that he is a college student," Claire began.

"What? Are you joking? An older man?" I asked.

"Yep. No joke. And he is like thirty years old too," Claire added.

"Uh uh, you are joking!" I doubled over screaming. I could not believe this!

"Yep and he thinks that she is the cat's meow too! It would make you puke to see them together. He fawns all over her like some blubbering idiot. And I really can't believe that her mother allows this. I bet you a million bucks that her mom knows nothing about it."

"I'd bet the same. This is absolutely hysterical. Is she still going to go to college? I mean, surely, she's not quick-hitch serious about him?"

I popped another chunk of cinnamon bun in my mouth and swigged it back with my café au lait. Claire folded her legs under her body on the couch and put her coffee mug on the table.

"No, no, I am sure she is going to college. She just met the guy. I'm positively sure she will dump him before the semester starts. She's just trying to yank his chain and her mother's, no doubt. I mean, it hasn't been that long since they met. It's just funny to see them together."

"Where did you meet him?" I wondered what other social events I had missed. I didn't seem to recall any parties that I was invited to and declined.

"Oh, we saw him at Gabby's house. Gabby had a pool party yesterday. Seriously, it was the lamest thing I have ever attended in my life. She had like a bag of pretzels and some sodas. Not that we needed some catered event, but throw us a sheet cake at least! She had her little brother there and he was so pesky, I was just wishing I had a giant fly swatter. You missed nothing, Alex."

"Well, why did she have the party and who went?" I unwound another piece of sticky bun and bit it off in another big bite.

"I don't know why. I guess to break up the summer a little. I mean, I wanted to take you too, but you were at the park with your Uncle. It was very last minute."

"Oh, and who went to the party?"

"The twins, of course. Although they stayed for about two-and-a-half seconds when they saw the sustenance that was being offered and decided it was not adequate. Tabs wasn't there. She was busy with some club thing. A few of the guys from the swim team and, I don't know, maybe some of her relatives. I mean, it was the worst."

"And there was Melanie with her man." I couldn't help but laugh at the sound of it. Melanie was the size of a peanut, so I could only imagine how it looked to have a giant standing beside a peanut.

"Yes, and *that* was the entertainment."

"What else is going on in the world?" I finished the last sip of my coffee and pulled on my fluffy pink socks.

"Yay, you wear those! I love those socks. I gave those to you for..." Claire paused to think, "Christmas, junior year, right?"

"I think so. I wear them all the time. They make me feel pampered. Anyway, how have you been? What else is going on?" I rubbed my legs. I remembered I had not shaved in several days; it just

had not been on my mind, like it is when I am on the boat every day. And then with the scars still healing, who cares?

"Not much, Alex. I really can't even think of anything else, it has been weird not having you running around coordinating all of our social events. We have officially decided that you are the event coordinator, and without you, we're just making bad choices. Gabby's party, case in point." Claire's eyes widened and looked right into mine with blame.

"I know, hopefully I can get back into some of that soon. I really don't know when Joe is going to leave again, and since I just found him, I want to spend every moment I can with him. I'm really having such a wonderful time." I thought of Joe. He had been absent from my thoughts ever since Claire showed up. I fell right back into high school drama when she arrived, and forgot the rest of the world.

"So are we ever going to meet this Uncle? More important, have you seen Lilly?" Claire noted that she did not see the type of food in the kitchen that Lilly left for me on a daily basis.

"No, I haven't. She is my next stop after you. I think I'll go over there today. Want to go?"

"I can't. I promised my grandmother that I would take her to the doctor today. I have been avoiding it at all costs, believe me. Seeing your grandparent slip naked into a hospital robe should be illegal. I mean, I just know I have a place in heaven for all I have already have done for her. Let's us not mention those things." Claire shook her shoulders as if she had the willies.

"I can only imagine, Claire. Bless your heart. Oh well, at least you have grandparents. I would trade being you for anything in that regard."

"Oh, I know. I'm sorry, Alex. I know you do. And I'm not complaining. It's just kind of weird seeing your grandmother in her birthday suit. The things that happen to our bodies when we get older are just heartbreaking. In any case, I have to take her, so I will miss the visit with Lilly. Tell her hello for me. I do have to run soon." Claire wiped the crumbs off her lemon yellow gingham top and reached over to pick up her giant mug.

"Well, I am glad we got to talk a little while. It seems like forever. Not being in school and not seeing everybody all the time is just weird." I yawned as I pitifully commented and got up and took my cup into the kitchen sink to rinse.

Claire followed me and rubbed my back, "Are you alright? Got things on your mind?"

"Honestly, I think I'm just missing my parents. You have heard it all before," I said, looking at the small tin-framed picture of my family on the windowsill. Really, I just wanted to tell her everything. I wanted to tell her about time travel, my Uncle, Laura, the whole enchilada.

"I know you are. Is Joe incredible, though? Good family? He seems like such a nice man from what you have described. I can't wait to meet him!" Claire jumped up on the countertop and begged for more information.

"He is the most wonderful person I could have imagined. He is so funny and energetic. Really, he reminds me so much of Mom."

"Well, all I know is that he sure seems interested in you. No one would just come in to your life like this and spend so much time with you if they didn't love you. I genuinely think that he wants the best for you, from everything you have said," Claire added.

"He's going to leave soon." I rinsed both coffee mugs and dropped them into the dishwasher. This was going to be tricky, I thought: how to explain where he was going and what he did for a living.

"Leave you? To go where?" Claire looked worried.

"I don't know. All he will say is that his career takes him away for long periods of time, and this time it will be for a long while."

"Oh. Where does he live? What does he do?"

"Oh yeah, he did tell me. He lives in Wilmington, of all places. Can you believe that?"

Claire hopped down from the counter and hugged me. "Oh this is wonderful news! Then you will be able to see him when you go to school. It's like a dream come true!"

"Actually, I'm not sure where he'll be."

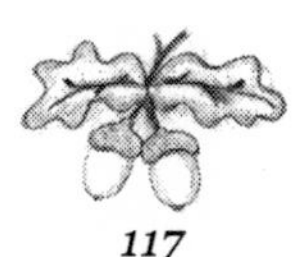

"Are you serious? I mean, that would have worked out wonderfully, don't you think?" Claire pulled her bottom lip down in a frown.

"Well, I'll take what I can get! Just like this morning. I am taking what I can get with you until your grandmother gets you for the rest of the day!" I hugged Claire back. I thought about telling her everything again. I could trust Claire. But I didn't really know enough yet. I should tell her about school, though.

"So what does he do?" Claire repeated.

"Well," I hesitated and tried to describe his passion in *normal* terms. "He is kind of a historical anthropologist. He does intense studies of focused periods of history."

Claire smiled. "Well that's right up your alley. I know that you like the historical romances more than any of the others."

"Claire, what would you say if I did not go to school in the fall? What if I went with Joe, where he has to go?"

"What do you mean?" Claire looked at me like she just heard the worst news ever.

"Well, I think I need to spend as much time with him as I can. I would regret it forever if I didn't. And school can always wait a semester? Right?" I looked at Claire, pleading with my eyes.

"Yes, I suppose. But I really need you. I can't make it through the first semester without you. We are supposed to be there together. What would I do? I know that sounds selfish, but we've been dreaming and planning this forever." Claire popped back up on the counter.

"Claire, you have always been my best friend, you and Tabs. If I decide to do this, I really need you to be happy for me. I'll catch up. I just might have to do this family thing for a little while." I went back to the windowsill and picked up my tiny family photo.

"I know you're right. I'm just not going to think about this right now. You're just talking it out. We don't know anything, yet, right? So let's just wait and see what happens and then deal with it. Okay?" Claire, the optimist, was obviously very disappointed and didn't want to deal any more with this possibility right now.

"Okay. I agree, let's wait." But I knew, right then, that I wasn't going to college in August, and maybe never at all.

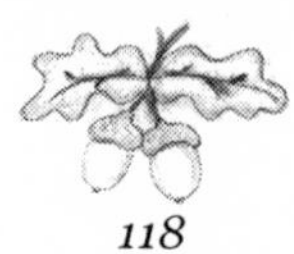

Chapter Fourteen

Lunch, June 22, 1989

My next visit had to be with Lilly. She had called me several times over the past couple of days. She was dying to catch up and find out what was going on with Joe and me.

I was hesitant to say too much to her; I didn't want to have to stretch the truth for any impossible questioning. I could just hear her now, asking me what Joe did for a living, just as Claire had. I now knew the real answer. I could not bear to lie to her about it, yet I could not tell her everything. I would have to think of something plausible.

I called her and set up lunch together. There'd been no further word from Joe for setting up plans. When Lilly got there, it was if I had not seen her for a year.

"Alex! I'm so happy to see you! How tan you have gotten this summer. Have you been out on the water with the boys a lot?" Lilly bounced into the house and hugged me. I always had to hunch over to give her a hug. She was only about 5'2" and lived in sneakers.

"Yes, the summer is certainly whizzing by. I'm sorry I have not seen more of you. It's not that I haven't wanted to. I've been so busy." I let go of her hug and we walked to the sun room.

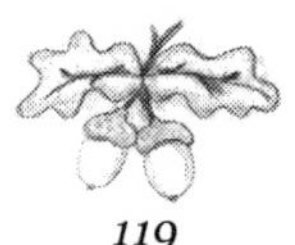

This was Mom's favorite room in the house. She loved going in there and reading. She was a book junkie just like me. We could devour books in one sitting in that room.

The walls were painted a pale aqua and always made me think of being at the beach. She had large, glass pedestal bowls that contained every sea shell she had ever collected. Best of all, there was the most comfortable white wicker furniture, with bright yellow and blue cushions on the chairs.

The round table in the back was our card table. We used to play Spades until the wee hours on weekends. Now the memory of those times was more precious to me than I can ever explain. Dad used to play Johnny Mathis and Nat King Cole over and over. Even now, when I hear those songs, I can think of nothing else. It takes me back to them, to that sweet and precious time, playing cards with my two favorite people in the world.

"Well, tell me everything!" Lilly opened a large box with the most unbelievable chocolate brownies inside. They were a dream; thick, moist chocolate drizzled with caramel and chopped walnuts on top. I grabbed one as soon as she offered it to me. I needed another sweet like I needed a hole in the head.

"It has been an exciting summer. Most days have been spent either on the boat with my pals or exploring the city with Joe. We've spent so much time together. I think I already told you about us going to the beach and to the park several times. I have really been catching him up on my life," I said as I took a bite of the brownie. The cinnamon buns were still hogging up my stomach. But, this is *chocolate.*

"I have been seeing the two of you coming and going, of course. I could tell it was a very happy time for you, each time you returned. Alex, I am so glad that you found each other. I'm sure it makes things better for you." Lilly grabbed a brownie and began working on the corners. I hopped up and went into the kitchen to pick up a couple napkins for us.

"Did you ever find out what that whole deal was about with his time running out? What does he do for a living?" Lilly hollered to me as I was still in the kitchen.

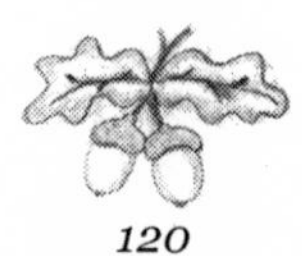

"No, I don't know exactly. I don't know when he is leaving or where he is going to go. All he said was a couple of months, but I have no idea of the exact date." I poured a glass of milk for each of us and came back into the sun room. The story worked once with Claire, so here I go again! "He's kind of a historical archeologist. He does research and then goes on site to get more detail."

"Have you really gotten to know each other? Are you feeling comfortable and at ease? Your history grades were always good, is it paying off?" Lilly was still working on her brownie, taking small nibbles. I have never known another person who eats in such small bites and as slowly as she does. I've heard it's a great diet trick.

"Oh, yes, I'm so happy that we have had this time together. He makes history very interesting and downright personal." I sighed and passed Lilly her glass of milk. Skirting the truth was hard.

Still, we chatted for hours, talking mostly about my time with Joe. Lilly wanted to know every little detail. You could just see her face glow with happiness. I know she was so comforted knowing that he was in my life and making me so much happier. Then she asked me about college. I don't think I was really ready for this. Claire had been difficult enough.

"So, what is the plan for orientation? When is it and can I go with you?" Lilly smiled, knowing full well that I had wanted her to be with me.

"I..." College was right around the corner, and I was pretty sure I knew what I was going to do. No time like the present to tell her.

"What is it?" Lilly looked more concerned now.

"I don't know if I am going to the first semester of college, Lilly," I said so softly that I doubted she even heard me.

"You don't know?" She had heard me. "You don't know what? You have already submitted your first semester's tuition!" Lilly stood up and looked horrified at what I was saying. I had never seen her like this before. She was always so calm and loving; this seemed out of character for her, an overreaction.

"Lilly, take it easy. A lot has happened over the past month. I'm not the same person I was back when graduation took place. I didn't have a clue as to what I wanted to do then, and now, maybe, I do."

"You do? What do you want to do, then?" Lilly sat back down and looked at me, her usually loving face, tense and worried.

"I have decided to go with Joe for a while. Not for a long time, but at least long enough to miss the first semester. I could possibly start second semester, but I'm not sure right now." Lilly started to cry when she understood my words. I think they completely shocked her, and it was just too much.

"Please don't cry, Lilly. I know you only want the best for me. And believe me, I want that too."

"Alex, I have been here for you since you were a little girl, and I'm always going to be here for you. But I know it was *firmly* in your parents' wishes that you go to college. I really can't believe what you are saying. I feel like I have failed them, and you. I've seen it too many times; grads put off starting college and they never get there. They get sidetracked and don't become what they could be.

You've said yourself that you don't know what your dream is. College will help you to explore all of the possible dreams you have to choose from. Whatever you do next, you'll be better prepared after college."

Amazed at her long outburst, I got up and walked around the room, twisting my long blonde hair. I knew that this would be hard for her to understand. I couldn't tell her the whole truth and even then, it probably wouldn't make sense to her if I did. I needed to comfort her and also make sure she knew I had made up my mind.

"Lilly, I hear how you are upset with me now. I know you don't understand my choice. But I need you to trust me and know that I am making the right decision. You have been there for me my whole life. I really could not have made it this far without you. But trust that whatever you have taught me, however you have guided me this far, it has made me the young woman who I am." I paused and could hear Lilly's heavy, upset breathing.

"I need to go with Joe. I am not going to miss this chance. College can wait a semester, or even a year, for me to get this figured out. Joe is offering a unique opportunity." As I stood there, now at a

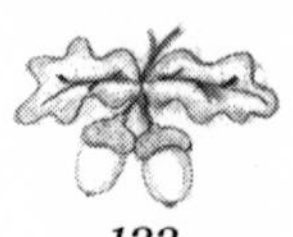

loss of words, I was feeling good about my decision. I felt resolute now, but still uncomfortable with Lilly's reaction.

Only moments later, Lilly walked up behind me and patted my back. "Do you know where I am?"

"You...you're behind me?"

"Yes. And that is where I will stay. I always have your back." Lilly turned me around and hugged me. She seemed to accept my decision. Now all I need to do is break the news to the rest of the pack. At least Lilly supported me, even if she did not understand, and I could move forward.

After Lilly left, Joe called and asked if I was ready to head to Wilmington the next day. He would pick me up first thing in the morning. After I got off the phone and started to think about it, I was *really* looking forward to it.

That night, I had another unusual dream. At the time, I couldn't make sense of it. It was such a strange dream, with no plot or storyline.

I dreamed about a large oak tree. I was walking through a field and came upon this tree, as if it was calling out to me. I sat down under the tree and looked out at the lush meadow, feeling relaxed and at ease. I couldn't explain it, but it went on for what seemed like hours. I sat under this tree, knowing I had made the right decision. It was as if everything I had been worried about had been resolved. I was happy.

Before long, I ventured into the woods, and found a large gray rock. The rock was twice as tall as I was, and there seemed to be a cavern just beside it. It seemed familiar, calling to me to come inside. I stood there, undecided about what to do.

I suddenly woke up. My dream seemed to comfort me but also left more questions in my mind. Where this place...and what was was inside that hole?

Chapter Fifteen

Morning, June 23, 1989

Joe arrived in his usual happy and chipper mood. It was a beautiful day. Sunny, but not as hot as usual. Summer days in the Carolinas can be absolute scorchers. But the wind was blowing and the rain from the night before had made the day refreshingly cool.

We drove straight to Wilmington, after our usual breakfast stop, of course. I think Joe got an extra egg on his plate. The waitress was certainly laying it on thick.

I was ecstatic; there truly are no words to describe the feeling. The top was down on the little blue Bug and my hair, although I had tied it a rubber band, was swirling all over as we buzzed down the highway. I think Joe wore a permanent smile for the whole ride. He was excited, the kind of excited like when a teenager is waiting in line to go to his first rock concert.

Lost in thought, I could not imagine what would happen when we got to Wilmington. I knew this was not going to be a touristy visit. It was the same feeling I had as a child, in anticipation of Christmas Eve. It was an excitement for what I knew was coming later that day.

As morning finally slipped into afternoon, we turned down a dirt road. The mailbox simply read "1266 Graham Dr"; its red flag hanging on by a thread. This was it; we were finally there. The excitement was more than I could stand.

The road was long and winding, with cotton plants thick and welcoming on either side. The drive down the road was uncomfortable. Pot holes caused us to bounce all along the drive. It was as though no one had traveled down the dirt road in a year of Sundays. To me, it already felt like we were going back in time, it could have been any year the way things looked around there.

"We have farmers who tend our crops year round. The family is great and I'll introduce them to you while we're here." Joe pointed out the tractor parked on the side of the field.

As we turned onto the last curve, I finally laid eyes on the house. My heart pounded with excitement. No words could explain what a magnificent sight was in front of me. I don't think I could have imagined it to be so overwhelming; it was beyond my dreams. In fact, I felt like I was in a dream.

The main house was situated at the end of the driveway. As we drove down the path, giant crepe myrtles hung over and shaded our car as it moved along with their hot pink bouquets offering us the first spray of brilliant color.

I could see the house, growing larger with each inch that we drew closer. It was an oversized, three-story, white house with black shutters. It was like the kind of house you would see on an old southern plantation, but on a much larger scale than I had ever seen. The antebellum plantation style house had a wrap-around porch on the first and second levels. The third level had a huge peak in the middle with two giant dormers. It was a mansion by anyone's standards.

The house was older; more like a historical site. An immense amount of landscaping was overgrown and strangling several parts of the house. There was a thick and heavy wooded area behind the house and two smaller houses tucked in between. I noticed a rock building on one side, which I figured to be the well house.

We drove right into a small carport and Joe hopped out of the car, still smiling from ear to ear. He slapped his hands together in excitement, and rubbed vigorously. "We are here, my dear," he said as he opened my car door, bowed, and held his hand out.

"Thank you!" I smiled with a shared happiness. "I can't believe how beautiful this place is. What an incredibly awesome home." I walk around the car port and could see the side of the house. There were several oversized hydrangea bushes that were drooping over, heavy with blue blooms. The surrounding large oaks had this easy moss trickling down their trunks like tinsel.

I didn't even know where to begin. I was too busy taking everything in. It was breathtaking, like being at a historical monument and getting lost in the stature of the building.

"Okay, do you want me to take you on a tour of the outside or the inside of the house first?" Joe's eyebrows perked up in utter delight.

"Let's start with the outside, since we're already here. How about that?" I didn't know where we should begin at all.

"Perfect!" And with that, Joe took my hand and brought me to the front of the house, clicking his heels together as if he was a soldier saluting his general.

"This is Holly. That is her name, the house, that is. Her name is Holly. Might seem a little silly, but believe me, she has a name for a reason. She is where it all begins for us. So the story goes, one of our great, greats named her Holly because he felt that Holly embodied the spirit of Christmas." Joe looked up at the house as if it filled his soul with goodness to be standing in front of it. Just to be in *her* presence.

Joe whipped around and looked at me. He grabbed my shoulders so that our faces were right in front of each other. Excitement poured off of him and onto me. "Can you feel it yet?"

"Yes. I can't explain it, but I do understand the importance of this place." I almost giggled and honestly felt weak in the knees. It was like Holly was speaking to me saying, "Welcome." Holly seemed like more of a presence, and not just a house.

"Well, lots to do. Let's get going on the tour. I feel like a kid in a candy store! I have never brought anyone else here. I've never had the fun of introducing Holly to anyone! It is such a sacred, special place for me. I'm thrilled to share it with you, Alex." Joe beamed at me as he spoke.

Now that I was there, I was overwhelmed and so excited at the same time. I just couldn't believe that Mom would not want me to be a part of this. I stopped to think of her, remembering her soft smile, hoping that she actually did want this for me after all. I stood there looking at the house, not knowing exactly what to focus on with all of its grandeur.

"Alrighty then, let's get going." Joe snapped his fingers and pointed at the smaller house adjacent to Holly. "Okay, so you met Holly, and we will be back here soon enough to go inside and explore. But let's get going on the tour of the outside grounds." Joe walked past the house and approached one of the smaller structures, a one-story, boxy, white house.

"This is one of the guest quarters. Basically, it is a mini Holly." Joe slid his hand over the door trim, apparently trying to find something by feeling along the edges.

"Ah ha, the key!" he pulled an old rusty skeleton key off the top of the door frame. After the door lost the argument to stay closed, he abruptly pushed it open. Sunlight filled the room and everything inside was light and welcoming. The home was pristine and immaculate, as if time stopped when the last guest left. Or, maybe I should say, the maid left.

We walked inside the tiny house and I took in the entire living area. The bedroom was open to the kitchen and a small living room. There was another door in the back. "It's quaint, I'll give it that. Holly can overwhelm you when you stay here alone, so I started living out here," Joe explained. "I guess you could say that this is *my pad.*" Joe's bad disco move was almost scary and yet too funny not to laugh at.

You could tell this was Joe's space. Everything about it made me think of him. The comforter on the bed was a red and blue plaid. It looked as if someone made it by hand. There were two brown couches, typical bachelor style. The furniture looked as if it had been salvaged from the 1950s.

In the kitchen, there stood a small round wooden table with two chairs. There was also clean and clear counter space.

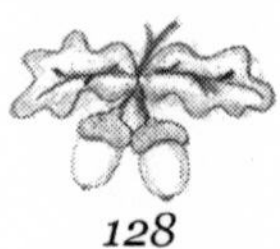

As I walked into the open room, I saw very few personal items. There was one side table beside the bed, with some framed photos, a yellow phone, and a dish with a watch in it. The living room, which again, was open to the rest of the house, only had the couches and one small rectangle coffee table with several sports magazines on it. I couldn't tell what year they were from, based on the position I was standing, but I thought of how perfectly suited they were to Joe's personality.

I quietly walked into the galley kitchen and studied the space. It was perfect for one person, I thought. Joe didn't say a word; I think he was pleased having a guest to show around. "It's cute. This is where you live?" I looked over at Joe. He was still standing at the front door.

"Yeah. I usually stay over here to sleep and relax, and then walk over to Holly when I am ready to work. Kind of like a working-at-home situation." He laughed as he continued to stand firmly in the same spot by the front door.

"Why not stay at the big house?" I still wondered what I was going to see once we finally got to explore Holly.

"Well, like I said, it can be a little overwhelming. There is a lot of stuff in there, and it's a big house. I needed something that I could pop in and out of. I hate being reminded that I am here all alone. This house meets my needs and seems cozy, comfortable. Don't you agree?" he asked rhetorically as he reached over, grabbed a ball cap that was sitting on the back of the couch and put it on his head. *Duke fan, figures.*

"Where are all your personal things, like clothes and photos, and stuff like that?" I looked around, trying to find evidence of anything else that truly belonged to him.

"I keep my personal things here in the closet, I don't know why. Maybe because I don't want to have too much to fuss over while I'm gone." He finally walked across the room and opened the one door inside the little home that I had imagined led to a bathroom.

There were two small boxes on the floor and about ten items of clothing hanging on a rack. Was this all he owned in this world? I thought to myself that material things must not be that important to him. I couldn't fathom putting all my worldly possessions into two boxes! "You have got to be kidding me. Where are the rest of your things?" I was still unable to believe that this is all he owned in the world.

"Nope. Only ever lived right here at Holly Plantation. After my parents took their last jump, I was the only one left to live here. They jumped one after another, and then it just didn't feel right staying in that big house all by myself. I can't really have company, so what is the point of having things around that I don't use? Everything I need is right here in this room." Joe walked out into the room and held his arms open wide, and spun around to face me.

I guess when your life's mission is to travel through time helping others, you are less infatuated with yourself, and really focus on what you *need* in life. I continued walking around and decided to open the refrigerator. It was empty. "What, no food either?" I chuckled.

"No, I eat. You already know that. But I only stock up when I'm here. While I was in Raleigh, I just stayed at a hotel and ate out or ate with you. No need to keep food here when I'm not here, you know." Joe opened one of the beige kitchen cabinets. It had a couple of dishes and cups carefully organized on the shelves.

"I just keep my basic dishes and what-not for when I'm back here. Remember, I am gone when I jump, sometimes for long periods of time. I've got to keep it simple. Does that make sense?"

"It does. I guess I'll have to lose a few things for sure!" We continued to laugh as a cardinal sat on the window sill, watching our conversation in its every detail. "Can I ask what happened to your parents? When did they leave you?" I hated to break the happy mood, but wanted to know everything that I could.

"Is this the time to hear about it? Or do you want to continue the tour?" Joe quickly winked at me.

"Yeah, I do want to hear about it. Can we cover it really quickly?"

"Heck yeah! Have a seat and I'll be back with some lemonade." With that, Joe pulled out a glass jug and put some powder in it. He made us lemonade and returned in short order to the couch, where I'd made myself comfortable.

"Alright, of course your grandparents were time travelers. My Mom was born into the family. She married Dad, who also became a time traveler. Mom used to say that they wanted lots of children, but they were only blessed with two, me and then your Mom."

"So you marry someone, they learn about the secret, accept it too, and gets to time travel?" I knew we covered it before, but I wanted to know more.

"Right. Anyway, they tried to spend as much of their lives together as possible, except when they jumped into the past. They thankfully never jumped at the same time, since your mom and I were growing up and needed at least one parent around. They missed a lot of time together. It was bittersweet." Joe paused.

"Why bittersweet?"

"We wanted to be with both our Mom and Dad, so bitter on that end of the deal. But when they got back, it was the best bedtime story of all! We got to hear how they went back in time. It made history come alive for us. And the stories were so cool. I could listen to them talk about it all day long. Hearing how they helped those people was really exciting and fulfilling."

"I can see what you are saying." I took a big gulp of the sweet lemonade, noticing the little yellow flowers etched on the glass.

"And so we had each other for the most part, me and your Mom. We grew up with so many fun things to do on this farm. Back then, we had animals like pigs, horses and chickens. It was a neat place to grow up. And my aunt and Uncle were still here on the farm. We had a lot to do. But as a child, it really did not seem like work. It seemed like having an adventure every day." Joe knocked his shoes off and put his feet on the coffee table.

"When you are born into this family, *it is hard to find a mate.* Not exactly a normal family to marry into, as you can imagine. Dad and Mom met in high school; they only ever dated each other. It is a love story worth repeating, but I will tell you the whole thing another time."

"Yes, please do. I want to know everything I can. I've missed a lifetime of stories, you know. But let me get this right, when you find someone you love, you can tell them you are a time traveler?"

"Right. Kind of. Once you're pretty sure that you are getting married, you take them to Holly. It's kind of an initiation thing. So far, no one has ever backed out once they knew. Time travel is a gift, Alex. But as I was saying, when you marry, you have children, and the children develop into the time-traveling mode, and so on and so forth, generation after generation."

I nodded, trying to understand all of this, patiently waiting for all the information to be explained. I *was* anxious to hear about how my grandparents fell in love, but I guessed that I would have to remind him about that later.

"I graduated from high school one year before your Mom. She had already met your Dad and our parents each had one jump left. I knew it would be soon that they would leave me. I guess I understood it was coming, but who can ever prepare you to lose your parents forever? Selfishly, I didn't want to know that other people, other families, would spend their lives with them and my life with my parents would end."

"I can understand that. It's sort of like knowing someone is dying from a terminal illness, and that you only have so much time before they die. They'll be happy in heaven but they still leave you behind." I put my empty glass on the table, pulled up my legs and sat back beside my Uncle.

"Exactly. Might as well have been death, since it sure felt that way. Mom went after Dad. I knew she was going to have the hardest time of all of us. Leaving your children cannot be an easy task. But she knew it was the plan. It was her calling in life."

"How did you know it was the plan? I don't mean that sarcastically. I just wondered how you knew." My analytical side needed to hear the science of how this worked.

"*You will know.* I promise you that. I can't explain it. But it is completely clear to you at some point before you leave on your first jump."

"Hmmm...guess I will have to take your word on that one too," I smiled.

"Like I was saying, Dad left to go back to save a girl from dying at the turn of the century. He lived his days out on a ranch with some missionaries. I have letters from his life after he jumped and he had been so much at peace with his decision to go there."

"I bet it is something when you know they jump and it all ends up happily," I added cheerfully.

"Exactly. And then Mom went a couple years later. I actually had just gotten back from my first jump and your Mom was already off and married to your Dad. My jump took longer than I expected." Joe looked over at me and pulled his knee up on the couch.

"Where did she go, grandmother, I mean?"

"She went out West. She rode on a wagon with a family of Mormons to Utah. We have her letters in the archives. They are just incredible. Life was really hard back then; there was a lot of sacrifice. Amazing how things change over time, progress and all that."

"Wait a minute, I thought you said not to go far. One hundred miles or less. How did she go out West? I thought that we needed to save local people." I was sure he'd told me that earlier about time travel.

"Oh yes, that is true. Mom and Dad both saved local people, but once they fulfilled their seventh mission, they were free to live or travel wherever they pleased. They both chose to go west. I did wonder if they ever contacted each other."

"That's wild. Living out your life before you are born. Do you think things are more stressful now?"

"It is a matter of opinion, I guess. Would you rather be stressed about which college to go to or be stressed about having no food in the winter?"

"I see what you mean." I was back on a wagon in the middle of the desert. Good thing I'd had that lemonade.

"Well, let's get going, I have a lot to show you. Maybe you should call Lilly and tell her that you got here safely. She does know that you are staying a couple of days, right?" Joe jumped up and waited for my answer.

"Yes, she does. Is that the phone over there, that huge yellow thing?" I laughed when I examined the large rotary phone sitting by the bed.

"Hey, don't knock it. It works!" Joe opened the front door and disappeared into the yard.

Chapter Sixteen

Afternoon, June 23, 1989

Lilly was glad to hear from me. While on the phone, I heard the sound of some motor growling along the back side of Joe's house. When I ended my call, I put our glasses in the sink, and headed out the front door.

There was a man standing with Joe and all I could see was the back of him as I approached. Joe looked over at me and smiled, "Alex, I have someone to introduce you to."

The tall man turned and I saw his face for the first time. To say my heart skipped a beat would be a lie; it skipped two. He was simply the most handsome man I had ever laid eyes on. Admittedly, he was dirty from head to toe. But his blue eyes pierced right through me. He had on old blue overalls and a ball cap, and looked to be about twenty. He took his hat off as I approached and moved to pull a white handkerchief out of his pocket. He wiped the sweat off his face in one big swipe.

Joe rushed over to me and put his arm behind my back. "I want you to meet somebody. Remember me telling you that we had farmers who handle all of our crops?" I seemed to be at a loss for words; I didn't respond to Joe's question. Joe took note of my silence, my stare, and the flushed look on my face and asked, "Alex, are you alright? Too hot maybe?"

Hot, heck, that wasn't even the start of it. Seriously, this guy was that perfect. Even the dirt wasn't bothersome.

The man opened his mouth to ask, "Miss, are you alright?" I could only follow his perfect lips up and down as he spoke. They were thick and pouty, and it was like the heat from the sun melted each word as it surfaced from his lips. OK, I was a goner.

"Alex, you need to speak," Joe commanded. Has the heat gotten to you? Are you sick? What's going on?" A minute had passed since his first sentence, and I was still just standing there, not even worried if my tongue was hanging out.

I finally, nervously, swept the bangs out of my eyes, looked downward, and responded, "Uh...sorry, I'm okay. I was just thinking about Lilly and our conversation. What were you saying, Joe?" I looked back up and I tried not to stare, but at this point, who cared?

"Like I was saying, I want to introduce you to someone. This is a friend of the family, one of our farmers, Jackson. Jackson Clark." Joe smiled with big twinkles in his eyes.

"Hello, it's nice to meet you. Sure heard a lot about you through the years," Jackson quietly addressed me. He knew about me? Good grief, where have you been all of *my* life? I quickly tried to seem busy by brushing off my shirt where a small gnat had landed. Honestly, I was making sure that I didn't have a hole where my heart had popped out, since it was beating so quickly.

I looked back up at the tanned Adonis. "Nice to meet you, Jackson. You...you farm? I mean, you help our family with the crops?" I don't have a clue where that dumb question came from. I was just blubbering now.

"Yep! He's the man. He keeps our crops comin' in. His family has tended to our family for generations. I am not sure what we would do without them." Joe smacked Jackson on the back like a football coach would do to his star rookie.

My question was directed to Jackson, but since Joe butted in, I had to think of another one, if for no other reason than to watch those lips move. His voice was soft and easy to listen to.

"Jackson, you live around here?" That was a good one. He will respond to this for sure, I thought, and then kicked myself for such a stupid question. Of course he had to live around here to take care of the place.

Joe interfered and answered again. "Yeah, he lives about a half-mile back the way we came. Nice brick house with a ..." I held my breath. Please don't say a wife! *Please don't say wife*! "...well, with a big, I mean huge, old dog. What's his name? Marmaduke?" With Joe asking Jackson a question, maybe I had a chance for a wonderful interlude between this dream boat and me.

"No, his name is Butterball. I can't tell you where that name came from, but it suits him just the way I like it, sweet and simple," Jackson answered softly with his smooth, light, wonderful voice.

I got your sweet and simple right here, Jackson!

I was in a cloud, drifting off the Earth. It was a perfectly awful feeling since I had never experienced it before and I was not sure when (or how) I was coming back down. This sick, happy feeling was so unexpected. I felt like I could walk up and kiss him without thinking twice. It was like my body was being pulled towards him but my feet were rooted to the ground.

Alex, the analytical, methodical girl, was having a very inconvenient episode. Why was this happening now?

Those lips moved again. "Well, it is certainly nice to meet you. Hope to see you in the future sometime. I got to get going, Joe," he said. I could see a second bead of sweat roll down his cheek and onto his neck. He held his hand out for me to shake. Dare I touch him?

I decided to do the polite thing and extend a hand. Strangely, he stood there a minute and we both looked at each other while we shook, well, really held, hands. Too soon, he let go and hopped back on his tractor heading out into the cotton field, waving good-bye.

"Well, I am glad you two met. You'll like Jackson." Joe motioned his hand to keep moving. I was testing my feet to see if the roots were still there. "Alright, so we saw my quarters, and there is

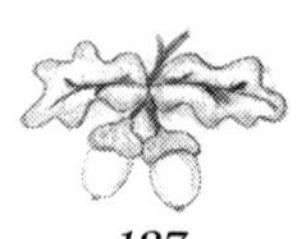

another one just like it. That one hasn't been lived in for quite some time. One of Jackson's relatives used to stay there when the Holly was full. And from time to time we have other people in his family live here, for security reasons, when I am away," Joe said as he felt on the top of the door frame of the other house, again for a key.

"What do you mean when Holly was full?"

"Years ago, there were a lot of people living here. We had aunts, uncles, cousins, sisters, brothers. At one point, we had a lot of people living here and we needed help. Help like cleaning and cooking, things like that. And this is where she stayed. Her name is Annie; she is Jackson's aunt. I was a boy at the time."

Joe finally pulled the key down and jammed it into the keyhole. A gray squirrel scurried up a tree and complained about the sudden loud noise as Joe forced the door open.

"Where is everyone, then?" I couldn't believe that the only people in our family who were left were standing at the threshold of this old house.

"Those who were left in our family all jumped back in time. And also, years ago, we had a barn fire on the plantation. We lost five family members. It was tragic. All the children, except your Mom and I, died that night. We were asleep in bed when it happened."

"Oh, my God! It must have been beyond horrible! So how is this legacy going to continue on when we are the only two?" I felt the pit of my stomach tighten, hearing about my cousins dying like that. Cousins. I used to have cousins.

"Alex, *you* are going to continue on for our family." Joe pushed the door further open.

"Me?" I felt totally shocked. How would I be able to handle all of this by myself?

"Settle down. You will learn. I trust you. But let's just not put the chicken before the egg. No, that's cart before the horse. Never mind. Once you see what I have to show you, you will feel better about this whole thing."

This house was dirty, dingy, and smelled a little damp. All the furniture was stacked up on one side of the open room. It was laid out

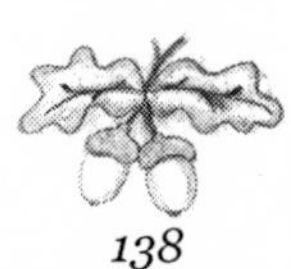

just the same as Joe's house, but this one had not been taken care of for some time. It needed sprucing up for sure.

"Yeah, well, this house needs some love, but it can be done." Joe stepped in and smacked away a big spider that sailed down from his web to greet him. Yuck.

After a couple of minutes, we both backed out of the house and closed the door. We continued walking along a gravel circle, passing Holly as we strolled along. I don't think I'd ever noticed how beautiful *trees* were until today. When you really stop and take note of nature's beauty, you can be surprised.

The backyard was completely overgrown with trees, vines, and shrubs. Honeysuckle dripped down every tree, as far as the eye could see. The back porch was covered with ivy that had made a complete canopy over the structure, like a green shawl on a lovely lady.

"That's the barn. Of course, it's the newest building on the property. We rebuilt it after the fire." Joe pointed to the building and we began to walk towards it.

"What started the fire?" I really dreaded hearing this story.

"The other kids had come outside, we think, to check on a cow that was due to give birth any day. I guess one of them had an oil lantern that tipped over. They had bolted the door from the inside, we think accidentally, and couldn't find their way out with all the smoke. The rest of the family was in bed and didn't know it happened until screams woke up your Grandmother. We all ran out and tried to put out the fire, but it was too late."

"I wish that you could have gone back in time and saved them. That is a very sad scenario," I said as I looked at the ominous barn.

"Alex, I know." He sighed deeply. "Just like we could not save your parents, we couldn't save them either. We can't do anything that is a personal benefit. Now I suppose another time travel family could pick us and make it right. But we can't contact, initiate or suggest that it happen." Joe pulled the large barn door open.

Just then a flock of Canadian geese flew overhead, announcing their departure. Their long necks were leading the way, as they headed south. "Another family? One of other time travel families?" And I did not mean the geese! I stepped inside the dimly lit barn. I heard something large rustling in the back of the barn. From the noise it was making, whatever it was, it clearly seemed agitated with our unwelcome visit.

"Yes. I have no idea where they all are, or how many, but we know there are more time traveling families. That was really the only way this would work, I guess, if you really think about it. You need people all over the world to do good for everyone and somehow you had to keep it all going through the regular tragedies of life." Joe heard the rustling and picked up a pitchfork that was leaning against the wall.

"I'm trying my best to keep it all sorted out. I guess that it's good that there are more families, right?"

"Right."

"But how do we know for sure that there are more?" I knew that I asked a lot of nit-picky questions, but Joe said that it was fine to be curious.

"You know, I really don't know the answer to that. Mom just told me that there were others. I guess the idea never bugged me." We heard the rustle again. It sounded like something pretty big. I was ready to leave. Really, no need in my mind to see any more of the barn.

"There was something that I wanted to show you."

"Can it wait? It sounds like there is a bear in here. Seriously, I don't want something jumping out at us." I stepped closer to Joe, feeling very creeped out about my surroundings.

"No, no, it isn't a bear. Don't think one would be able to get into the barn." Joe moved cautiously with each step as he poked the pitchfork in the air.

"Maybe I should open the barn door wider so we can get a better look." I went back and pulled the door all the way back and allowed the sun to pour into the dusty room.

"Ahhhh!" I screamed so loud, I am pretty sure I must have roused my departed ancestors. There were bats flying out of the barn and several smacked into the wall and door in their haste, scaring me half to death.

Joe came running out and burst into laughter. "Alex, you are a riot! You scared *me* half to death with that howl you let out! You are alright!"

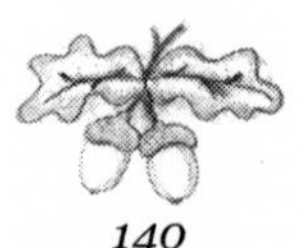

"It did not sound like bats in there. It sounded like..." and in mid sentence, a tall, skinny, gray-haired man came walking out. We were barely able to see, after the blinding sun.

"Benjamin my man, I thought that was you." Joe laughed again, brushing off the hay from the old man's shirt.

"You mean, you knew he was in there?" I puffed out.

"No, well, maybe, but you can never tell about these things. That's why I grabbed the pitchfork." Joe poked at the air near Benjamin as the old man stood there yawning, unimpressed.

"Hello Missy, who are you?" The old man spoke to me in his thin, scratchy voice, as he rubbed both of his eyes.

"This here is my Alex, my niece." Joe stood shoulder to shoulder with me and squeezed me closer.

"Yes, I am his niece. That's me," I blubbered as I smiled stupidly, feeling certain that the unhappy odor I was getting wind of was clearly the unbathed man in front of me. I'm sure some cheap rot gut liquor he had indulged in for breakfast contributed to the stench as well.

"Alex, my girl, this is Benjamin. He is our traveling friend. He makes a stop whenever he can, and simply parks wherever that happens to be." Joe looked at me and winked.

Yuck. A rogue alcoholic. What is he doing in *our* barn?

"Well, my dear, as they say in the movies, I'd better be on my way. The missus, my wife that is, will be thinking I have a girlfriend." And with that, Benjamin waddled out and through the pasture.

"See ya, man," Joe yelled, lifting his hand high in the air to wave good-bye, as Benjamin ambled away.

"Why was he in your barn?" I quietly asked, still not understanding who the man was.

"Well, Alex, you have to be accepting of all types of people. Benjamin was a prominent man in our community, Chief of Police, some years back. But then his son was kidnapped and murdered. He never recovered from that. His wife left him, after a few years of dealing with his drinking.

And now we find him all over the place from time to time. Once, he was in the bushes of the Anderson house. They just walked past him that Sunday morning and headed on in to church. It is a pretty regular occurrence around here. You just live with it and try to be understanding." Joe still had me firmly clenched up beside him. "You okay? Those bats really got you going!" Joe laughed.

"Yeah, yeah, laugh if you want." I was still perplexed as to why someone would sleep in the barn. And even more than that, what a horrible thing that had happened to this man. I couldn't imagine.

Joe asked me to come back inside the barn; he still had something he wanted to show me. I had forgotten all about that, after the bats and the drunkard. In the back of the barn, against the staircase, was a quilt covering something rather large. Joe quickly pulled the quilt off, making a cloud of dust and debris fly around the room. "Ta da!" Joe was smiling like a kid with a new toy.

"A piano? Man, that thing looks pretty old and beat up. Does it play? How old is it?" I was only mildly intrigued at this point.

"I don't know for sure, it has been here forever, but it plays. Want to hear?" And with that, Joe pulled out a rickety piano bench, plopped down, and began to play. Half of the keys were missing, but it seemed like he knew it and played something that didn't seem to need those keys. Wow.

I scooted beside Joe on the old seat and listened as he played. I didn't know the songs, but man, could he play. "How do you know how to play so well?"

"Practice."

"You took lessons?"

"Nope, I play by ear and I just practice. I hear a song and then I try to duplicate it on the piano."

"This piano? Don't you have another one? One with all of the keys?"

"Yes, there is one in the house, but this one is just fun. It's all out of tune, doesn't have enough keys, but it makes a difference playing in a barn, don't you think? Couldn't you see an old fashioned barn dance in here? People hopping around back and forth? Heehaw!"

I *could* imagine it. People waiting all month to come to a dance. Dressed in their Sunday best. And once they were here, they'd dance until they couldn't breathe. The piano would belt out one song

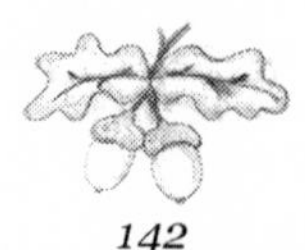

after another in cheerful harmony with the dancers. "I bet it was such a wonderful thing back in the day," I said, dreaming of the crinoline dresses flinging around the room.

"Yep, back in the day. Speaking of which, we need to continue on. There's a lot to cover." Once we stood up, Joe pushed in the bench, grabbed the quilt, and draped it back over the piano.

"Where to next?" I asked. Joe bent his arm and held it out, as if we were leaving a dance together. I was in the spirit, took his arm, and we sashayed out of the barn. Once outside, we discovered that the wind had picked up a little. The cool breeze was so inviting after being in the stuffy barn. Joe closed the barn door and began heading toward the back yard.

"Okay, we have hit the highlights on the buildings, with the exception of the inside of Holly, of course. Now I need to take you into the woods." Joe skipped ahead.

"Into the woods? What's back there? Goldilocks and the three bears?" I couldn't imagine what I would need to see in the thick woods, and Holly was still such a mystery. I figured a bear was a real possibility.

"Just trust me. It's one of the main reasons that I brought you here, aside from my smashing bachelor pad that you certainly *had* to see." Joe snapped both his fingers and pointed both of them right at me like two guns.

I rolled my eyes. "Yes, the bachelor's pad. That was something." The woods quickly mentally enveloped me, and I had barely set foot in them. What in the world would be back there that I needed to see? Not grave sites, I hoped. That would give me the willies for a week. Maybe I could ask more about this little field trip. "What's back there? I don't want to see any more winos, ah, sheriffs, or bats!"

"I promise there won't be any of those things this time. Could be snakes, though." Joe started to grin. He must be joking. He picked up a stick and rustled it on the path ahead of us.

"Snakes! What? I hate snakes! Are you serious?" Now I was scanning the grass for any signs of movement.

"Not to worry, I'll walk ahead of you. I'll get it before you even see it, if one comes along. I promise, Alex, this will be worth it. You'll be okay." Joe held his hand out and I stood there.

"Snakes?"

"Come on, I said I would protect you, and I will." Joe extended his hand for me to take.

"Okay. But I will *never* forgive you if you mess with me!" In actuality, I really was very afraid of snakes and there was not a single way to fake that. I didn't have a brave bone in my body when it came to those slithery reptiles, not that I ever had a bad experience with one.

We walked for what seemed like a mile. I know it was probably about a quarter of that, but I felt tense as I scanned the ground for fork tongued creatures and listened for a rattle or whatever sound a snakes makes. Even though it was sunny and I could see most everything, the umbrella of shade the trees created made shadows that caused me to continuously take a second look at things.

A stick, for an instance, looked just like a snake at the right angle. I would jump and then stop. Joe stood firmly, as if he had just crawled out of an alligator-wrestling contest as the winner. He was fearless. Again, it reminded me about my original impression of him, being an animal park or safari tour guide.

"Ah, we are here. We made it. Really!" And just as I was feeling relief that we were at the end of my panicked journey, my heart stopped again. Three times in one day. First Holly, then Jackson, and now...

It was as if I was witnessing a miracle. Maybe it was like someone seeing the Grand Canyon, up close and personal, for the first time. It was just simply a miracle that no words could adequately describe. Standing several stories above me was the most magnificent tree I had ever seen. It was the most beautiful living thing I had ever gazed upon.

At the bottom, the roots locked into the earth. Once the trunk took over, it coiled all the way up to its branches in one large swirl around itself. I had never seen a tree that big, wound up into one twist like that.

The branches were broad and heavy with millions of green leaves. As the wind blew, it sounded as if the leaves were having a conversation. We stood there in awe. The limbs were thick and heavy, low to the ground. No acorns yet this year, but I could tell by the rounded, sculptured leaves that this was a mighty oak.

Joe, with both hands on his hips, was staring up at the branches. I could tell he was lost in thought. He had no words at this moment. And neither did I.

The trunk was massive. I could only imagine how old this beauty was. Hundreds of years old, that much was certain. Joe finally looked over at me, beaming. "I need to show you something. Come over here." Joe held his hand out and I walked over, still admiring the coil of the tree.

We walked around to the other side of the tree; I concentrated carefully on my feet, watching where I stepped to avoid tripping over a root. And then I noticed the most magical thing I had ever seen. In the trunk, there was a large hole, almost as if it were hollowed out, naturally, as it grew. It was gnarled and knobby around the opening. It looked as if the tree was yawning with a great misshapen hole in the middle.

But because the tree was so large, the hole was big enough to actually walk into it. I looked over at Joe and he nodded his head, obviously understanding that I was curious about looking inside. As I stepped forward, I could see that there was a simple, little wooden seat that someone had placed on the interior wall.

"What's that for?" I asked, pointing to the small bench.

"This, my dear Alex, is how we time travel." Joe calmly approached me, taking a deep breath. Simultaneously, I began breathing in the earthy tree smell. But my scientific mind couldn't put it all together.

"In a...tree trunk?"

"It's what was intended. It's the instrument which we use to travel through time. Our family has been traveling through time inside this tree since the 1700s. Your super duper great-great-something grandfather, Oscar Shannon, found the tree. The whole family came over on a boat from Ireland based on a very powerful dream he had. I guess the tree called out to them," Joe said as he lovingly rubbed the outside of the tree. "It's estimated that this tree is over one thousand years old."

"What do you mean that it called out to him?"

"Well, I guess God kind of appeared in a dream and told him that he had to find the tree. Lucky that his wife, your great-great-granny, believed in him. That's what I call standing by your man! Anyway, they brought a lot of the things that we use for time travel with them. You'll see soon."

I continued examining the seat and the carvings inside of the tree. Several people had carved their names in the tree. "I hope you won't do that," he laughed.

"What? Write my name?"

"Yes, I always worry it will damage the tree, hurt her in some way. I have taken great care of our *Evening Oak.*"

"Evening Oak?"

"Yes, that's her name. You see, you can only time travel at night. You can't be caught climbing out of a tree in broad daylight, you know." Joe and I laughed. I guess I understood that much. I'm glad someone figured that out a long time ago.

"If you think about it Alex, trees have been around as long as there has been mankind and even before. They have witnessed *everything*. They have witnessed *all the history* that has happened on this earth. Trees provide comfort and reassurance that life will go on. Have you ever had a bad day, and then just went outside and sat under a tree?"

"Yes, at the park, plenty of times." I could readily think of a few instances off the top of my head.

"A tree not only gives life, it also soothes what troubles the living. It puts things in perspective. So it is no surprise that a tree was chosen to help facilitate what we have to do."

"I guess so. It does make sense." I continued watching Joe gently rub the bark of the tree. "It is simply incredible. I have never seen anything like it. I mean, the coiling around the trunk and all the way up, it just seems unreal." I backed up to look at the tree.

"It's a miracle. Just like you and me, Alex. What we do and will do is a miracle." Joe stepped back and stood with me.

"I am truly in awe." I walked forward with the weirdest sensation in my body. It was like I wanted to listen to the tree breathe. I walked right up to the tree and put my hand on it.

My hand felt the tree. It wasn't cold or hot, just the same temperature as my hand, body temperature. I put my other hand on the tree and pressed my head to the trunk, closing my eyes. *This was the tree in my dream.* This was the one that I had sat under, pondering for hours.

This *was* my destiny. I finally knew it. I now knew, beyond a shadow of a doubt, that I would be a time traveler. The tree was speaking to me. But not it a way that we all use words, but in a feeling, an overwhelmingly happy, intense feeling. I felt pain in my chest from the overpowering, rushing, and crushing sensation that the tree was trying to share with me. I had connected to my family now in a way that I finally understood. I had a heritage.

I turned to look at Joe and instantly dropped to the ground.

Chapter Seventeen

Evening, June 23, 1989

I cannot tell you what emotions flowed through my body that day. Whatever gift the tree gave to me, it was so powerful that it caused me to lose all function and I passed out. That had never happened to me before.

I can remember turning and looking at Joe, and then it felt like small flickers of light were flying in front of my eyes. I got dizzy and lost strength completely, falling to the ground in one quick motion.

The next thing I knew, I was lying in an overstuffed, goose feather bed. I could barely see the floor from where I was lying, the bed was so high. I pulled off a washcloth that was on my forehead, hearing a cheerful whistling in the background. Slowly, I sat up and looked around. Did I go back in time?

The walls were covered with low-hanging pictures. There was a dresser with a large round mirror, a lovely tortoise shell comb and brush set carefully arranged on top of it. The four-poster bed had elaborate wheat carvings in the posts and was several feet off the ground. The goose feather mattress felt like I was lying on a cloud. Where was I?

I pulled my body over to the side of the bed, noticing a small stepstool on the floor. As I was just about to step on to it, Joe called out to me, "Alex! You're awake? Are you okay?"

"I think so. Did I pass out?" I rubbed my head, still not having my bearings on where I was, but very relieved to see Joe.

"You did." Joe flipped a kitchen towel over his shoulder and grabbed my hand. "Now I want you to take it nice and easy, and let's see if you can walk. You feel up to it?"

"Oh, I can walk, I feel fine. Well, actually a little embarrassed... Where are we?"

"Alex, meet Holly. Well, one of Holly's rooms, I should say."

"For a minute there, I was afraid I had traveled through time." Joe pulled my hand toward his and helped me down the stairs, one at a time.

"Nope. Not today. No time traveling today. And by the way, just for the record, I passed out too. Not that it is any kind of bragging rights, more like a rite of passage, but we all do it. The tree has a power; I guess you found that out the hard way. Not that there is an easy way."

"We're inside the big house then, inside one of Holly's rooms?" I was still scanning the room as I questioned.

"Yes, this was my mother's room, your grandmother's. She was an amazing woman, someone who I loved very much." Joe paused his flow of conversation, still assisting me through the room.

"She constantly teased us that she was going to end up in the Gold Rush of California, and so we all just believed it and then one day it popped up, out of the blue, and she said she was going to Utah."

"So this is where my grandmother slept?" I shook my head. "I'm standing in the house where she lived. Wow. I wish I'd known her."

"Hold on, here's a picture of her." Joe pulled down a large black and white picture off the wall. She was looking to the side, slightly smiling. Her hair was pulled into one big braid all the way around her head. Although you couldn't tell the true color, it seemed light brown or even blonde. She had soft, gentle eyes, with long lashes; she was gorgeous.

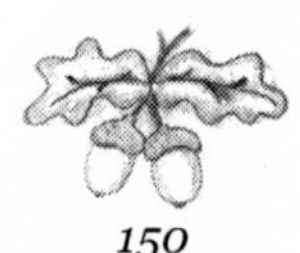

"She was a beauty, huh?"

"Yep, that's my Mom. I spent a little too much time in front of this photo when she left. I missed her so much it almost overwhelmed me. I thought a lot about going to Utah to be with her. I just couldn't live without her." Joe was scratching his chin nervously.

"What did you do? How did you overcome that?" I could see Joe's face turning red.

"I just did. I had to."

And with that, Joe hung the picture back on the wall and put my arm over his shoulder, helping me down the hall to the kitchen. "You look like you needed a little help still."

"I'll be fine," I began, when I stopped talking to examine the room we were in.

I immediately felt like I had walked into a time warp, one that took me back to the 1950s. The entire room was bright yellow, including the walls, the curtains, and even the rectangular yellow table that had a silver rim around it. There were six chairs that looked like they had giant yellow candies for seats. Yellow glass containers of lemon drops covered the counter top, as well as several yellow tin canisters and a large yellow breadbox.

The ovens were also older models, but shined to pristine condition, as if they had never been used. The refrigerator was a tiny ice box with silver legs that looked like it could get up and walk away at any moment.

The room made me feel cheerful the moment I stepped into it. "I can't believe this place. Is this the main kitchen?"

"What else would it be, my dear? Sure isn't the bathroom!" Joe gave his quirky little grin at me.

"I just mean, this does not look like a kitchen that anyone has ever used. It's like a model from the fifties. Like one of those commercials from the *Wave of the Future* kitchen exhibits."

"I know, I don't use it much."

"It's a very unique kitchen, I must say." I continued examining everything in the room, down to the black Felix the Cat clock on the wall. Its tail clicked back and forth with the passing seconds.

"Your grandmother renovated the kitchen in the 1950s. She always wanted a modern kitchen, and my Dad gave it to her. I just kept it this way. Why would I change it? It works, I guess."

Joe began stirring vigorously whatever he had boiling on the stove top. I was starving and glad he was preparing something to eat. "Hungry?" Joe asked.

"You took the words right out of my mouth. I could eat a buffalo." We laughed and Joe continued working on his dish as I sat on one of the yellow gumdrop chairs.

"Well, let's take care of some supper and then we can continue on with the tour of the house if you are up to it. Sound like a plan?" Joe poured the steamy mixture into a colander in the sink.

"Sounds wonderful. This day has been whirling by at the speed of light anyway. I guess we are staying over here at the house tonight?"

"Yes, I think so. You saw how big my pad was."

"Well, we can stay there too. I am happy either way." And I was happy. I couldn't stop thinking to myself that only a few short weeks ago, I was taking my final math exam, and now I am learning about time travel.

My mind began to reflect on our day together when Joe interrupted. "Hope you like spaghetti, because it is just about the only thing I know how to make from scratch." Joe poured the sauce over my noodles.

"I love it. This is perfect." I couldn't wait to send those carbs into my mouth. Breakfast had worn off long ago, and I was famished.

"Joe, can I say something?"

Joe passed me my fork and sat down beside me at the table. "Sure, what is it?"

"Thank you."

"Thanks for what? Scaring you half to death with a swarm of bats or carrying you back to the house?"

I looked at him with the most sincere intentions. "No, thank you for believing in me."

"Alex, I do believe in you. In fact, it is more than that. I am *counting* on you. I know you will be just fine once you learn everything, and then you will be changing the world to make it better."

"I sure want to," I replied emphatically as I spread the sauce over my noodles.

We ate quietly as I was thinking through the day's events in my mind. I wondered how the tree knew where to send you when you time travel. What happened to Laura? What is Jackson doing? How does it all work? My mind was lost in a myriad of questions.

"Like my pasta?" Joe slurped up his noodle. Why do men eat so fast and with so much noise?

"Yes, I was hungrier than I thought," I picked at the pasta before selecting the right one.

"Well, like I said, it is my specialty," Joe complimented himself, grinning with sauce on his chin.

"I was wondering..." I propped my hands up on the table.

"Yes, what is it?" Joe continued shoving food in his mouth, wiping the dripping red mixture off his chin with the back of his hand.

"Alright. I was wondering, how does the tree know where and when to send you?" I took a mouthful and began chewing.

"Well, we're going to get to that. I really have to show you, instead of telling you about it. Can it wait until after supper?" Joe was almost half way done with his spaghetti. It had to be a record in eating, I would bet. He should definitely get into professional food eating contests.

"Yes, that's good for me. Well, how about another question then?" I couldn't imagine he would refuse.

"Shoot."

"When are we going to talk about what happened to Laura? You were going to tell me about that today, right?'

"Well, not tell you, again I have to show you. There's a lot more to come before that, though."

I thought through more questions, wondering what I could ask at the supper table. "How do you make your living? Like, how do you have money to go back in time or to live in this time, for that matter?" Surely I have hit on a question that could be answered now.

"Now we are getting somewhere!" Joe stuffed the last forkful into his mouth, jumped up out of his chair, and rinsed his plate at the sink. He looked like an oversized squirrel, standing there, with two large nuts in his cheeks. It made me laugh.

"What?" Joe turned around and saw me giggling.

"Nothing, you are just a nut."

"A nut?" he continued chewing and finally swallowed. "A nut?"

"Yes, you are always in such a good mood. How hard is that to pull off every day?"

"Not hard at all. I love life. I look for the best in every situation. Life is good. And no matter what, I just keep moving forward. It's all right here, Alex." Joe rubbed his chest and stood there smiling. "But let's not get lost here. You asked about how I make my living, and I intend to give the little lady what she asked for."

Joe immediately whirled around and began pulling all the lower cabinet doors open. As he did, I noticed that there was a sea of aluminum coffee cans neatly stacked underneath the counters. Each was facing forward, in perfect sequence. He plucked one of the cans out and sat it on the table. He turned his chair around and sat on it with the back of the chair against his chest. Dad used to call that cowboy style. Mom would always add that distinction, "Yes, Alex. Cowboy, not cowgirl. It isn't ladylike to sit cowboy style."

Joe tilted the can forward so that I could read a small piece of tape with the numbers "1902." He popped the can top off and dumped out the treasure inside. "This is how we live in the past."

"Cash, that's how we live." Joe starting fanning out the cash from inside the can and I could see it was old money. Money from 1902.

"We got it covered. It's kind of like a winery with fine wines. Only it is a bank of sorts with cash from every year that we would possibly need." Joe pulled out another year and opened the can, again fanning the money.

"Incredible. Are you not worried about someone taking this money? It doesn't seem really *safe in a coffee can*." I must admit, I was honestly intrigued that someone would really stash money in coffee cans like this. It was a vault of money.

"It's as safe as Fort Knox here. No one's going to come in this house. It is very well protected."

"How? We walked right up to the house with no..."

"Ahhh, now someone came quickly to find out who we were, didn't he?" And with that, my mind instantly went to Jackson. Ah, sweet Jackson.

"So when you said that Jackson's family..." I started.

"Exactly. His family has a jack of all trades. We got your lawyers, we got your farmers, we got your cooks, we got your security. You name it, we got it." Joe smacked his hands together loudly and I jumped. My mind had already sailed off on a boat named Jackson. Yes, we got your bodyguard, I hoped.

"They watch over this place 24/7. I'm not one bit worried that anything will happen to our sweet Holly or any of her contents."

I surveyed the cans as we continued talking. "Alex, I don't think I have told you this, because I think I was waiting." Joe put the cans back in the cabinets and closed the doors.

"Told me what?"

"Your family, uh, our family, has enough money. There is no need to worry about anything that you may need." Joe sat back down in his backward-facing chair. "I mean, time traveling is your job."

"This is *all* you do?" I asked as Joe nodded. "How's that possible? It can't take up *all* your time." I was steadily working through my dinner now, trying to talk between mouthfuls, immensely curious about his answer.

"Yes, this will take up all your time. This is all of your life." Joe cocked his head to one side.

"No. How could it be all of your life?" Up until now, I was beginning to think that you live quite a life as a time traveler.

"Alright. Step one, you read. Step two, you research more by reading. Step three, you read and research even more. Step four, you make up your mind. Step five, you travel back in time. Step six, you come back. And then six more times, you repeat steps one through six." Joe used his fingers to demonstrate as he went through each step, counting finger by finger.

"What is this, time travel for dummies?" I reviewed my plate and finally scraped the last of my meal onto my fork.

"No. I'm just saying, it takes up an awful lot of your time. It can take forever to make a decision, because you have to crawl through history to find the one right event and the circumstances that fit." Joe took my empty plate.

"You see, an event I might pass over, you may feel very passionate about going back to correct. You could feel the calling to help someone that I did not. It's very personal, and takes a long time to decide about. And then, you could be in the past for a week or two years. It depends on how long it takes to achieve your goal."

Joe flipped the towel off his shoulder that had been perched there like a pirate's parrot the whole time. He dried my plate and quickly sat it on the stack that was neatly piled in the cabinet.

"Well, why is it all the rush, rush, rush of getting done so quickly?"

"It isn't really the rush, rush, rush. It is the study, study and wait."

"Okay, that is going down like a lead balloon. Study, study and wait? Wait for what?" Somehow, his explanation was lost in translation.

"You have to wait until the time is right and then you can travel. You can't just go whenever you want to."

"Is this one of those things that you just have to show me?"

"Yep. You got it." Joe got up and began walking toward the hallway.

"After you, my dear." He motioned to me with an extended arm.

"Where are we going?" There was so much about this house that seemed like a mystery. There we so many places that I wanted to be let loose to explore, but I had to learn patience as my tour guide led the way.

"To the library."

My mind was filled with curiosity. A library? Joe motioned me to walk up a small flight of stairs from the kitchen and we were suddenly in a very large room on the third floor.

It was one great big room, one entire floor of the house, and it was filled from floor to ceiling with books, papers, journals, magazines,

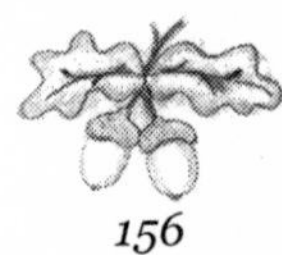

maps, and more. Some sections seemed a lot older, based on the bindings that were sticking out, and others, new and colorful. It was a sea of literature, periodicals and papers.

There were rows and rows of books around the perimeter of the room, and single standing racks in the middle of the floor. The walls of the room were completely covered; you could not spot a single inch of open space except the few windows. Books were stacked back to back on elaborate shelving that wound around the entire room. The deep, rich color on the shelving only added something to the intricate carvings which gave an old-world feel to the room.

As I stood there, I took a deep breath and could literally feel the history filling my lungs. It was a thick, earthy smell that immediately beckoned me inside the room.

"This, my dear Alex, is our library. Now do you see why this could be a job in itself?" Joe looked around as if he was a proud father, happy but stoic at the same time.

"I think I *am* beginning to get the picture." I continued scanning, walking slowly into the room. It was unbelievable. It was like being in a library, but different, more like being inside a historic landmark filled with precious artifacts.

There were stacks of periodicals in nests here and there along the floor. Heaps of letters were tied up with twine or ribbon. Newspapers were rolled and placed in various baskets and wooden containers all over the room.

As I continued to survey the room, I spotted a large oval desk. I don't think I had ever seen an oval desk before this day, but it was more than that in its uniqueness. While walking up to the desk, it occurred to me that the desk was one perfect cross-section cut from a very large tree. Someone had crafted it so that it was oblong instead of perfectly round. Either that or it came from an oval shaped tree. I simply could not tell.

There was a tall, ladder-backed chair that was pushed up against one side of the desk. Void of any drawers, the heavily lacquered top proved to be a beautiful, but very simple, piece of furniture.

"My goodness, it's incredible," I said as I reached my hand out to touch it.

"Yes, I've had many a happy hour behind this desk. Glad you like it." Joe smoothed his hand over the top while he seemed to be thinking about something. The top was flawless, as if no one had ever used it before.

"You mean it has been used? That can't be possible. It's immaculate." I scanned the top again to see if I could spot signs of use.

"Generation upon generation has used it," Joe commented, gently rubbing the top of the immaculate desk.

"How could that be? It doesn't appear to have *ever* been used before."

"Like I said, we take care of things to make them last." Joe smiled. "What do you think about the room? The library?"

"I can't put it into words. It's simply amazing. I can't wait to have time to see what is hidden in these walls." My eyes gleamed in delight with the thought of endless days of reading.

"That will come, I promise you."

"It's already coming together. I mean, earlier today we were sitting down to eat breakfast, and I knew nothing about how all of this works. Every minute seems like a new wonder unfolds. I really can't believe how incredible it all is."

"It's a lot to take in. Why don't I leave you to explore awhile, and I go down and get things ready for our adjournment for the evening?" He switched to a fake English accent, "Feel free to touch, read and look at anything you would like. I shall return." Joe bowed and went down the stairs, leaving me in a complete trance. Where would I begin?

I turned around from the desk, my eyes glazed over in book heaven. I looked at the shelf that was at my eye height. "North Carolina History, Years 1935-1937." Not that one.

"Maps & Charts - Appalachian Mountains." No, not that one either.

"The Civil War." Yep that's the one. I pulled out the desk chair and began to read. Maybe I would spot some bit of history that would help me understand Joe's story with his Laura. As I scanned the pages,

I did not see anything that related to any Laura. It appeared to be a history on guns used during the Civil War.

Sometime later, Joe resurfaced carrying two sodas, one in each hand. "Figured you could use a drink. I know it gets a little stuffy, but we really can't open up too many windows when it looks like it is going to storm."

"Storm?" I looked up from my history lesson to review the windows for signs of clouds outside.

"Yep. I can tell its coming, I hear the thunder. You didn't hear it?"

"I guess not," I said as I reached out to grab the cold drink.

"Well, it's on the way." Joe took a quick gulp of the bubbly soda.

"I was just reading about the guns and artillery that these guys used during the Civil War. I don't understand how in the world they could do go through all those steps just to shoot a gun. Guns today, you just load and point, right?" I continued sipping my soda.

"Yes. There's a lot to learn. Well, I know I promised you that I would give you some answers about Laura, and more about how we time travel. Are you ready to continue on?"

I was literally walking my mind through everything I had seen that day and could not imagine how much more I could handle. Everything was so overwhelming, but at the same time, so thrilling and captivating. Could I handle much more in one day? Maybe I should pace myself. A couple of hours in the library and it would be bedtime. Tomorrow, maybe tomorrow, we could move on.

"Would it be horrible to start again tomorrow? I know you are pretty anxious to share more with me, but I feel like I am on overload. Can I absorb today and start again in the morning?" I looked at Joe with a questioning expression while holding my fingers firmly in the book.

"Yes. I actually am glad to hear you say that. I would really enjoy a little down time. Do you want to stay in the library or come down and play a game of cards?"

Hmmm...trick question. But the books *would* be here. I would share the rest of my life with these treasures, but Joe would be gone. I

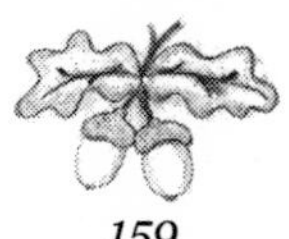

should be with him. I need to spend as much time as I can in his company.

"Hearts? Rummy? What will it be?" I stood up and replaced the book on its shelf.

"Old Maid, maybe?" Joe laughed and followed me down the stairs.

That night, there was a storm, just like Joe said there would be. Summer storms seemed to come in quickly, roar loudly, and then disappear. This one was no different. While there was a brilliant display of fascinating lightening, the thunder gave me the willies. Thunder reminds me, with great angst, of the night my parents passed away.

Again, I took refuge in my grandmother's bed. There was so much to review. This was the analytical part of me that was conflicted with the physical needs of sleep. I lay awake for hours. My brain was not about to let my body go to sleep when there was work to be done. I had some heavy sorting out to deal with before sleep.

One thing was perfectly clear. This place, Holly, was truly magical. No words could sum it up. And as each new development unfolded, the parts were beginning to make a whole.

It *was* like standing on the edge of the Grand Canyon. You can't believe what your eyes are taking in. You blink, but it is still there. You can't imagine this beautiful, wonderful thing being as vivid and breathtaking as what you are witnessing.

The tree was so powerful. I could never conceive that a tree could hold the secrets of time travel, but it makes perfect sense once you know the secret. Of course trees know all, they have *seen* all.

As the minutes let go and allowed the hours to continue on, my mind inevitably trailed off to thoughts of Jackson. I wish I had not met him today. But his image was there, standing in front of me. And I felt that his eyes just begged for more conversation. Or action?

The trick was that I knew this was like getting a new puppy. You have to know what you are investing in before you invest. Love was something I could not invest in right now. Maybe it is nothing. Maybe it was a quick and very short-lived fascination.

Evening, June 23, 1989

I wanted to see him again. I wanted to know what he was doing. How could I control myself from getting too close to him, talking to him, learning more about him? I *had* to let go. I needed to remind myself constantly of what Claire went through. Love is painful. No need for pain while I am in the most beautiful place in the world.

Chapter Eighteen

June 27, 1989

The next morning I could hear Joe in the kitchen, tinkering around. I couldn't imagine what he would be cooking for the both of us, considering he already made his one specialty the night before. "Coffee?" Joe extended a hot cup to me and offered up some scrambled eggs.

"Thanks. Well, I didn't get a lot of sleep last night, so this coffee is definitely going to help wake me up." I took my first long sip of the hot brew and took my plate to the yellow table.

"Why is that? I slept like a baby!" Joe grinned while he poured himself a cup.

"I guess I have a lot going on in my mind. I'm trying to keep everything sorted. You can imagine it's a lot for any one person."

"Yes, yes, I can. You are handling it well. But there is more to see today. You up for the challenge?" Joe waited as I took a long pause to answer. He scraped the last of the eggs onto his plate and sat beside me.

"I *am* ready. I can handle it." I laughed just looking at him with his goofy hair and mad scientist expression.

We continued chatting through breakfast mainly about the crops that our acreage held, and the history of the plantation. Joe was very detailed and quite the professor. He explained to me about Oscar and Maren Shannon, my great plus, plus grandparents who built the great Holly. I had so many questions, but he said that much more would be revealed later. It was impossible to tell me everything about our family's history in a couple of days.

We talked a lot about Holly. The house was so secluded from everything else. Holly is situated in, what we call in the South, *the boon docks*. The farms that were near ours belonged to families who had lived there for generations. They are safe, trustworthy families. Joe hoped that this would not change in the future, as there would be continued growth in the area.

"So, what do you have planned for us today?" We finished our simple breakfast and I was ready to take a hot shower once I knew the game plan.

"Just get ready and I will meet you back here in a few. And by the way, Jackson brought those eggs over this morning. I didn't want to wake you when he got here." Joe dug both his hands in his pockets and leaned against the yellow cabinets.

"Thank you for your kind consideration, Sir." But I *did* want him to wake me up. I didn't want to miss seeing Jackson again. How could I achieve that without telling Joe how I felt about the dream boat?

In the bathroom, I jumped into the shower and realized that the plumbing was less than desirable. I felt like I had to dance around just to get a water droplet to hit my body. Okay, it wasn't quite that bad. But I might have to do something about that if I am to stay here for any length of time. A girl needs good water pressure.

But as I let the water trickle down my face, I wondered what Jackson looked like today, when he dropped off my eggs. Had he in his overalls or something else? I had never seen his face clean and clear. His eyes were certainly inviting. Inviting! Alex, I told myself, get your mind off the boy. Focus. Today is the big reveal about Laura. You need to keep your eye on the prize. What a prize Jackson is...No! No, the prize is finding out about Laura. She is where your thoughts need to be.

Have you ever felt like you just lost an argument with yourself?

When Joe and I met in the kitchen, I was still having a battle my own thoughts. It was overpowering. I had heard that the heart wants what the heart wants, but doesn't the brain, the intellect, get a vote in there somewhere?

"Alright, I promised I would continue on with answering all of your questions. Is there anything that you want to start with today?" Joe smiled. Jackson's phone number, maybe, we could start there?

"Nope, Joe, just lead me in the direction you intend and I will follow."

"Well, let's get going. There's a lot to cover." Joe was wearing a pair of khaki shorts, the kind that barely touch the knee. His bright red shirt was a sharp contrast. He looked like he was ready to head out on a Boy Scout hike up a mountain.

With that, we were both up and walking across the worn floorboards of the hallway that popped and snapped with each step. It was to be expected with a house that dated back to the century when the Declaration of Independence was signed.

"Now you asked me yesterday how the tree knows how to send you to when and where you want to go. You ready?"

"Yes, ready."

Joe walked ahead of me to the end of the long hallway. There was a large, white door that was closed, with a glossy, white doorknob smack dab in the middle of the door. I thought it was a strange place for a doorknob.

Joe asked me to close my eyes. He held my hand to guide me through the doorway. I could hear him opening the door.

Walking into the room, all I could hear was what sounded like wind chimes, lightly making music. The room was much cooler than the rest of the house. The air was crisp, though, and it almost burned my lungs as I took a breath, like breathing pure oxygen.

"Alright, you ready to open your eyes?"

"Yes, ready." I smiled at the drama.

"Open your eyes!"

I don't know what I thought it was that triggered time travel. Lying awake last night, several things came to my mind. Maybe there is a potion that you drink before you jump? Maybe there are special poems you have to read to activate the tree's powers? Click your heals, maybe? I really didn't know. But nothing came close to what I saw when I opened my eyes that morning.

As I slowly lifted my eyelids, I saw a profusion of sparkling glass saturating the room in a glorious sea of crystals and light as far as the eye could see. The entire length of the room was a myriad of sparkling diamond-like crystals. A stream of sunlight poured in from the windows and bounced off the glistening gems.

The crystals were all shapes and sizes and encompassed the entire room; it was like one giant chandelier. "Oh my goodness," I quietly commented after moments of sheer astonishment.

"It *is* amazing, isn't it?" Joe smiled at me. "Let me explain," the tour guide coming out in him once again.

"Please do," I quietly commented as I clapped my hand over my mouth.

"Well, you have to have a key to unlock the energy from the tree. You do that simply with a crystal." Joe walked over and pulled one off a hook that was holding it to the ceiling. "This crystal has the ability to take you through time, back to where you are going. This little jewel is all you need."

"The crystal activates the tree? Is that what you are saying?"

"You got it." Joe placed the crystal in my hand. "A long time ago, one of our great Uncle's brought over some of the crystals from Ireland. He was a glassmaker, and knew what to do to design the crystals. He was very important to the history of time travel for our family. Every crystal in this room has been lovingly polished to a glossy finish and was brought in here to hang. And then...it waits for you to choose it."

"What do you mean, choose it?"

"You have to have a crystal to make the tree work. Once you decide on where and when to time travel, you come here, select the right one, go to the Evening Oak, and off you go. It is as simple as that."

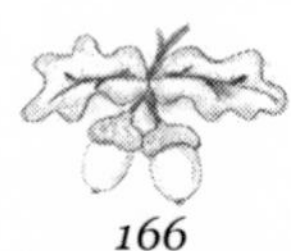

I walked forward, looking around at the ceiling and rubbing the crystal in my hand. It was incredible. The beauty was breathtaking, just like the tree. "The crystal gives the tree the information to go to the right time and place."

"How does the crystal know what you are trying to do?" I asked sheepishly.

"I wish I knew. I don't." Joe hesitated and started again as if he wasn't sure how to answer my question. "It's like it just calls to you. When you know where you are going, it calls to you. Something happens when you are truly ready to time travel and then you enter this room. You will know which one to pull down." Joe picked another one and reviewed it closely in his hand.

I held my hand up in the air and gently touched the crystals as I slowly walked along. It felt like the power of the universe was in this room. I could feel the pulse from each crystal, like each one had its own beating heart. And as my fingers made contact with the crystals, it was almost like I could hear them...giggling?

"Can you hear them?" I turned around to look at Joe as he asked me this, since that was my exact thought at that moment.

"You hear it too?" I pulled my hand back.

"Everyone in our family could hear a tiny, high-pitched giggle when we touched them. It was like they are being tickled. I mean, the crystals are not alive, but they sure feel like it."

"I thought I heard it too, but I guess I couldn't believe it." I looked back at my hand in astonishment.

"Believe it. This is the real magic. This is where dreams come true."

"It feels like we are in a cloud, like when a rainbow is shooting through. I don't know; I am just spell bound."

"I knew you would feel this way." Joe hung his crystal back up on the ceiling and pulled out two black wrought iron chairs from a nearby closet. They were perfect for this room. They both had a winding back in the shape of a heart. The seats were one large, curly heart. We both sat, as I continued to stare at the ceiling.

"So here is how it works. After your research is complete, you will make a decision on where you are going in time. You come in here and you wait until you hear one of them speaking to you, almost calling out to you. And then you take it."

I looked at the crystal in my hand. It was so simple. It calls to you. The tree transports you back in time. *It is magic.* It is the place where dreams come true. I was so overcome with finally learning all of the truth about time travel. Never in my dreams could I have imagined such power, such enchanting possibilities, could be on this earth.

Life had seemed so painful to me for so long. No answers, just questions. The *why's* take over your mind and you can never resolve them. And here I sit, knowing that there is a destiny for man that we can change. There is a breathtaking reality of hope. The knowledge that Joe was giving to me was dreamlike power harnessed in a tiny crystal.

"Are you able to take just one anytime? Anytime that you are ready? Is there a trigger that once you take it, you have to jump?"

"No, and I wish it was, because that would make your life predictable. You could plan your travels around your life. Unfortunately, the crystal tells *you* when it is ready. And it could be right then, or a year from right then. So when you make that decision, you have to be ready."

I looked around the room again. The crystals were *alive?* They spoke to you? My mind went back to something that Joe had said to Lilly on that first phone call. "So why did you say that you are almost out of time?" I brushed my bangs out of my eyes uneasily.

"That's what I don't know. So I plan for it to be soon, and hope that I have more time. I have made my decision on who I'm helping for my last jump. I have already taken my crystal. And now I wait for it to happen. Alex, all I can hope is that I have enough time with you to give you what you need to carry on. I hope I'm given the time."

"How does the crystal tell you its ready? How will you know?"

"It glows. And like I said, it sort of speaks to you. It's a weird feeling the first time it happens. Almost like the tree thing. But then you know. And it doesn't wait around. When it's ready, you have to act sooner than later."

"Okay, that's going to have to be one of those see-it-to-understand it things, I guess."

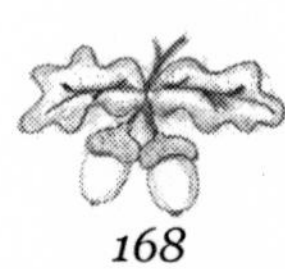

"You think you can handle this? Do you want to be a time traveler, now that you know?"

"Yes, I think I'm going to keep our family's tradition strong. I can do this. I'm not going to let this gift be wasted. I know you don't know me very well, but Alex Charles can handle anything. I think I've already proved that in many ways." The passion was pouring out from my heart as I spoke. I wanted to be the one who keeps our family's purpose moving forward. There was no other choice. How could I sit among God's beauty and not choose to be part of it?

"I'm so glad to hear you say that." Joe rubbed his chest as if easing the pain of all the worry he had held inside these recent weeks.

For the first time, it was *all* clear to me. I knew what I needed to know to time travel. I now had a clear resolution to spend every moment with Joe, and help him leave the present with the peace in his heart that our name and our God given talents would be put to good use.

"I was wondering when you would share the story of Laura?" I batted my eyes at him. The wait had been hard enough. I was ready to know the truth.

"Well, I'd like you to read something. I want you to read the letters from Lucas and the diary of the Confederate soldier who stayed on Chestnut Plantation. Do you think you'd like to do that?"

"Yes, I'd love to read them. Is this what you read to make your decision to chose Laura?"

"It is. And I think it will help you understand even more," Joe added.

We went back to the library and Joe knew exactly where to find the letters. They were worn, but still very legible. Joe handed me the delicate stack as if they were the most fragile items he had ever held.

"I will leave you to read. Please be careful with the pages. As you can imagine, they are very precious to me. Come on down to the kitchen when you are done. I definitely want to hear your thoughts on what you read." Joe hopped down the stairs, and I turned to the pages in my hand.

The writing on the outside of the first letter simply read "Laura Chestnut, Chestnut Plantation, Bentonville, North Carolina." I immediately read the signature. I knew that this was the letter from Lucas to Laura while he was still in the war. It was yellowed and weathered, smudged with the ink from his quill.

Dear Sister,

March 1862

I hope this letter reaches your sweet hands, as we never know from one post to the next what will be taken by the Union bandits. It has been a long hard winter and now spring has given us some hope of the War coming to an end.

Not to worry on it, but I was injured this past month by a wild shell that hit my leg. I am doing some better now, but it has been a tough go of it over many weeks. I was not sure I would keep my leg, but now it is on the mend.

I die of news from home. I only wish I could hear something from my dear sister and mother. It is a spoil when letters are passed out and there is none from home. I pray for news each day, as I can only imagine how our crops need to be planted soon in this warm Southern sun. I hope our livestock are fat and happy.

I will see you soon, as I am sure the South will prevail and win this awful war. Though this war has made its mark on so many, we will never know the pains that some have endured. I have certainly seen enough bloodshed and pain for one lifetime.

I regret I have not been paid as of yet and have no money to send home. We are fed about half of what it takes to keep a man whole. And some days not at all. Rations are constantly running out, but we continue on as cheerfully as we can. Bread and water is about the best we get somedays. Each of us waiting for papers to be able to return home, even for just a short time.

I regret that this Post is so soure, but my heart can only extend the warmest affection and yurns to see you both soon.

With love,

Lucas

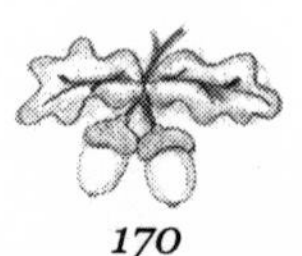

June 27, 1989

I carefully folded Lucas's letter and began reading the next series of tattered pages that were folded together.

Diary

March 19th, 1865

I know not who will care or take a care to read the ramblings of an injured soldier. But nonetheless, it helps pass the time to get my thoughts on paper. I have been injured and taken ill at this nearby home, Chestnut Plantation. The owner and her daughter, Miss Laura, have earned their place in heaven, no doubt, with the things that they have so unselfishly given on our behalf.

I have enjoyed meeting Miss Laura, as her sweet nature reminds me of my good sister. I hope to see my sister someday soon and be rejoined with all of my family. As of today, I am not sure what will happen to any of us. The war has been a terrible thing to live through. Most of us have only the shirts on our backs and have no idea on when we will have help. This whole war has been a waste for all of us. I have lost many a good friend and neighbor. Most died from illness, which has been my biggest worry during the war. I would like to see my family again and go on with my life.

I was shot on the first day of battle. My Major, General Robert Hoke, sent injured troops here for rest and recovery. We hope to be moved to a better hospital soon.

March 20th, 1865

Today was a hopeful day as many of the soldiers were able to finally carry on by foot. No hope for me at this point, as I lost one arm and leg and they are having a terrible time of healing. I remain still on my cot and thank the good Lord for whatever food and water is given me.

The lady of the house has taken ill too and has been unable to leave her room. Miss Laura carries on and all we can do is offer our sincere thanks for the help that she gives us. The weather has been hot but bearable.

March 21st, 1865
The Battle of Bentonville has been lost to the North. We are in great pains to know that our losses have been in vain. I would be a liar if I did not say that we feel like we downright failed. We didn't think this would be the way the war would end.
A horrible thing happened last night. As one of the men were going out to relieve themselves, they heard Miss Laura crying out from the barn. Some yellowered, nasty Yankee rascal took a hold of her and violated her. Thomas Lloyd said he fount her there with that nasty Yankee on her. I wished I could take the life right out of that old buzzard! But I reckon Thomas and company took care of him and the matter is settled. He ain't comin' around here no more.

March 22nd, 1865
Today is my last post as I have some rotten news, to be sure. There was a horrible fight last night with the lady of the house and Laura. I can only reckon that Laura's episode in the barn was revealed. Well, I guess her mother's mind was gone, she just went into a plain old fit. We seen her dragging poor Laura out of the house and into the back woods. The woman came back ranting that she would not have a Yankee bastard in her house. I knew what she done. She took that poor girl out and had the last of her. But what could I do in my condition?
Laura has not returned, and with the woman of the house taken ill in her room, we can only imagine that we have seen the last of that poor Laura. And it is a crying shame there ain't nothin' that can be done about it.
I am leaving my pitiful words here in the hopes that Lucas, her brother, will return and know what happened to his family. God bless.
Cadet Edward Clayton

I had to read the diary twice, as my mind was still lost in "had the last of her." She was left tied to that tree to die. And did Lucas return from the war and find his home in this incredible state?

I decided to find Joe and get more details.

"What happened to Laura's mother?" I found Joe outside standing beside a swing at the front of the house. Among a sea of pink

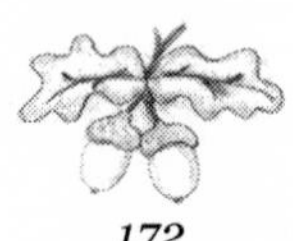

cone flowers, a large oak tree held two large ropes with a wooden seat tied at the bottom. I could see the bees dropping in on one flower after another, busily doing their jobs.

"Oh, that was fast!" Joe yanked at the swing rope.

"Well, I had to stop and find you. I have a few questions. I can't stand the suspense."

"Sure. What is on your mind? I will help if I know the answer." He looked at me, curiously.

The swing looked so inviting, I decided to hop on and swing as he talked to me.

"What happened to Laura's mother?" I kicked my legs out to gain more height. I could see over the field and over the roof of Joe's house. I was beginning to think I might spend some serious time on this swing. It was lulling, calming. Reading those letters broke my heart. And there was more hard news to hear.

"How about I make it short and simple?" Joe rubbed his hands together.

"Okay, go ahead."

"Lucas returned home a short time after the diary was written. He was finally released and made it back. He found his mother had locked herself in the potato cellar and an empty house. She survived but could tell him nothing of what happened. She had totally lost her mind, I suppose. He learned what little was explained on those diary pages."

"At least they both survived."

"Yes, they did. Lucas carried on at the plantation with a woman who he married."

"At least Lucas carried on."

"They all *carried on.*"

"Oh yes! None of this really happens. It's so hard to pull myself away from the tragedy."

"Exactly. And then you make it right. You make it the way it was supposed to be." I continued to swing in silence for a few minutes.

"Joe, what does Jackson do for the farm?" I asked as my blonde hair flew in my face. I needed to dig out of the sadness that I was feeling.

"He takes care of all the farming for us. He plants and harvests all of our crops. He's really a very good farmer for someone so young."

"How old is he?"

"He's twenty."

I hesitated to ask, but I really wanted to hear his thoughts, "Do you think that is too old for me?"

"For you? Why are you asking?"

"I guess I'm just curious, that's all."

"No, he is not too old. You are almost eighteen, so I would think that you are old enough to make your own decision about this, Alex."

I continued swinging and then we both decided it was time for some lunch. We retreated to the blue Bug and headed into town. Wilmington still feels like a hometown. It's kept its southern charm and creates a very welcoming place for UNC college students.

My friends will be here soon, for college, just like I would have been. I guess I needed to start figuring some things out. Where will I live? What will I do when Joe leaves?

"How about Bubba's Café? You'll love the fried chicken."

"Sounds good to me."

As we sat in the tiny diner, there was a lot on my mind. The waitress brought us each a large plate of fried chicken and mashed potatoes slathered with white gravy, and a mountain of biscuits.

"Through the lips and over the gums, look out stomach, here it comes!" Joe grinned as he forced a very large fork load of potato into his mouth.

"How old are you, again?" I smartly asked as I thought about how much I would miss his humor when he was gone. He made my soul feel happy when I was around him.

"Now, getting back to Jackson, what's the deal?"

"We don't really need to really talk about that. And by the way, when will you tell me about what happened to Laura? I'm dying to know!" I slathered butter on a southern biscuit. Is there anything tastier on the planet?

"Well, I can't *tell* you about what happened. I have to let you learn by other means. Just trust me, all will be revealed tonight. For now, we can relax and talk about your interest in Jackson."

"Is that weird, though, me asking about Jackson? It isn't like me at all."

"No, I don't guess. What do you want to know?"

"Have you known him his whole life?"

"Yes."

"How big is his family?"

"I couldn't tell you. Why, when you consider uncles, cousins and all, it is a big family. He has two little sisters. His Dad, Bill, and his Mom, Allie, are the nicest people you would ever want to meet."

The waitress interrupted to pour us both more sweet tea. She had a bluebird pin on her dress that winked. "I love your pin," I told her.

"Oh yes, had this a while. It is my little bird on my shoulder. I guess like a guardian angel. A good friend gave it to me many years ago. Seems to have worked so far; I have had a good life." She smiled and walked on to her next customer.

"I guess that is what we are; a little bird on someone's shoulder." I smiled at Joe.

"Yes, that is exactly what we are. Did I ever tell you about our crops, what we grow?

"No, what do we have?" I was curious about that and it was off the subject of Jackson.

"We have soy beans, corn, wheat, cotton and peanuts. We also have a pretty big vegetable garden in the summer. Lots of things that are ready to harvest now, actually."

"Wow, how did we come up with that combination?"

"I don't know; we have always had those crops, and they all pay very well. They rotate to keep the soil in good condition. I love having the farm. I like spending time out there with Jackson and his family when I am home. Growing something and getting your hands in the earth feels right. My parents taught me the meaning of a hard day's work."

"Does Jackson's family know everything?" Oops, back to him again.

"Yes, they do. And they will be a big help for you down the road. They have been very loyal and good to our family. We could not do what we do without them. So, it is important to keep that relationship strong."

And with that, Joe slid his plate forward and wiped his mouth. I hadn't even gotten halfway through my meal and he was already done. It's like eating with someone in the Army!

"What do you know about Jackson personally, though?" I risked the topic one more time.

"You mean, does he have a girlfriend?" OK, Joe. Cut out that big smile!

"Yes, I guess that's what I mean. And really, any other bits about him such as what he likes, he dislikes, those kinds of things." I shoved a mouthful of the crunchy chicken in my mouth.

"Well, let's see," Joe started as he stretched out lengthwise on the booth seat, picking his teeth with a toothpick. "He likes sports, I know that; Jackson's a big college basketball fan. I can't think of a single girlfriend he has ever had. But that's not to say that he hasn't had romances in high school."

"No college then?"

"Nope. He stayed here to work with his family. I guess the way he figured it, he would tend our farm the rest of his life. No need to go off to college to handle that. He's taken some specific advanced courses but has no interest in a piece of paper, a degree. But who knows?"

"Okay. Well what about his personality? Kind, hot tempered or what?"

"Well, girl, it's hard to say what his genuine temperament is, since most men will show another side to their ladies than they will, say, to a neighbor."

"Don't make this so hard for me! You know what I mean. Is he someone who you could see me getting along with?"

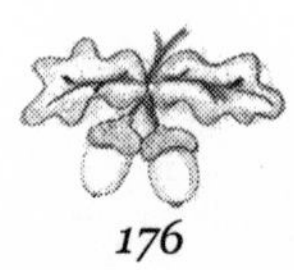

"Of course I could. He's a good guy, Alex. I hope you become friends. By the way, what are your plans with your friends back in Raleigh?"

"That's simply something I have not worked through yet. I'm missing the first semester of school, obviously. And I told Lilly already, and Claire, but I've not told everyone else yet."

"Big decisions are ahead of you. I know I have laid out a lot of responsibility. But we will work through everything. It will feel right when the time comes."

"I know now that it will. But may I tell you something?"

"No! Absolutely not!" He smiled with his devilish grin. "Of course, what is it?"

"I *am* a little scared. I'm scared that any minute you are going to leave me and then what? And honestly, I'm just tired of family leaving me alone." We both paused and Joe seemed to understand my concern. He sobered up for a moment. "Not to worry, we have some time and I will teach you what you need to know. You are going to be okay. Like you said, you are strong. You can handle this," he reassured me.

I finished eating and we continued our conversation as we went back to the car, talking about a bunch of funny things that have happened in Joe's life. I asked him about where he went for all of his jumps, and he gave me a general idea about a couple of them. I wanted to know a lot more though.

He also told me about some of the tricks to remember for time travel, like how to blend in with the time you are in. One funny thing was how to dirty up your teeth. He said you have to carry a small can of brown candle wax. It works perfectly to make your teeth look darkened, if you go far back in time.

When we got back to the farm, the afternoon moved along as slowly as honey dripping off a bee hive on a warm day. We relaxed on the back porch, the one that was so heavily covered with ivy. The summer wind relaxed both of us and gave us a chance to talk more about Joe's travels.

If I picked up anything from Joe over the weeks we had spent together, the main thing would be that he is so relaxed, so at ease, so comfortable with his life. That was what I was hoping for, to have a life that I could be proud of, but would not drive me nuts. Hearing him talk about his travels gave me a firm sense that he was proud of his life. He was completely happy with the choices he had made, that those lives were forever changed because of his good work.

A sense of purpose is all anyone wants in life. Life should feel like it was all worth something: the sacrifice, the hardship, the loss. Was there a point to all of it? With most of my life ahead of me, that was the $64,000 question. I hoped that I would discover the meaning to it all through serving others.

I shared with Joe a lot about my life with Mom, his baby sister. I could tell that he missed her and wanted to spend more time with her than he had.

The sun went down and darkness began to envelop the house. I was already having anxiety about going to bed that night. The evening before had not provided me with such restful sleep. If I could just get my mind to quiet all the questions and allow me to rest peacefully.

We had a simple dinner: tomato sandwiches and milk. My stomach was thankful after our very large and greasy, but yummy, lunch. Simple and easy was what we needed. After we ate, Joe took me back into the crystal room.

"You wanted to know what happened to Laura and now it is time you are *witness* to the truth."

Joe pulled a crystal from the ceiling and checked it carefully before passing it to me. Engraved on the crystal it read, "Ella Laura Chestnut, 1865."

"Does every crystal say something?"

"No, only when you get back from your time travel. You engrave the year on the crystal from your time travel so you know which memory belongs to that crystal. You can relive the experience. I'll show you how to do that later."

"Relive?"

"Yes, tonight, keep this crystal in your hands as you sleep. The truth will be revealed to you in a dream. You will see exactly what I saw...and feel as I felt."

"How is that possible? I may only sleep for hours, you were gone for..."

"Almost a year."

"A year? How could that work?" I looked down at the crystal as if it would answer my question. The room was dark now, and the glitter of the crystals was more like icicles dripping off a tin roof on a winter's evening.

"I don't know how it works, only that you will see exactly what I saw from the time I walked out of the tree until I returned."

"I am excited! I can't wait to see what happens to Laura." Now I was rubbing my hands together like Joe does, and actually looking forward to bedtime.

"Yes. And just so you know, you can see any time travel in this room, anytime you want to." Joe put the chairs from our earlier conversation back into the closet.

"Wow, that is incredible. You can see anyone's time travel?"

"You got it." Joe began down the stairs, with me following right behind.

"Well, I guess it is getting to be that time of night. I'm hitting the hay, so wish me luck." I took a deep breath and smiled at Joe, as I had not a clue what I was getting into.

"One thing to remember, like I said, you will feel as I felt in the dream. Don't be surprised if you wake up with a heap of emotions. Since this isn't my first rodeo, I know what happens. So just call for me in the morning when you wake up and we will talk it through. It's going to be heavy. It's a 3-D movie with smell-o-vision."

And with that, we were both off in our own directions to bed. I would finally know how he saved Laura and I would know how he fell in love with her. The waiting was already more than I could bear.

Chapter Nineteen

March 19, 1865

I climbed into Grandmother's tall plantation bed and covered myself with the cloud-like down comforter. I took a deep breath and grasped the crystal tightly in my hand. I was surprised that I was so nervous, having anxiety about what would happen once I fell asleep. I slowly closed my eyes, and shockingly, I was instantly asleep.

I opened my eyes abruptly to see that it was night, and I was inside the Evening Oak. I remembered that I was seeing things through Joe's eyes. For that matter, I was feeling his nervousness right away. I wondered why it was so dark, but then I remembered that Joe told me that you have to travel at night, so no one can see you suddenly appear or disappear in the tree trunk.

Joe moved out of the tree and looked around anxiously. He instantly took inventory of what he had brought with him. He checked his clothing to make sure he had everything he intended. His pockets were full of money, bills and some small gold coins, a pistol, his brown wax, some letters and a folded parchment.

He pulled a small sack of clothing off his back, a sack of food, a mess kit with a frying pan and a rolled wool blanket. He took his time laying everything out in front of him. Looking down at his body, he was wearing a standard gray uniform. I could sense his apprehension, his fear of meeting someone and fitting in with this time. I felt his worry about making sure that he accomplished his task.

Once he packed everything back up, he headed out on foot to find a place to rest for the evening. Looking back at the grandness of Holly in the distance, he silently prayed about his mission. His stomach was a knot of emotions and it took him a while to settle in for the evening.

As dreams typically do, time flew by and I began to think about the fact that I couldn't divide one hour from the next. One day he was sleeping in a meadow, and another day he was sitting by the road, humbled, eating a meal that a neighbor shared with him. He was heading to Chestnut Plantation as quickly as he could get there on foot.

Many times he was stopped on the road and folks inquired about who he was and whether or not he was a deserter. He always produced his trusty release papers, proclaiming that he could not wait to get home to his beloved family.

What I observed more than anything was the devastation: so many burned buildings, so few crops, so many hungry men, women and children. There was death everywhere you looked. Everyone seemed exhausted, worried and starved. I had to remind myself that more Americans died in this war than all of the Americans who lost their lives in both World Wars. A combination of old-school thinking and new, more effective weapons had created a devastating war.

Joe met many families who shared their stories with him. Every family had lost a son, brother or father. Some were still hopeful about the return of their loved one. Even so, Joe's mind was ever-focused on getting to Chestnut Plantation. He walked until the sun went down and started again at sunrise every day. It was almost as though I could feel his conviction to get there on time, to serve his purpose.

On the day that he reached Chestnut Plantation, Joe pulled out a letter from his backpack, portraying that he was a currier. It was his angle, his reason for showing up on the plantation as a relatively physically preserved man. He wrapped his arm in a sling, for injury appeal.

Joe walked up the long driveway, taking note of the great crepe myrtle trees that lined the drive. There were several apple trees sprinkled along the path, bare and poorly tended. As Joe approached the main house, he could see soldiers stretched out all over the lawn. It was an unwelcoming site, but one that Joe had prepared himself for. The stench was something else.

The plantation house was tall, two stories, white with black shutters, and long columns in the front. There were several large barns further in the back. It reminded me of Holly at first glance, only on a much smaller scale.

"March 19th, 1865," Joe whispered to himself, arriving exactly when he planned to be there. I could feel Joe's hesitation about seeing Laura for the first time. He was still calculating his introduction to her.

Joe walked up on the first soldier lying on the lawn. "Joseph Cain, Corporal. This Chestnut Plantation? I'm here to see Miss Laura Chestnut. I have a letter for her."

The sickly soldier sat up and shook Joe's hand explaining that his name was Charles Allen and that Joe had the right place, Chestnut Plantation. He took note of Joe's arm. "Injury bad?" Charles slunk back into his lateral position and swatted a fly from his face.

"Yeah, almost lost it, but I am doing better," Joe rubbed his arm as he spoke.

"Fortunate. I lost mine. Guess you just got lucky." Charles looked down at where his arm used to be.

"Glad to know I got to the right place. It's the hospital, right?" Joe continued surveying the scene.

The soldier sat up again and looked around before responding. "Not rightly a hospital. Yes, we have been fed and watered but too many folks here for what they got. The poor Misses of the house doin' the best they can. They are kind folk but there ain't much to go around for all. You got the right place though."

"I can imagine. I'm sure they just aren't equipped to be a hospital. Where is the man of the house?" Joe knew the answer to this question, but it was the gentlemanly thing to do.

"He ain't here. Dead and gone, I reckon." Charles scratched his scruffy beard.

"Death everywhere you go, huh? What a shame," Joe said, adjusting his backpack.

"Yeah, we just left the battle. Came here to get help, but I reckon it will be a few days." As Charles spoke, Joe could hear the guns popping in the distance. The battle was just down the road and fresh fire was at hand.

"Well, best of luck to you, Charles," Joe said as walked on down the path. His mind thinking for a moment about what he would say to Laura. He felt sick in the pit of his stomach. Even though he had rehearsed this meeting in his mind a million times, he was still nervous.

He felt locked in fear suddenly about meeting her, so he decided to go sit under a tree and collect his thoughts. He had been waiting for this moment for a long time. Being a young man, and going into his first jump, he was anxious and wanted to do all the right things. If he did not complete his mission, he knew what fate awaited Laura. I could sense his inner conflict.

As he looked over at the grove of hickories, he was contemplating his choice, praying that he would be able to fulfill his goal. Joe wilted in the heat sitting against the apple tree, collecting his thoughts. He pulled a twist of tobacco out of his jacket and picked off a piece to put in his pipe. Puffs of smoke circled his head and it seemed as though the thick cloud softened his anxiety. After finishing his pipe, he propped his head on the tree and was soon fast asleep.

A large beautiful moon greeted him as he awoke. He immediately thought that nighttime was not the time to approach Laura. Looking up at the house, he could see the warm light pouring out of the windows, but the air was filled with fouled-mouthed injured soldiers. There was a sour, unwelcoming fog that hung over the house. It was the reality that he was expecting. From so many years of studying and researching the war, he knew what atrocities laid ahead of him.

Gazing up at the moon, he decided to head to the pond to wash off. He was hot and sticky from his extended nap. As he came around

the house and moved towards the pond, he stopped and listened. Frogs were croaking their nighttime songs, the crickets singing and the wind softly moving through the trees.

The pond was small but the moon had just enough room to create a lovely mirror. He could see the water reflecting the full face of the moon. It was such a serene picture, one that Joe took in deeply and admired.

Undressing, Joe took off everything except his white underpants. It was a swim that he was going to thoroughly enjoy. At the edge of the pond, he walked into the water and began to sink into the southern clay under his toes. The water felt so refreshing, so invigorating, his body welcomed the coolness that was enveloping him.

Joe drenched his body completely into the water and surfaced with a quick blow of air. It was a luxury to relax in the water and let all the worry rinse off his body. He floated along the water and suddenly heard a rustling by the pond's edge. He looked around and realized quickly that it was a turtle digging a hole, and he quickly went back to swimming.

And then again, he heard another louder noise but continued to pull himself out of the pond and sat on a large log on the bank. He allowed his body to drip dry off and when the noise he heard earlier came closer to his quiet retreat and Joe stood up with his gun in hand.

Pointing his weapon in the direction of the noise, he quietly called out, "Is anyone there?" His heart started to race.

No answer. He did not want to hurt anyone, just thought he might need to be prepared for some rogue Yankee. He walked closer to the edge of the pond and heard a sudden splash. Instantly, there was a small body floating on top of the water, skimming along like a leaf that had just fallen from a mighty oak. Joe watched as the body moved closer to him.

As the floating leaf drifted over, Joe could see that it was a woman in her white undergarments. He didn't know what to do. Should he introduce himself now and scare her half to death? No good could come of jumping out at a lady in the dark while she is alone.

Joe picked up his gear and uniform and moved behind a large tree, hiding himself from the uninvited guest. She continued on, swimming quietly and peacefully. The figure did not seem hesitant, obviously unaware of not being the only one out that evening.

Sometime later, the figure gingerly moved through the water to the edge of the pond, her white garments clinging to her bare skin. She had a small, thin figure completely visible by the moonlight. As he watched her, he was entranced by her every move. Her small body was not more than five feet tall. As she rung her long, black, curly hair out on the bank of the pond, he could not imagine anyone being more enchanting.

She was incredibly beautiful and Joe admired her body. Gently humming, she carried on about dressing, placing a large black dress over her white garments. She pulled her hair into a bun on top of her head with a small wooden stick, and headed back along the path to the house.

Joe contemplated the entire time whether or not to come out and introduce himself. He didn't want to scare the young woman, but he was rapt by her beauty. He wondered at every moment whether or not he would talk to her.

I could feel that it was somehow a magical moment for him. Whoever this woman was, she had already captivated Joe. He slunk down beside the tree and continued to think. Who was this woman? He dressed and fell asleep by the tranquil waters and waited until morning to return to the house.

Chapter Twenty

March 20, 1865

As Joe walked back to the house that morning, it was a beautiful, bright, sunny day. Even though the sorrows of the infantry were still floating thick in the air, he could tell that it was going to be a wonderful day. He would think positively; he would be helpful and he would make himself an integral part of the operations of the plantation. Above all, he would succeed in his mission.

Joe arrived on the porch, perfectly dressed as if he was reporting to work on his first day into battle. He had his "injured" arm wrapped and rubbed his full-grown beard nervously with his other hand.

He stood on the porch, looking around uneasily at the men who were staring at him. Two of them were sitting on rather large rocking chairs. One was on the porch swing with his leg hiked up on the arm of the swing, whistling "Dixie." Several others were simply propped up against the house. Their butternut gray uniforms were tattered and filthy.

"Ain't no need to knock," reported an elderly man on the porch swing who seemed to track the comings and goings at the house. The

Missus is 'round back pumpin' water out o' the well. She don't answer the door no ways, we just keep a comin' from battle. What er ya here for, anyway? Don't seem like you got much to worry 'bout with those two strong legs." Since he seemed knowledgeable, Joe inquired further.

"Good morning, Sir. I am, uh, pleased to meet you. I'm Joseph Cain, Corporal. I have a letter for Miss Chestnut." Joe paused, reviewing the rotten lot of men. "And you?" Joe extended his fit arm to the nosey man.

"George Wilson. And I reckon you are lookin' for some food, but there ain't much and I would keep on a travelin' if I were you. Since you can walk, I would keep on a walkin'." George picked at his teeth with a small stick.

"Well, I am not here to be a burden, like I said. I am a courier and have a letter for Miss Chestnut. Although, I would like a word with the man of the house. Is he around?" Again, Joe already knew the answer to the question.

"Ain't nobody here but us vermin and the two Missus of the house. We been hangin' out here till our regiment sends the wagon fer us." George finally swung his body around and faced Joe.

It was clear that this man was still healing, as his leg had been amputated and was wrapped with bloody gauze. He scratched feverishly at his scalp. The man closest to Joe looked up and smiled, his teeth rotten and black.

"Yeah, lice, it's real bad. And I reckon I smell like a dead possum, but that's just the way it is." The soldier smiled, his drooping mustache choking his thin lips.

"Well, pardon me. I'm going to see if I can find the missus. At the well, did you say?" Joe looked back at George.

"Yep, she's aroun' there somewheres in the back, just keep on a walkin'." George pointed to the back yard.

Joe walked back down the porch stairs and followed the clay path around to the back of the house. He could see the well house further along, but no one was there. He continued, checking each possible place, finally deciding to look in the tobacco barn. Two soldiers had caught a rabbit and were making a stick rotisserie pit to cook it. Joe wanted to stop and inquire on how they caught the animal, but he continued on.

As he opened the door to the barn, he thought it was such a sorrowful sight to see that tobacco barn empty. There was no tobacco, no wheat, no animals. There wasn't a thing in the barn but a bunch of sick and injured soldiers lying around waiting to be saved.

Joe did pause to think about the fact that this is where Laura was taken by the Yankee. It made him sick and more convinced about what he had to do. She would never have to go through that pain.

Joe walked back to the front of the house and walked straight inside this time. The room was open to a stairwell, and there were two small rooms on either side of the stairs. The space on the right had several tables and cots lined up with soldiers lying on them. The area to the left had one soldier after another on wool army blankets. The sight was horrific, to say the least. None of the men even looked conscious. The smell was unbearable. Joe backed out and went through the front door and closed it behind him.

"We can't rightly handle the smell either," the rotten-toothed man looked at Joe, again as if he read his mind.

"I know it. I'm sorry for all the losses and the suffering of those men. I guess I will just go on out to the yard and sit until I see the Misses around." Joe advanced forward and the soldier grabbed his leg.

"Thought you was gonna head on down the road, seeing as you ain't found the Missus yet?" he questioned sarcastically.

"Oh, I'll find her. I'm not leaving until I find her." Joe yanked his leg out of the man's hand.

"You's awfully clean there, soldier. See any battle or break that arm on fixin' a wagon?" another soldier asked in a mocking tone. All the men burst out into laughter.

"I was in battle. I injured my arm in battle. They put me on courier assignment to finish out the war. I guess they thought since I was unable to fire weapons, I was no use on the field. But I'm still serving my country and I still take baths when I can." Joe's voice was hard and almost sarcastic as he spoke.

"I don't expect you seen much of anything," the soldier added, continuing with his wicked laugh. The men reminded him of high school bullies who would instigate anything to pull someone down to their level.

"I'm not sure what you meant by that, but I assure you that my intentions here are truly honorable. Now if you will excuse me." Joe was visibly agitated with the soldier's remarks and started to leave the porch when George spoke to him again.

"Where 'bouts are you from, Mister?" George entered back into the conversation.

"Raleigh. I'm from Raleigh. And I'm ready to get back home too." Joe hoped he could continue on walking back to his apple tree without any further comments. He walked forward and noticed something he had not seen before.

There was a chicken coop directly on the other side of the house. He walked towards it, though there were no chickens in sight. When he approached the small building, he could hear something muffled inside. He hesitated a moment and then slowly opened the door.

He never expected to see the same attractive woman who had been at the pond last night, sitting on the ground with her hands covering her face. As cracks of sunlight crept into the small building, he could see that chicken feathers covered her gorgeous black hair.

"Please leave me for a moment. This is the only private place I have on my father's land. Could I join you momentarily?" The woman asked in a soft and mellow voice as she sniffled, her hands gently covering her face.

"I mean you no harm, Ma'am. I was looking for the lady of the house," Joe continued as he stood in the doorway of the coop.

The lady removed her hands slowly, revealing her porcelain white face and picked her long black dress up as she began to stand. She wiped her face again and finally looked at the man in the doorway, her eyes filled with tears.

In an instant, all Joe could feel was passion for this woman; he was overcome with her beauty which was so clear in the daylight now. His heart quickened.

She was a young woman with large, brown eyes and a small round face, which was now suddenly flushed and pink. To Joe, she

looked exquisite. He only had a glimpse of her beauty the night before and now he could see the sweet enchantress in full daylight.

"I beg your pardon, but *I* am one of the ladies of the house. What a sight I am for sore eyes, I can only imagine you are thinking at this moment." She curtsied and fluffed her dress out.

"Not at all," Joe paused, trying to think of what to say next. "Can I assist you, Ma'am?" Joe held his hand out to help her.

"Yes, please. Thank you, Sir. I'm afraid I made a mess of myself and was not very ladylike with my earlier request. A southern lady wouldn't do such a thing under normal conditions, but you have found me in a state," she said as she finally met Joe's eyes. She was so small, so frail looking.

"I've been looking for you, but didn't imagine you'd be in with the chickens, er, I guess the missing chickens," Joe smiled.

"Me? You were hoping to find me? You must mean my mother, the lady of the house. I'm the daughter of the owner." She stepped forward and into the warm sunlight, revealing to Joe how absolutely gorgeous she was. Her skin was as white as driven snow, flawless perfection.

"Let me help, if I may. You have a few feathers here," Joe began plucking them from her hair. He remembered how beautiful her hair was in the moonlight.

This was Laura. He could not believe it. He had not expected to be attracted to her. That possibility had never entered his mind. He just knew he wanted to save this woman. He had no idea what she looked like or how he might feel after laying eyes on her.

"Please excuse my manners, Sir. My name is Laura Chestnut. And yours is?" She brushed at her dress to remove the dirt from the coop.

"I'm Corporal Joseph Cain. A pleasure to meet you, Miss. I think I got all the chicken feathers out of your hair." Joe stepped back to look at her and took his hat off. He was unsure about asking her as to why she was crying. Would that be the gentlemanly thing to do?

"It is a pleasure to meet you, Sir." Laura looked so sweet and innocent while she bowed again, as a southern lady would do.

"Might I ask as to whether you are hurt or injured, as you seemed quite upset?" Joe decided to head into the question, hoping it would not offend.

A crow dropped down and sat on the coop. He seemed perfectly annoyed that he did not have a crop to feast on. He began cawing out at the couple.

"Sorry to disappoint you, but I will not be seeding any corn this year, Mr. Crow. So you can continue on your complaining, but we have nothing for you to eat." Laura looked up at the bird and flung her arm in his direction. "I guess I should have some compassion, since he is hungry just like the rest of us."

"Are you alright, Miss?" Joe repeated his earlier question.

"I'm not hurt, Mister Cain." Laura continued wiping dirt and feathers from her dress. She sat down on a tree stump just outside the chicken coop. "Just another moment, if you please; I need to get my thoughts together before I have to go into the house again. I had a very long and unpleasant evening last night." She dropped her head as she spoke.

"Of course. May I inquire as to why you were so upset just now? I know it is none of my affair, but I am not used to seeing a lady in tears. Well, the truth is, I have not seen many ladies at all for some time." Joe tried to press her for more information, twisting his hat nervously in his hand. The day was cooler than yesterday, but the heat was beginning to beat down on his head and created long beads of dripping sweat.

"Mister Cain, I don't wish to burden you with my problems, but as it were, you've asked. My brother is off to war and well, I'm so worried that he's dead or injured. I can't help it, I just know it. I guess I just thought of him being injured the way some of these men are injured. I have never seen blood like this. What these men are going through is inhumane." Laura wiped her face again.

Joe offered a handkerchief that he carried. "Are *you* injured?" Laura looked back at Joe's arm and accepted the cloth he offered. She wiped her eyes and whispered, "Thank you."

"I have an injured arm, but it's on the mend. It really doesn't need to be wrapped anymore, truthfully. I'm on my way home. But I

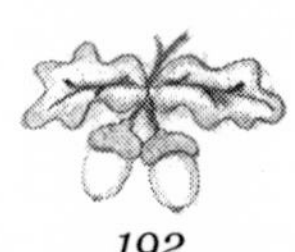

heard about this place from a fellow soldier and wanted to stop for a meal and maybe a night of lodging possibly?" Joe wanted to say more about Lucas, but didn't think the timing was right.

"We don't have much room, I'm afraid to say. We don't have room for the men we have here as it is. The poor things continue to stream in by the hour. You seem able to walk. Pardon me for saying this but maybe you should keep going, if you know what is best for you. This place is becoming a burial ground. Maybe it's cursed." Laura pointed to the field with several small crosses sticking out of the mounds of newly loosened earth. She saw another wagon heading down the driveway and let out a big sigh.

"It's not cursed, Miss Chestnut. We are at war and people die. I'd like to stay and help, if I can be of any assistance." Joe took his handkerchief back. He admired her tiny hands once again, trying to imagine them delicately placed on his own.

Internally he wondered why he was having such feelings. Seeing this sweet creature crying was enough to send his heart sailing on a ship with two passengers, him and Laura. He wanted to take her away from all of this.

"It certainly feels like this place is cursed. We don't have much to offer, but you are welcome to find a place to lie down where you can. It has been a pleasure meeting you, Mister Cain. I'll be heading back to the house to get some soup in the kettle for suppertime and need to receive these new soldiers coming this way." Laura stood up again and Joe tucked the handkerchief back in his sack.

"Is there anything I can do to help you right now?" Joe watched as the wagon passed with more soldiers. He knew this was the way to prove his worth by helping them in every way possible.

"Yes, if you don't mind, just follow me," Laura moved to a standing position and continued to walk toward the house. "Kindly, if you would like to be of assistance, please tell these men that there's no more room in the house. They'll have to find a place in the yard. If you could, try and find the medical attendant and tell the soldiers to do what they can while I go inside and start some supper." Laura continued into the house.

Joe completed the task she requested of him and then retreated inside the house to the kitchen, which was located in the back of the house. It was very simple, with a large cutting block in the middle of the room and a small, black wood-burning stove against the side wall. There were several small cabinets. A large bowl with a pitcher sat on the counter and several mounds of bloodied gauze lay on the center of the table.

"My apologies for the disrepair of my home. You never know what you might walk into at any moment. We need to make room for the new soldiers, but I don't know where. If you wouldn't mind, would you help me pick this table up and put it against the wall, please?" Laura grabbed one end of the table and Joe used his one "good" arm to move the table to her desired location.

"I gave up on caring about material things after our second Yankee raid. They only want food or loot. We didn't have much, but whatever we had is pretty much long gone now. But I'll make do with what we have." She put the large kettle on the countertop.

Joe's heart was filled with compassion. It was hard for him not to think about what was about to happen to her. He had to be successful in his plan. He had to save her. He would prevent that awful night from ever happening. He had to keep her as close to him as he possibly could. He had to make sure that her mother believed Lucas was coming back. It was his focus, and *he could not fail.*

Joe felt sick again. He had to eat something. He was not used to eating so little. As he looked at his body, he knew he had already lost considerable weight. "Miss Chestnut, would it be alright if I had a bite to eat?"

"Yes, Sir, I do have bread." Laura pulled out a small pan with several slices of bread. They were not very appetizing, as flies were all over the house, constantly landing on everything in sight.

"Thank you. I appreciate it." Joe began eating and unbuttoned the top button of his shirt. The kitchen windows were open, providing the slightest breeze, but his uniform was still horribly hot.

"Where are you from, Mr. Cain, if you don't mind my asking? Not from around these parts, I'm guessing?" Laura began pouring water from the giant pitcher into the kettle pot.

"From Raleigh. Got a ways to go to get home. But I look forward to seeing if my family fared well, or I guess I should say, if they fared at all. I have not heard from them in some time and don't know what tragedy awaits me." Joe continued taking large bites of the bread. Hunger took care of any queasiness about the flies.

"Raleigh. That is a place I have never been. Did you love it there when you were at home?" Laura procured two small potatoes and began slicing them into the pot, skin and all.

"I did, I do, love it there. It is a good place to have a family." Joe finished the last of his piece of small meal.

"I'm sure. I hope to have a family one day, if you don't mind me saying so. I guess that it is so far away from where I am today, I can hardly think of it." Laura continued cutting the potatoes as she shuffled back and forth, as if she were dancing.

She seemed easy to talk to, perhaps needing a friend to confide in. Joe could not believe how optimistic she was, even after such a recent tearful episode. She seemed hopeful and committed, despite her frail physical appearance.

"Should I go back outside and help with the soldiers coming in?" Joe was not sure how she was handling the flood of sickly men.

"No, the sawbones and his assistants should be handling most of the work. I've just been handing out water and soup for two days and trying to stay out of their way. It's the best I can do for now, with so little. I need to get this pot on the stove and get it cooked. Then you could help me deliver the food, if it pleases you." Laura stirred the soup with a large gray ladle and placed it on the stove.

Joe was not sure about the right time to talk to Laura about Lucas, but he needed to let her know that Lucas was alive. He decided that there was no time like the present.

"Miss Chestnut, I know we have just met, but I have news from the war. I was in a local hospital for some time and met a man," Joe hesitated to say too much but he knew that time was not on his side. He needed to earn her trust as quickly as possible, and there was no need for her to worry one more minute about her brother.

"This man who I met was on his way to deliver a message to you. But I am afraid he expired before that time and I decided to

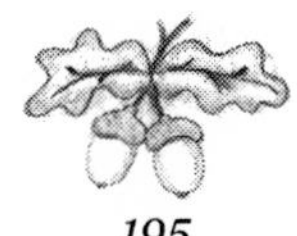

complete his mission." He looked at Laura hoping she would believe his tale that substituted for the truth. "This man knew your brother, Lucas Chestnut. And he wanted you to know that he was alright, and that he would be coming home soon."

Laura instantly turned around and sat directly beside him at the table, pushing the heap of gauze aside. "Did you meet him? This soldier knew my dear brother?" Her eyes were wide with interest and longing.

"Yes, he knew your brother. We were both in the hospital. It was there he told me about your plantation and of what he promised your brother. I did not have the chance to meet Lucas. But as I mentioned, the soldier passed before he was able to tell you in person. I vowed to continue on with the news to your family. No one should have to worry about such a thing."

Laura got back up and looked at Joe, "Oh, bless you, kind Sir! Our prayers have been answered! My mother won't believe this happy news!" Laura clasped her hands together and walked back over to the pot and put the top on. "We have been praying everyday. But Mother has taken ill the past couple of weeks. Excuse me, while I share this glorious news with her!" She quickly moved out of the room in a joyful comfort and left Joe sitting there at the table.

Suddenly the back door of the kitchen flung open and two soldiers who were carrying an injured man burst into the room. Joe instantly stood up and assisted them in getting the man on the table.

"Please don't take my leg. It ain't that bad. Don't you rascals take it!" The injured man pulled at his appendage and let out a pitiful cry.

"Just calm down now, we ain't the sawbones. We'll see if we can get you some help." And with that, the man with the patched eye looked at Joe.

"Where's the man of the house?" he said wiping his forehead with his sleeve.

"I believe the missus of the house will be back in a minute. I don't know where the sawbones or the assistants are. Can I help you?" Joe folded up the injured man's hat and placed it under his head, as the poor man continued to wail.

"Jeb, I'll be back. Stay here with this man and we'll git you some help. Don't go nowheres." The man with the eye patch and his partner left the kitchen.

"Who are you?" the injured man asked.

"I'm Joseph Cain, Corporal. And I'm sorry to see you in pain. Were you just injured?" Joe began to fold back the pant leg off the man's wound.

"Yep! And we ain't won the war, even! All this for nothin'. Where's all those folks who were yelling about the Cause now?" The poor man gritted his teeth, obviously in horrible pain.

"I know it. Try to stay calm. Can I get you some water?" Joe couldn't think of much to do to help him at the moment. It was such a shock to see an injured man like that. He could only imagine what the pain was like for him as the blood steadily pumped out of his leg.

"Yes, but ain't nothin' gonna help me now. I just know they're gonna take my leg!" The man blindly held out his hand for the cup as Joe hurried to pour him some water.

Laura came into the room, accompanied by the two soldiers.

"Where's the surgeon, Miss?" the eye-patched man asked.

"He should be in the front yard. We're just doing the best we can." Laura walked over and inspected the injured man's leg.

"Please, Miss, don't let them take my leg. It'll get better; I *just* got shot, so it might take a minu..." the soldier said just as he passed out from the pain and now lay limp on the table.

"I don't have any pain killers or anything to assist in surgery. Our home has been ravaged by the war and we don't have much to offer. We have one meal a day, if it lasts." Laura's hair stuck out in every direction while the bun quietly rested on the back of her head; she looked worried about the man.

Standing in the kitchen with the group of soldiers was very awkward. Even though Joe felt he could pass for a soldier, pretending to be someone who he wasn't troubled him. He always followed a personal code of honesty and integrity, but going back in time instantly created a façade that must be upheld. No one can know that you are from the future. Who would believe it, even if you told them?

Joe examined the soldier lying on the table, and noticed that he was holding a picture in his hand. He reached over and looked at the black and white oval. It was of a small child, maybe two or three years old. He thought that it must be the injured man's child.

"What are you doing?" the eye-patched man barked.

"I was just curious as to what he was holding." Joe pushed the photo back into the soldier's limp hands.

"Now I won't abide by stealing. I can't have you take another man's things. 'Specially one who is in such bad shape as this one is!" The eye patch man moved forward as if he was going to hit Joe.

"Gentlemen!" Laura called out. "I think there is no call for that in this house. Corporal Cain was simply looking at his picture. He was not planning to take it. He's a friend of the family, and I believe him to be an honest and upstanding man. So please refrain from any further arguing on that point.

We have a sick man and need to take him into the front of the house to await medical attention. There's nothing further that we can do for him in this kitchen. If you please, let's get him there quickly." Laura motioned for the men to pick up the soldier, and she disappeared out of the room with the men.

Joe sat there analyzing his next move. Things were happening so fast now, and he didn't want to lose sight of protecting Laura. He thought about the fact that he needed to find a hiding place for his gear, needed to roll up his sleeve from his one good arm and do the work necessary to help Laura.

Laura swiftly came around the kitchen door, pasting her hair back on the sides of her head. "I'm not sure if we have anything else to add to this pot. I think I'll go out and see what I can scrounge up from the yard." Joe sat there, not knowing what to do. He was concerned about leaving his personal items anywhere, in case someone should get a case of sticky fingers.

"If it's alright by you, I'd like to take a look around your plantation," Joe requested nervously.

"Of course. Take your time. I'll be working on the last of the ingredients for this pot as it is. We should be ready to eat by noontime. Help yourself to the bread if you need more," she offered with her voice

was so calm, so sweet. No one was going to get the chance to hurt this delicate creature, he thought.

He went out to the tobacco barn and looked around for a hiding place. He spotted stairs going to a small loft at the second level. He moved up the wooden slats until he came to the area. It was almost bare, but the rafters were dark and even with the light of day, no one would see something tucked behind them. He left all of his belongings except his frying pan and mess kit. Coming back down the stairs, he examined the area again to make sure that it was, in fact, a hidden spot.

The breeze was rustling around his hot, nervous body, and he looked up at the oak that was situated beside the tobacco barn. The leaves moved with the wind and somehow reassured Joe that it would all be okay. It gave him renewed strength. He took a deep breath and looked up toward the house. The tall white structure with the black shutters seemed to epitomize the old South. It reminded him of Holly, of his home.

Back in the kitchen, Laura had incredibly managed a couple of bacon slabs for the soup and continued stirring the liquid. "You're back," she smiled.

"Yes, I am. Miss Laura, I would like to talk to your mother. Would that be possible?" As Joe spoke, Laura turned and brushed her hair out of her face.

"I guess it would be *possible*, although, she has not been out of her room today. She says she's not well. Although I did share with her the joyous news of our beloved Lucas." Laura went back to stirring. He noticed how thin she was in the face, how tired she looked and how perfectly beautiful she was. He was so thankful he chose her. He knew it was the right thing to do. But he also had to reach her mother. He had to make sure that the older woman still had hope.

"Okay, let me go tell her that you would like to see her. Maybe she will be happy to have a visitor and that will get her spirits up even more." Laura left the room quietly. As Joe sat, he could hear the screams of the injured man from earlier. They must be taking his leg, he thought. He put his hands into the bowl on the counter and splashed water on his face. Combing his hair back with his hands, he thought about how uncomfortable he was.

It was some time later when Laura came back. Joe was standing beside the kettle, stirring the soup. It smelled wonderful, despite its lack of ingredients. Then again, eating just one apple a day could make mud look appetizing.

"She *would* like to talk with you. I was surprised, I must admit, that she would even see anyone. Despite the news about Lucas, she is still grieving for some reason. I think she has lost sight of who she once was." Laura looked at Joe with tears welling up again. "With our home in a shambles, it's hard to see a future."

"Please don't cry, Miss Laura. *It's going to get better.* It is going to be alright and Lucas is going to come home." Joe smiled and continued to feel overwhelmed with his desire for her. He knew he had to stop these feelings that were overwhelming his heart.

"I certainly hope you are right. We have been praying for his return above all else. And I do appreciate your kindness. Shall we go see Mother?" Laura turned and directed him to follow her. Through the house, Joe took note of the lack of furniture, the excess of injured men and the overwhelming smell in the house, thick and salty.

When they reached the room where her mother was sitting, Joe knew that this was the moment of truth. Joe began to think that even if he kept the Union soldier from taking control of Laura, her mother may still be capable of doing harm to herself or her daughter.

As they carefully walked into the room, Joe examined everything with his eyes. He noticed the large framed picture of a man on the wall, a beautiful desk in the corner and a small table in the opposite corner. There sat a gray-haired older woman, but just as attractive as Laura. She was in a black dress, much the same as Laura's, but pristinely clean. Her hands were gently folded on top of her dress. She was sitting on a chair and turned to look at Joe.

"Who are you?" she scowled.

"Mother, I told you, this is the man who wanted to see you," Laura pleaded.

"Who?"

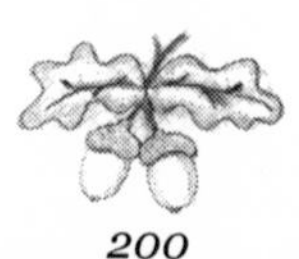

"This kind man would like to help comfort you. He believes that our dear Lucas is coming home soon, remember?" Laura smiled at her mother with such excitement in her eyes.

Joe knew that he might have only one chance to make an impression on this woman. He needed to gain her trust. He needed to bring her back to reality. He would not leave her and he would do whatever it took to make her better. He would save this family.

"Who are you? Why are you here, and what do you want?" the woman fired out again.

"My name is Corporal Joseph Cain. I'm here to help." Joe pulled her hand into his hand. She looked up at him, with her braid lying on her shoulder like a snake. It twisted around and sat there as she blinked relentlessly. "Gentle and kind lady, I have good news for you. Your son is alive and coming home; think about what I am telling you."

"You know my Lucas? You know my boy?" Her voice was dry as her breathing slowed down.

"I don't know him. But I met a man who did know Lucas and wanted me to make certain that you and your daughter knew that he is coming home. You are going to be alright and I'm going to stay with you until his return." Joe continued holding her hand.

"You are? Why? What do you want?" Her blinking was more intermittent now.

"I'm just a man, an honest man who wants to help a family in need. I can only hope that you will accept my help and allow me to stay until your son is safe, back in his home." The wailing from an injured soldier was more pronounced now and distracted Joe's thoughts.

Joe pulled a small ladder-backed chair from the desk and sat beside her. Laura entered back into the room moments later and offered water to her mother, who seemed absolutely deprived of it, judging from the way in which she drank it.

Some hours passed and a dark cloud moved over the plantation. A low thunder began to rumble. After little conversation, Joe rested his eyes and waited for the lady of the house to wake from her sleep. Laura checked on the pair several times, at one point

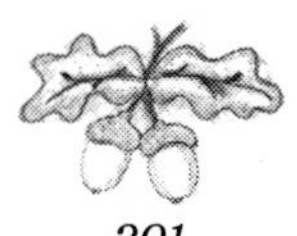

bringing bread and soup. When night fell over the house, Joe said goodnight and went downstairs to sleep. He was terrified that Laura would leave the house and the soldier would meet her.

Where to hide? Where could he go and watch that Laura did not leave the house? Joe decided to simply sit on the stairs and stay vigilant all night. If she tried to leave the house, he would know. Time crawled by and exhaustion caught up with Joe, making his eyelids heavy and impossible to keep open. Soon, Joe was fast asleep, perched on the stairs.

Chapter Twenty-One

Twilight, March 21, 1865

Hours later, the door opened and soft candlelight illuminated the step that Joe was seated on. Laura moved passed him and out the door. Several minutes later, Joe woke suddenly and realized that he had fallen asleep. He jumped up and checked Laura's door, feeling sick that he had allowed himself to fall asleep. The door had been left slightly open and Joe peered in to see one person in the small oak bed.

"Oh, my God," he said quietly. Laura was not in the room. He immediately wondered where she was as he moved about the house looking for her, with only a small candle to light the way.

Several soldiers rustled and let out groans, as candlelight bounced against the walls in each room. Joe was wide awake now, and overwhelmed with concern. Of all nights, how could he allow this to happen? Regret was rampant in his thoughts, when he suddenly stopped, realizing that Laura must be on her way to the pond! He immediately ran out the front door.

Scrambling down the front porch stairs, he panicked as he tried to remember which direction would take him to the pond. "Where is

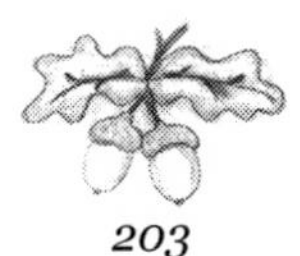

she?" he cried out, in weary frustration. Soldiers littered the front of the house and sat up watching his frenzied movements.

"Who you lookin' for there, soldier?" a low voice crept out of the dark.

"Miss Laura. Did anyone see Miss Laura?" he choked out.

"Who's that?" another yelled out. "The lass who brought you water and soup", yet another replied.

Joe quickened his pace once the stranger's words registered in his mind. She is the one I am here to save! His stride accelerated into a sweat-streaming run to the pond. Quickly examining the water and the surrounding trees and bushes, he could see no sign of Laura.

"Laura? Miss Laura, are you out here?" Joe yelled at the top of his lungs, with no response. Where could she be, he panicked and then suddenly thought of the fact that she could already have been dragged into the barn. Could she be in there with that soldier? Could he have ruined his chances to save her? All of this time preparing and waiting, and only a few hours of sleep devastated his plans to save her?

Joe circled around the pond and headed straight to the tobacco barn, deep in anxiety about the possibility that he would discover her assaulted and in pain. Flinging the door open, his worst fear was true. Laura was being held on the dirt floor by a blue coated Yankee. And as he stood at the barn doors, poison began running through his veins, a poison named vengeance.

"Get off of her!" Joe yelled and flung himself on the Yankee stranger, knocking him off Laura and into the wall. With the advantage of surprise and quickly regaining his balance, he aimed his swings at the man's face. The adrenaline was pumping through his body as if he could not be defeated. The Union soldier tried to defend himself. Their fight pulled a hatred and vengeance from Joe that struck home blow after blow. Joe wasn't going to allow this man to get away with what he knew had already happened. This dog was never going to try anything like this again!

Moments into the fight, two heavy hitting Union soldiers pulled Joe off the unwelcomed outsider. Joe immediately moved over to Laura. The terror of what might have happened to her was pumping through his veins and he picked her up and carried her out of the dark and putrid barn.

Laura lay there, motionless in his arms. He held her close to him as he moved out of the barn and into the clear moonlight. Laying her on the pump house bench, he gently slid the black curls out of her face. Total fear overcame him. "Laura, Miss Laura, are you alright? Please answer me," he begged.

He could hear her shallow breathing and reviewed her dress for signs of blood. Picking up her small hands, he could see no signs of injury and couldn't imagine why she was not responding. Was she in shock? Did she have a concussion?

He tenderly rocked her, saying, "Laura, please come back to me. I know you can hear me, please come back. I should never have let this happen to you. It's all my fault. I was sent here to save you and I failed." Joe could not decide what else to do.

"Oh, what's going on! Oh, help!" Laura finally gasped, pushing Joe out of her face.

"Settle down, it is me, Joseph, Joseph Cain," he pleaded.

"Help! Help! Get off of me! Get away!" She continued screaming as she thrashed around and pushed Joe away from her.

"Calm down, please, Miss Laura. I'm here to help you. We are here to help!" Joe tried to yell over her screams, but moments later the Union soldiers came running out of the barn.

"What is going on?" the man with a bloodied nose shouted.

"She's in shock. She doesn't know what's going on," Joe held his hand out, stopping the soldier from advancing. "Give her a minute, she needs to get her bearing," Joe said, clearly concerned about the terror that was on Laura's face.

"What happened?" the other soldier howled.

"I don't know. I just found that nasty creature on top of Miss Laura. I beat his face as best as I could. Where is he?" Joe questioned.

"Joseph? Joseph! Oh, thank God!" Laura seemed to have cleared her thinking and identified Joe. She grabbed his neck and started sobbing.

"Where is he? Where's that villain?" Joe scowled.

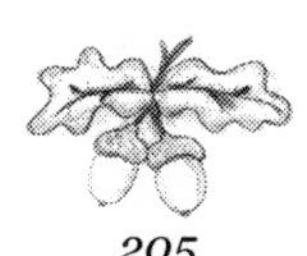

"He ain't going nowhere! I'm going for the chains," the soldier announced, and marched past Laura and Joe.

"We might not need those chains. We took care of him right!" the second soldier proudly added. "He might already be dead and rightly so."

"I'm going to take her back inside. I don't know exactly all that has happened but the sooner I get her inside, the better," Joe said as he picked Laura back up, her arms still wound around his neck, leaving the lone soldier behind.

Joe carried her up the stairs, all the while hearing her hushed weeping. "It's going to be okay, I promise. I'm here and I won't let you go."

"Why? Why did this happen? Where did he come from? What did he want? I was only trying to go for a swim. Is that so wrong?" Laura looked into Joe's face for answers.

"No, no, that wasn't wrong. Hush now, you must calm down. I'm going to take you to the kitchen so I can see what is going on with you."

The dimly lit kitchen was the one place in the house that no one else occupied this night. He had privacy to talk to her about what had happened in the barn. He sat her down on the kitchen chair and quickly moved to the seat beside her, while pushing the candle closer to them both. "Are you alright? Tell me what hurts, what injuries do you have?"

"Joseph, thank you for being there." A sob and a deep breath competed for expression. She reached out for his hand. "I'm sorry I was yelling at you. For some reason, I didn't understand what was going on for a moment there. Why was he trying to hurt me? What did I do? What did he want from me? I don't have any more food!"

"I don't know. He was a Yankee, and he is not going to make it through this night, if I or that other soldier have anything to do with it." Joe tried to control the raging temper he felt toward this man. He had never experienced such a murderous rage. He had never been certain that he *was* capable of murder until now.

"I cried out, but no one heard me," she said softly, trying to stop her tears.

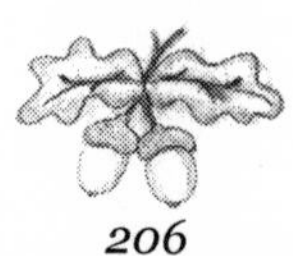

"Please don't cry, Miss Laura. You're safe. I'm here now. I should have been there for you to avoid this whole situation!" Joe became more animated, torn over whether to leave Laura and go outside to check on the Yankee dog.

"Why is *all* this happening? I don't understand," Laura said as she wiped her face with her skirt. "We are not in this wretched war! Women are not supposed to be part of this nightmare! I have not done anything to harm anyone!"

"I know. This shouldn't have happened. But I must ask again, *are you all right*? Are you injured in any way?" Joe moved closer to Laura examining her dirty face. There was a pause, as if Laura was thinking about each body part, connecting her brain with her limbs, one at a time. "*Are you hurt*? Did he...?" Joe paused, not sure that he could bare the answer if he had been too late.

"No, no, I don't think so. I'm a little rattled, but not hurt, I don't think. There wasn't time," she said as she rubbed her neck. "He'd only dragged me into the barn and wrestled me to the ground when he was flung off me. That was when you came to my rescue, dear Joseph." Even in the dim light, he could see her eyes focused on him.

Relieved, Joe dropped his head backwards and looked at the ceiling. No words could explain the relief that he felt at this moment. She was relatively unharmed. He had succeeded in a small way.

"Now you, Sir, do look injured. Your nose is still bleeding," Laura said as she pointed to Joe's face.

He had not taken a moment to think about his injuries or the fact that his face was cut and dripping blood down his neck. He had not felt anything. Joe went to the bowl and pitcher of water, and splashed his face. The sensation of pain began to connect as the water made contact and he felt that his nose might be broken. Of course, none of that really mattered right now, since all he could think of was Laura and getting her safely back to bed. She was thinking the same.

"I just want to get back to Mother. I'm going to rest with her. Thank you, thank you for...for being there," Laura said, her voice more level and clear.

"You're welcome. I'll make sure that you can sleep at ease." Joe dried his face with the white linen from the counter. He didn't want to let her leave him, but that afforded him time to go back to the barn.

He escorted her to her mother's room and heard her lock the door. He would gladly have talked to her longer, willingly stayed right beside her as she slept. The guilt of not adequately protecting Laura created an internal battle of guilt, relief and *I told you so's*, as well as immense suffering about what might have happened if he'd been too late.

Joe went to the barn and talked to the soldiers who had gathered around. The Yankee was dead. And nothing would bring him back to tell the tale of why he attacked Laura. Joe wasn't naïve. Laura was a beautiful young woman. Rape had been the ultimate insult and power play in war, for as long as there was written history. The dead body was taken to the horse and wagon and taken off the plantation.

Joe spent the rest of evening seated on the floor in front of Laura's doorway, quiet and thoughtful. Pulling his tin-can candle closer, he rehearsed all the events of the day as he watched the flame die out. He could hear Laura pacing inside the room. He wished he could hear her thoughts, to know how she felt and to comfort her. He could only comfort himself with the thought that she was scared, but safe and unharmed.

Chapter Twenty-Two

March 21, 1865

Sunrise came and he began to see the light creep into the house while rifle pops echoed in the distance. The battle had started again. "Can you get me some water, Mister?" croaked a young boy who was leaning against the stairwell.

"Yes, my boy, I'll be right back." Joe knelt down and comforted him. "Me too!" another man screeched, causing others to call out in an eerie synchronicity.

Joe retreated to the kitchen and returned with a full pitcher and a small tin cup. He poured and watched as each man drank the cool water in large gulps. One pitcher after another he filled and emptied until every man on the bottom floor had been given refreshment.

"Thank you, thank you, thank you," the grateful soldiers called out. He managed to help a few of the men to their feet and allow them to use him as a crutch as he escorted them outside to relieve themselves.

"Thank you as well," Laura echoed from the top of the staircase.

"You are also welcome, Miss Laura. Are you well this morning? What can I do for you?" Joe wanted to rush to the top of the stairs and hold her in his arms. From this moment on, all he could do was serve her and make sure she stayed safe under his watchful eyes.

"You have already done so much. I'm quite well today. I can only imagine that you did not sleep all night. You should try to rest." Laura looked around in the room. The candles were all used, leaving heavy wax pools on the floor.

"Yes, I could use some rest. Do you mind?" And with that Laura shook her head so that Joe could rest at the apple tree once again. He was afraid to leave her, but felt comfortable that she would not venture out alone with the wagons coming in by the hour. Complete exhaustion would not be any help for either of them.

Another wagon made its way up the road to the plantation, waking Joe from his short nap. He immediately jumped up and began directing the steady flow of victims to their temporary resting places. Men were in the worst possible physical and mental states. Some had been shot multiple times, others experienced heavy shrapnel wounds; it was hard to tell what they once looked like. Some were in shock and could just not believe what they had seen. Joe felt nothing but compassion. Until this conflict, there had been a certain glory and honor associated with the War. When it had started, picnic outings were planned by the local civilians, both men and women. A regimental parade and mock fighting had been expected as the entertainment. Those days were gone forever. Joe could hear the guns of the new war, a very cruel war.

"Who are you?" the healthier soldier hopped off the wagon, belting out his inquiry at Joe.

"Corporal Joseph Cain. I'm here assisting the ladies of the house."

"Let me see your papers, soldier!" he scowled at him.

Joe pulled his assignment papers out of his jacket and saluted the superior officer.

"Why are you here? Are you on route to make a delivery?" the man loudly questioned.

"Yes, I delivered a letter and planned to head home, but as you can see, there's work to be done here. If I can't fight in the war, but I

can help those who are in need." Joe pointed to the growing sea of patients in the yard.

"Hmmm...well, seems strange that you are so suddenly side tracked." The man was hulking over Joe as if he was trying to intimidate him into saying something he shouldn't. "You aren't trying to take advantage of the women here, are you? I'll kill any man with my bare hands if that were the case!" His eyes bulged out, his face red with anger and frustration.

"The ladies here are in bad shape, but not by my hand. One is laid up in her bed and the other is barely surviving, her food rations are so low. She is trying to tend to the injured soldiers with water and soup, when she can get ingredients together. They need all the help they can get. I'm a good man, Sir, and I would also bury any man who injured a woman in any way." Joe tried to defend his honor. It was the first time he worried that he might be discovered as fake. There was a good long pause as the man contemplated what Joe said.

Finally, "Carry on soldier!" the man said, seemingly at ease with Joe's presence.

Joe felt sick again. Lack of food, lack of sleep, the ungodly amount of blood everywhere, and the stench were catching up with him. Male body parts were exposed in every way, a sight that Joe could barely stand. He had to keep reminding himself that he was there to set only certain things right. It was the price he had to pay. He would endure and carry on.

The day consisted of carrying, moving and situating soldiers into a resting place in the house and all around on the lawn. Several men died in the house, so replacing those spots with new injured soldiers seemed constant. He simply lost count of how many died and how many would soon pass away, and how many more arrived and how many more were expected.

He watched as Laura went from man to man, serving soup and water. The officers who were providing medical attention had few supplies and used everything from curtains to old clothes for dressing wounds. Wagon after wagon filtered in as the clamor of war continued in the background. A steady sound of fire and horses hooves clotted the air.

Joe kept a steady eye on Laura and made sure that her mother also received visits. She remained in her bed and only got up to use her chamber pot. Laura commented that her mother seemed calmer and more hopeful that she would regain her strength.

That particular day seemed to go on as if the clock was moving backwards. Although busy, Joe was watchful of Laura's every move. He didn't want to take any chances that he would lose sight of her again. Finally, night began to settle in on the plantation. After Laura went to bed, Joe sat on the floor outside of the ladies' bedroom. He had so little rest the night before, he hoped she would not mind him making a bed on the floor.

Earlier that day, he had suggested, "Miss Laura, I'm worried about you and your mother. There are so many wild men running around from both sides, and I would not trust anyone with the temptation of two lovely women up here alone. I plan to sleep outside your door."

"That would be a comfort, to be honest with you." A soldier needed moving just then. Laura lifted the man's feet as Joe grabbed his arms and helped transport him. The last wagon had rolled into the yard and the men were again lined up even further out from the house. Joe nervously scratched at his beard and smoothed down his growing whiskers.

"You have been a wonderful help to the men and me." Laura rubbed her hands together as if to get the filth off. "I don't know how we would have made it without you."

"Thank you. Please be expecting me in a while. I'll knock three times, so you will know it's me, before I set a place to sleep up in the hallway. Can I do anything more for you?" Joe loosened up the man's shoes to help him be more comfortable for rest.

"No, Sir," Laura said as she began walking back to the house. "But..."

"But what? Name it, and I will be happy to attend to it." Joe ran up and stood beside Laura. When he looked into her eyes, he felt like a lost puppy, and just wanted the warmth of her gaze.

"I want to know what has happened to Lucas. I feel more dreadful with each passing day. What could have happened to him?

Can't you write when you are in the field? Not every letter could have been intercepted by the Yankees, right? I just can't understand it. Were you able to write your family and keep their worries subsided?" Laura looked as if she was ready to cry. She picked up her bloodied apron and stared at the stains.

"Yes, I know, it is hard when you don't know what is going on. Out in the ranks, when supplies are low, there is little food, let alone paper and pencil. Usually these things are luxuries and you have to swipe them off a dead soldier, if you can believe that. And the truth is, I know that he's alive and he will be home soon. I need for you to believe it too."

Joe reached over and pushed her hair out of her face, ever so gently. He immediately second guessed this action, as the passion filled his heart again.

He wanted to hold her. Joe was already feeling so much love for this woman that he couldn't bear the thought of leaving her for one minute, much less forever. He decided to stay with her at all times now. He couldn't chance a mistake until the war was over and someone else was there to protect Laura.

That evening, Joe made a comfortable place on the floor with his blanket. It proved to be better than the stairwell. Laura slept with her mother again, and for the three of them, there was a night of peace.

•

Chapter Twenty-Three

Surrender, March 22, 1865

Morning delivered itself on the plantation similar to the day before. The Confederate troops, leaving a single Calvary detachment, retreated from the field. The guns were silent, but men, per the norm, remained hungry and in pain. As in the day before, the wagons came and went, delivering the wounded and burying the dead. Joe made his rounds just like Laura, tending to whatever dressings could be changed with limited supplies and providing as much food as was available.

The soft wind carried the thick odor of death all over the plantation. It slowly drifted into the house, but went unnoticed due to the ghastly stench already present. At moments, Joe gagged; he had never before seen anyone rotting away. He attempted to do so many things to help the men, knowing full well that these may be the last hours they had on earth. Knowing that he could not comfort them all, he focused on doing simple things, such as a quick damp wipe down, for as many soldiers as possible.

If only I could do more, he kept thinking. Six hundred thousand will die from this war. The losses are too much to bear. Joe began to feel like he *could do more,* and so he continued applying every bit of medical care he possibly knew. He applied pressure, kept wounds clean, and advised the medical attendants on how to save limbs when possible. It was not always necessary to amputate, if they could just get the bullet out and the keep the wound clean.

He supplied fresh water from the creek constantly. The water was essential not only for drinking, but keeping tables clean and sanitizing all the gauze with boiling water. Joe was feeling a renewed strength this day, if for no other reason than he knew Laura was safe in his keeping. He would help the soldiers all that he could, but most importantly, he *would accomplish his mission.*

"Mister Howard, can I offer you some soup, Sir?" Joe assisted him in sitting up, and poured the liquid nourishment into his mouth.

"Ahhh, thank you. I much appreciate your help, Corporal. I see you have been keeping busy these past few days. How bad are things? As you can see, I can't get around too well." The solider had lost both of his legs and had a shot shell in his arm that was festering. "It is a cryin' shame that so many young boys are here, helpless and at their end. I'm long in the tooth, and have lived a good life. Wish I had taken better care of myself, and sure wish I'd not scolded my children as much, but I feel complete if the good Lord sees fit to takin' me." Mr. Howard laid his head back on the log.

"I understand. Can I get you anything else?"

"Any chance of a brown liquor shot?" His jack-o-lantern teeth were glaring out between his gums with glee.

"Nope, don't have a drop. Now rest some." Joe continued on.

Laura came running up to Joe, hot and sweaty, and loudly announced, "It is over, oh thank God! It is over."

"What on earth do you mean, Miss Laura? Slow down?" Joe placed the soup kettle on the ground.

"The Battle of Bentonville is over! I can't say as I'm happy about the outcome, but it's over. There's an end to this massacre!" Laura spun around and loudly crowed, "It is over, men! The battle has come to an end! Sherman's taken his troops off in another direction."

How would things change from this moment forward, Joe thought? Would he be able to harness his feelings and not allow them to surface to Laura? There was a mix of relief and disappointment among the ranks. Joe heard the men's comments. The South did not prevail. It was a bittersweet moment for everyone.

"Miss Laura, I know you are grateful for this news, considering what you have been dealt with here at the house, but there is still much work to be done. We need to stay ever ready to assist the Confederacy in whatever way necessary. I'm going to continue my rounds with the soup pot and then check on your mother." Joe picked up the pot and walked away.

Chapter Twenty-Four

March 31, 1865

Over the next week, the steady flow of men leaving the plantation alive was a welcome site. Laura's mother continued to improve. She ventured outside on the porch when the soldier count had gotten down to about fifty. She seemed able to handle being around others for short periods of time and took to eating more frequently.

She began calling Joe her son's name, Lucas. It was unsettling for Laura, but she kept quiet about it, as it seemed to help her mother feel better. It seemed to be that in her mother's mind, her children were with her, and she certainly seemed more tranquil.

Joe continued the manual labor on the farm, as well as cleaning and removing the injured men, and many other ongoing tasks. He was simply doing whatever was necessary to get everyone through the next few days. His body was becoming accustomed to working every waking hour.

On one happy morning, coffee and apple butter was available to the men. The strong, delicious aroma instantly calmed the souls. It was a treat like no other. The men's spirits instantly revived with only

a sip or two. That day, both the coffee and the apple butter were enough of a luxury to make them believe it was Christmas morning.

Before long, all but a dozen men had left, and the days were sliding by as quickly as butter melting off a warm biscuit. There were so few men by this time that everyone was able to rest inside the house. Some were even able to do some things for themselves.

The days were filled with constant rain, creating a mud field out of the front yard of Chestnut Plantation. It became impossible to maneuver there with a wagon. Joe developed a routine of taking care of Laura's mother and tending to the men. Laura was able to spend more and more time getting her home back into order: scrubbing the floorboards, cleaning up stains, straightening what furniture was left, and washing and mending clothes.

Every once in a while, Laura would notice Joe looking at her. He must have been lost in glances, as he was mesmerized by her movements.

One afternoon when Laura and Joe were working in the rain, he approached her. "Miss Laura, I need to talk to you when you have a moment, if that would be okay." He scraped the bottom of his shoe with a stick. The mud stuck to his shoes like spackle.

The rain was drowning Laura and she stood there, soaked to the bone. "Yes, Sir, I will be back inside soon." Laura pulled her bun down and let her hair cling to her shoulders. Joe looked at her as though she was the most beautiful creature he had ever set eyes on.

He could not help his feelings. He adored the way she swept in short choppy strokes, never getting anything really clean as she swept along. He loved her delicate hands and the compassion she poured into the soldiers, along with the water or soup into a poor man's mouth with a long stemmed ladle. He loved watching her comb her hair at the end of a day.

And most of all, he loved that she did all her work without a murmur of complaint.

Days earlier, Joe finally met Cadet Edward Clayton, the soldier who wrote the diary from his archives. "Cadet Clayton, how are you?" Joe asked as he busied himself with ripping the white linen in strips.

Wounds needed constant bandaging and there never seemed to be enough clean dressing.

"Not so good. I've seen better days, that is for sure," Cadet Clayton pointed to his injured legs.

"Glad we can be of some assistance. We have a place here next to the desk. Let me help you get comfortable," Joe quickly responded, as his only thought was to help Cadet Clayton relax and have a quick stay on the plantation.

Joe made sure that Cadet Clayton had all he needed to write and keep himself busy. They passed time in the evenings by playing cards and throwing jacks. Joe felt it a true pleasure to spend time with the young, high-spirited man. In a different world, in a different time, they could have been friends.

At the end of his stay, Edward gave Joe his handwritten pages and when the wagon came to pick him up on the last day, a wave of relief came over Joe. Edward thanked everyone and commented on the kindness that Laura and Joe had shown him.

Joe's heart was full of satisfaction. The diary was never written with those horrific words about Laura and her mother. Those horrible things never happened the way he had read them in his library back home. *It was the first time he had changed the course of history.*

His mission, his great task, was almost complete. Joe breathed a deep sigh of relief. Laura was not violated by that Yankee soldier in the barn. Her mother did not lose her mind. In fact, her mother was on the mend, day by day. And lastly, Edward carried on with his life without leaving the horrible diary pages for Lucas to find.

Joe felt it was an honor to have preserved Laura Chestnut's safety. His pride in keeping her virtue intact and her life out of harm's way was more than a miracle for him. Each time her head hit her pillow gave him another night of peace, and determination to continue. He was making a new history for the Chestnut family.

Everything was complete except one final charge. Joe could not leave now; he had to finish. He felt that his one last task of seeing Lucas safely home would have to occur before he left. In waiting for Lucas' return, he would help rebuild the plantation.

On that rainy day, Laura complied with his request to see her. "Apologies, Sir, for the delay. You wanted to see me?" Laura found Joe in the kitchen, washing the kettle.

"I did. I need to talk to you for a moment, if that would be okay." Joe offered the chair at the kitchen table. It seemed like yesterday when he had walked in this room for the first time. They both sat down and Joe noticed Laura had changed into her only other black dress, a dry one.

"It sounds as if something is wrong. Are you alright, Joseph?" It was obvious to Joe that Laura had gotten comfortable being around him.

"I'm fine, Miss Laura. I know we have accomplished a lot here. I want you to know that it has meant so much for me to be able to help. I hope you will allow me to do something more. I hope you trust me." Joe pulled out a small stack of Union bank notes that he had taken from his pack hidden in the barn.

"Oh, my dear Lord, where did you get those?" Laura was suddenly shocked with the vision of money on her kitchen table.

"I have had it since before I arrived on the plantation. I hid it when I left home, before the war, and recently retrieved it on my way to the plantation. And I know that maybe we could have used it to help the men, but I wanted to use it to rebuild your farm. Its spring and time to plant crops. You won't survive another winter with what food you have left." Joe pushed the money forward to Laura.

"I, I just can't believe this. How could I accept any more than you have already given? I'm at a loss for words, my dear Joseph." Laura felt the money in her hands.

Joe's mind froze with her sentence. Dear Joseph? *Am I dear to her?* The words dripped off her tongue and Joe accepted them so willingly. He had no understanding of her feelings for him. He had secretly hoped that she felt the same for him, but what if it *was* true? What could be done? He belonged to another time. He knew that he could not stay and build a life with her.

"Am I *dear* to you?" Joe slowly and very sheepishly asked his secret love.

"I feel ashamed to have these feelings, Joseph. I hope you don't mind me calling you Joseph. I cannot tell you what your being here has meant to me. And not just saving me on that wretched evening. I never knew such sacrifice was possible from anyone." Laura looked down at the money without acknowledging Joe's facial reaction.

Joe smoothed down his blonde hair, taking a heavy gulp. He could not imagine feeling more excitement with what she just said. What do I do? How do I respond? I can't accept this love now. I can't mislead her. I can't hurt her. I have to stop. I have to stop. *I have to stop.*

Joe stood up and paced back and forth slowly.

"Have I said something to offend? I have been too forward in my words. I'm sorry if I have caused you any embarrassment." Laura continued to hang her head low.

The feelings of love and pure passion were pumping steadily through his veins now. He felt overwhelmed; his emotions boiling over and wanting nothing more than to grab Laura and place his lips on hers. He was overcome with desire.

Joe swept over to Laura and picked her face up to look at him. He dropped to the floor on his knees. "Miss Laura, I do want to help you and your family. I want to be a good man. I want you to know that you are not offending me. It is just..." he paused. The words that he wanted to say were not the words that he knew he *could* say. He was breathing heavier and heavier with each passing moment.

"It is what, my dear Joseph?" Joe's heart was pumping even faster with the delicate words coming out of her mouth. He did not know if he could take another moment alone with her. He had to back off, step away and regain his composure before it was too late.

Joe stood and clasped his hands behind his back, "I believe that getting a crop going and making sure that your mother continues to mend should be our focus. We can't allow our feelings to take control. I want to help you and I will be here until Lucas returns. You can count on me being here for you. *I will keep you safe.*" Joe stood up and walked back around to the other side of the table.

His heart ached with the painful words he had just said. He wanted to share his true feelings with her. He wanted nothing more than to take her in his arms. He wanted to hold that gossamer cloud that had floated along the pond. He wanted to be her strength, her rock. But not one of those things could he do without making a mistake, without hurting both of them.

"I don't understand." Laura continued looking at Joe. "Do you not feel as I do? Do you not have a pain in your heart that cannot be described? Do you not want gentle admiration from me?"

Joe's head spun with confusion. *Yes, yes, yes!!* He wanted to say yes to all of those things. All he could think of was to run out of the kitchen and avoid saying anything else. He walked out the back door, out to the back yard, out under the moon's glaring disapproval. He ran to the barn and dropped to his knees.

"God, I'm lost. I did not intend for this to happen. I had no idea that I would feel this way. What am I to do? If I stay until Lucas returns, will I have the power to contain my feelings and keep my heart under lock and key? Give me strength! Help me." Joe sobbed uncontrollably. "I know I have to leave, even if my heart is left behind."

It was a mixture of hurt, passion and confusion. He had worked so hard to make sure that everything had gone smoothly, and he felt as though this love could easily cause everything to fall apart. He could not control the feelings he had.

Joe sat for hours in the barn, thinking over the situation until his body and mind had calmed. He decided it best to go back into the house to find Laura and apologize. By now, the house was dark and Laura was not in the kitchen; surely she had already gone to bed for the evening.

He felt lonely and empty. He slumped into the same chair he had sat on so many hours ago, before she divulged her feelings to him. It seemed like an eternity. And his mind reviewed, over and over, whether or not he should just leave.

He knew that Grant and Lee had signed the papers for the surrender of the Confederate Army today. The news would spread throughout the country over the next few weeks. Maybe it was time to go before any hurt had time to develop between the two of them. He always felt so guarded with his emotions, and he felt that with Laura he would never be able to mask his feelings for her. Then he realized that it was already too late.

He glanced at the kitchen table and saw his hat neatly propped up. He lifted the hat and saw a clean folded handkerchief draped over his stack of money. “L” was hand embroidered on the top in black. As he picked it up, he pulled it to his nose, breathing deeply.

Joe remained awake all night, sitting in the corner of the kitchen on the wooden chair. He was unable to calm his feelings, even staring mindlessly at the white linen handkerchief. When the morning sun finally awoke the bluebirds, he decided to leave his temporary home and head to the storehouse to make his first purchases.

Chapter Twenty-Five

April 10, 1865

After several hours of travel on foot, Joe reached the small general store. The red building, worn and hunched in its stature, was a welcome sight to him. Its tin roof, rusted and bent, did the best job it could to protect the goods within. A field of cheerful flowers waved to Joe, welcoming him inside.

A jovial, bearded man greeted him at the door and filled his order. Joe paid for a small wagon of items with the Union bank notes and headed back to the plantation in haste. He pulled the wagon back to the plantation and arrived in the foyer, excited like a child buying his first toy.

"Miss Laura, please come down. I have something to show you," he yelled at the bottom of the stairs. The vision that had kept him up all night floated down the stairs and met him eye to eye. "I have returned!" She took her last step and smiled delicately at him. "Hold out your hand and close your eyes." Joe put a large jar of molasses in her hands. "Open your eyes." He stepped back, grinning from ear to ear.

"Oh, molasses! What a treat! Thank you, thank you. It's wonderful, Joseph," and with those words she ran into the kitchen with her gift. Joe followed, dragging his small cart and shared his excitement with her.

"I have more!" Joe exclaimed. "We have seeds for planting." Joe brought out bags of seeds and stacked them on the table. "I have some other things for you. Let's see, a ham, some eggs, tin-canned goods and a sack of sugar." Laura took the items with wonder in her eyes and cheerfully kissed each item.

"I can't believe we have food! I can't wait to make our supper today!" Laura was so relieved to see all the treasures. "Thank you, Joseph. Is it proper to call you Joseph now?"

"It is. I would like for you to call me Joseph. As far as our new riches, I want to do this for you and your family. I want to help you and I will continue to do so as long as I can." Joe emptied the wobbling cart. "You do not owe me anything, Miss Laura, you should only feel that you deserve this. We still have more work to do. You have to help me get this crop planted!" Laura gave a sweet, simple giggle. "Okay now, fair is fair, call me Laura."

"How can I ever repay you?" she continued. "What could I ever do to thank you for all you have done already? Before you came, my mother almost lost her mind. I had no time to tend to her; the battle consumed me. I felt so alone and my courage felt like it left on the floor along with all those horrible limbs. It just all played on my mind, thinking that Lucas, our sweet Lucas, would be dead and gone.

But with your cheerful spirit here, looking after Mother and me, I felt whole again. You have helped me to believe he will return. And if all the labor you have contributed isn't enough, you have also given me such courage to be strong, to move forward. I don't know how I could ever thank you."

Laura's cheeks were flooded with tears and she stood up, looking at Joe in such a way that his heart began to pound again. He could not bear the conflict, the conflict of loving her and not being able to tell her or show her. It seemed too insurmountable a task.

Joe dropped his head down. "Miss Laura, sorry, Laura. Please don't cry. I can't handle you feelings hurt, in any capacity. You are too

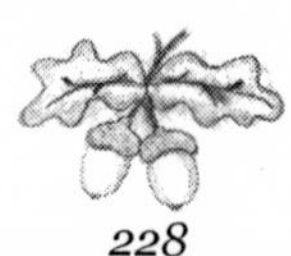

precious to me to cause you any harm." Joe wanted to jump up and take her into his arms. She just needed comforting. But how could he hold her and ever let go? He had to be strong. He had to keep her out of harm's way by not allowing her to fall in love with him.

"*Am* I precious to you?" She sat back down. Joe took a deep breath and looked at Laura.

"Miss Laura, we cannot allow our emotions to take over. We have to be strong." He paused and ran his fingers through his hair. "No matter how we feel about each other, I will have to leave this home and return to where I belong. And as hard as it is to hear, that's the truth. I can't run the risk of hurting you. I can't do that to you."

"Why? If you feel as I do, then why? Maybe Mother and I are supposed to leave this place and join you wherever you are going." Laura's eyes were still full of tears.

"No, it isn't. It can't be," Joe quietly answered.

"Is there a beloved who you left before the war? Is that why?" Laura wiped her eyes with a kitchen towel that she had been holding for some time.

All Joe could think was that he could answer yes, he could lie to her. That would keep things at a distance. But the truth was there was no other woman. He had never known love like this before and had not expected it. He did not know what to do with the feelings that he had.

How could he answer her? What would he tell her so that they both could just continue to tend the farm and wait for Lucas to return? He decided that simply telling her the truth was the best thing to do. He would not lie to her again.

"You are the most kind and loving woman I have ever known. But you need to know that I do not belong here and you do not belong where I have to go. We have to cherish the time we have, however little time that is. I will do all that I can to help get the farm back in working order, and I will not leave until Lucas arrives. That is all I can promise you." Joe's heart felt like it was literally pumping out of control. He was trying to keep his emotions from scattering everywhere.

There was silence.

"I will honor your wishes," Laura murmured. "You will have me by your side, and I will not leave you until you say our time is at an end." Laura quietly left the room and went upstairs to check on her mother.

Joe closed his eyes. He had never felt so horrible in his whole life.

Chapter Twenty-Six

April 11, 1865

During the early morning hours, Joe went to the marketplace and bargained for a mule and a horse. He needed help plowing the field. Since he was not exactly an experienced farmer, his thoughts were filled with how to accomplish his task. Two men, former slaves by the looks of things, were there and asked Joe if he needed help, taking note of his obvious discomfort. They requested food and a place to stay in turn for their assistance. Since it was not his decision to make, he brought the men home and asked Laura.

"Yes, yes, this would be just like our home used to be! We were never comfortable with having slaves but we did hire people to help us from time to time. I'm so thankful that you have brought them to join us, Joe. It is with high hopes that our relationship will be considered a mutual partnership. Introductions, if you don't mind, Mister Cain?" Laura nodded happily to the two men. Joe was surprised by the formality of it all.

"Isaiah and Samuel, this is Laura Chestnut. Now I hope you boys are good Christian men and don't have any ill intent for this family." Joe looked at the two thin, dark men, knowing they needed him as much as he needed them. They both agreed to work hard and do everything they could to make the plantation what it once was, including watching over the women of the house. On this point, Joe made himself very clear, once they met privately without Laura.

Isaiah the taller of the two men, seemed simple minded, but he sure knew how to plant a crop. He was a man who seemed cheerful no matter what the course the day took. He whistled constantly and kept a piece of hickory twig in his mouth that he worked over persistently. Whenever asked to do something, he immediately responded, "As you wish, suh!"

Samuel was shorter and rougher around the edges. He had a large scar over his left eye that when asked about, he only replied, "Bad times." Joe could only imagine that he had been in some mess of a fight with the outcome being less than favorable for Samuel. He was easy to work with, but wandered off occasionally to sleep or fish. He got the day-to-day tasks done; he was dependable for that, but not much more. Considering their wages, Joe had no complaint and was delighted with the growing family.

Over the next few weeks, Samuel and Isaiah taught Joe more than he ever intended to learn about cultivating crops. Before long, the seeds had been laid to sprout from the contented earth.

Isaiah and Samuel were welcome comic relief, never letting much time go by without a song or a story. They certainly kept Joe and Laura's spirits high with their cheerful demeanors.

One telling of their "tales" was about Samuel being hired to catch and pluck chickens. He wasn't fast enough to catch them and once he did, he didn't have the stomach to kill the chicken and pluck the feathers. He laughed as he told of how ugly and pathetic he thought a chicken was with no feathers, the poor thing. He remarked that it was the shortest job he ever held and still to this day, didn't think he could get rid of that chicken smell on his hands.

Every evening after the meal, everyone assisted in cleaning the dishes and tidying up the house. Only four soldiers remained, waiting for their orders to be moved to the hospital in Goldsboro. They seemed to be very comfortable with each other, a small motley group.

Even Laura's mother was calmer, and becoming healthier every day. She continued to call Joe, "Lucas"; however, Joe could not determine if she did this out of habit or if she really did not realize that he was not her son.

Laura spent her evenings by candlelight, knitting and mending clothes. The men continued playing cards, while keeping everyone's spirits high. It was a simple life, but created a time of relaxation after a hard day's work.

"Good night, Miss Laura," Joe commented and smiled as he walked down the hall towards his guest room. By now, he was getting very comfortable with his quarters, Lucas's old room. He did not worry that Laura would venture out on her own at night.

"Joseph, wait just a moment, please," Laura said, gliding down the hallway towards him.

"Yes?" he nervously answered, not comfortable with the two of them being alone in the dark hallway. If he had done one thing well over the past couple of weeks, it was to avoid being alone with Laura.

"I wanted to thank you. These past few months have gone by so quickly, and I never seem to have a moment to talk to you. I just thought I needed to tell you that." Laura turned and walked down the hallway.

"You are welcome. *And I love you*," he very quietly whispered as he watched her disappear into her room. He then turned and retreated to bed for the evening, without her hearing his loving words.

Chapter Twenty-Seven

June 1, 1865

Joe's mind was clouded with thoughts of Laura, even more passionately than any day before. He had escorted her to the pond that morning, and although he waited just down the road, his thoughts were heavy with the first evening he saw her out in the moonlight.

They walked down the path together so closely that Joe could feel the heat from her hand near his. Oh, how he dreamed of holding her exquisite hands. He wanted to pull them up to his lips and kiss them ever so sweetly. As he sat there, he was totally lost in a sea of emotions.

Most days, when she was escorted to the pond, either Joseph or a soldier named Talley brought her. Talley was one of the soldiers who had been recovering from pneumonia and was unable to get around for many weeks. Being outside really cleared his lungs and he enjoyed the walk with Laura.

Talley had grown so fond of her, Joe was sure that Talley had feelings for Laura that she was absolutely unaware of. Joe kept an eye on their interactions from a distance, and wondered if Talley would be a good match for his dear Laura.

As the days unfolded predictably like a napkin does at the dinner table, Joe watched as his seeds grow into beautiful plants. His only hope was that he was creating a crop that Lucas would be proud of. He continued to watch Laura's every move: her gentle walk, her easy voice, her loving ways. These were actions he would find difficult to remove from his thoughts.

When they weren't tending the garden, Isaiah, Samuel and Joe spent their time repairing all sorts of things on the plantation. One day it might be a roof, another day the chicken coop. The war was over and the South was rebuilding. Summer was settling in on a new world. And a man with a little bit of money could do a lot.

"Samuel, I have to check on the fence in the back property. It should take me a full day, so please look after the Missus," Joe directed. "I will be back as soon as I can. We can't have any cows in there until that fence is mended. I hope to be back by dusk." Joe lifted his new hat up and slowly walked down the driveway with his backpack.

Laura was standing on the porch, and she could see Joe talking to Samuel. He would have to leave her this day, she thought, there was work to be done. He glanced back and held his hand high as she waved to him.

The southern heat was sweltering and Joe was thankful that he had invested in a new set of work clothes. Joe figured it was about a hundred degrees out in the field. There were no shady spots along the fence line and, even without the wool army uniform, Joe had to take several breaks to rehydrate and shade himself from the sweltering heat. He spotted a tree deep in the woods, one tall and majestic, somehow calling out to him.

He walked inside the canopy of tree limbs and reviewed the oak's stature. It was a mighty oak, like one on his family's land. Relaxing, he ate his apple, inspecting his handy work on the fence.

Joe fell asleep and when he awoke, it was already evening. The fireflies flew around in every direction as if they were sending out an SOS to awaken him. Joe was disoriented and concerned about being gone this long. He knew he had a trip of at least an hour ahead of him before arriving at the plantation.

Grabbing his backpack, Joe hurried through the woods without watching where he was stepping. An oak branch whipped back and hit him in the head, blinding him for a second as the momentum of his stride continued. And then suddenly he was falling.

"Ahhhhh!!!" He heard himself yell as he landed on something soft and slimy, his hands moving around in the muddy mixture.

Joe had fallen into a sinkhole, a rotten pit in the earth that had never been occupied by man or beast. He was lying face up, trying to think through what had just happened. He had dropped about fifteen feet into the earth.

"Where am I?" Joe said out loud. With the evening sky above him, and the earth below his body, he quickly realized what had happened. He couldn't believe it. In his disorientation, he did not know what to do.

Sitting up carefully, he moved his body slowly, feeling all around him. He felt the cold mud sloshing around his feet as he apprehensively tried to get his bearings. He could not make out what the rotting leaves in his hands were, as he nervously felt around. He grabbed a strong root and pulled himself up. Looking up at the night sky, he had no plan on what to do to get out.

Joe felt around for his backpack; it was still with him. Inspecting the walls of the pit, he could not make out any way to hoist himself up, despite his constant attempts at new ways to achieve that goal. There were no rocks or tree limbs to use as leverage. The roots were thick and menacing as they grabbed at him no matter what direction he took in the small hole. It was no use; he decided he had to wait until morning to develop a strategy to get out. He propped up against the mushy earth and tried to rest.

The sunbeams finally found Joe's muddied face at dawn. Waking abruptly and immediately standing up, again with the help of the root system, he could see more of the pit he'd dropped into. He found that his night detective work was true. There was no way to get out. He already knew that he did not carry any rope, but he opened his bag and took inventory of what he did have.

He began talking to himself out loud, "Alright, I have a hammer and a wedge. They are no use to me now, unless a tree falls in the hole.

Water, at least I have my canteen, and I did pack a lunch. Thankfully I only ate the apple." He leaned back against the larger root. "How did I ever get myself in this mess? Or better yet, how am I going to get myself out of this mess? I can't believe I did this to myself."

The hours crept by, marked only by the changing shadows from the sun as if each hour took a full day to complete. He reviewed every possible scenario on how to get out. The recent rain had muddied the hole, and without much sun coming in, he could find no way to get the earth dry enough to climb. The exposed root system was thick and winding, but who knew if they would hold a fully grown man trying to climb the wall? He had already tried several times unsuccessfully. On top of that, no one seemed to hear his cries for help.

At the end of the first day, Joe felt as though he now knew what a prisoner in solitary confinement felt like. He was uncomfortable and angry at himself for getting into this situation. He was wet, dirty, and worst of all, getting hungry.

Chapter Twenty-Eight

June 2, 1865

On the morning of the second day, Joe decided to start screaming for help as soon as he detected the sun's arrival. If anyone were to pass, they would surely hear his cries. He rationed out his last bit of pork, savoring every bite as if it were his last. The rest of the time he continued his pattern of yelling, "Please help me!" accompanied by quick screams. Several times he threw things out of the hole, by chance they caught someone's attention that happened to be passing by.

Intermittently, he would whistle tunes that Isaiah had taught him to keep his mind busy. There was nothing left to do but hope. If Samuel and Isaiah were the men who he thought they were, they would come looking for him. *Unless they thought he left for good.*

Joe's mind started playing tricks on him as the days unfolded. He could hardly keep up with how many days he had been gone. Time seemed to move in reverse, and he would lose track of how long he had been down there. He thought of his father and how disappointed he would be that Joe never came home, and no one would ever know why he didn't.

Two days, three days, and soon he had been gone five days. All he could think of was Laura. Was she okay? Was she worried that he had abandoned her? Would she come looking for him and something awful would happen? He could not quiet his mind and had no other way to keep his thoughts busy.

He smelled of urine and earth rot, which made him sick to his stomach. The mud had thickened with the lack of rain, but it formed on his body like thick pudding. He cried, he yelled, he hit the muddy walls. Now he fully understood how Laura's mother could have lost her mind. Loneliness and despair can drive a person crazy, he thought.

At the end of the fifth day, Joe awoke from a nap to hear a faint, "Joseph" in the distance. Someone was calling his name. He jumped to his feet and began belting out a thin, scratchy, "Help, I'm here!" From days of yelling and lack of water and food, Joe was almost totally dehydrated and with little voice, his body barely alive.

"Here! I'm here, please hear me, I'm in this hole in the woods!" Joe strained with every ounce of energy that he could muster and looked for more things to throw out of the hole.

"Joseph!" It was coming closer and he continued yelling out. He could hear someone in the woods, the leaves crunching, twigs snapping as the person moved closer. "Joseph!" Soon a dark face looked down on his muddied skin. Joe's limbs relaxed in total relief. He had been tense for so many days that his body literally collapsed. He was found. He had never had a happier moment in his life. Until then, he was not sure that he would make it out alive. It was horrifying to think that he would die like this.

But he was found, and now he had to get out of this dreadful place and back to his Laura. He had to know that she was okay, that she did not think he had abandoned her. Joe looked back up at the dark face and realized it was not Isaiah or Samuel. Who was this man gazing down on him?

Chapter Twenty-Nine

June 5, 1865

The man looked down and said he would be back soon with help. "No! Please don't leave!" Joe wailed.

"Suh, I's gonna be right back. I ain't got nothin' to pull you wif. You's is gonna have to trus' me." The man quickly left and Joe could hear him running away from his muddy prison.

Who this man was, Joe could not imagine. Nonetheless, true to his word, the man returned some hours later. He threw the rope down and Joe tied it around his waist. He tried to pull, but he could barely anchor his feet on the wall of the pit to leverage his weight for the man. After much work, Joe was out of the hole and he could finally examine his rescuer.

The man was a tall man with no teeth. Although he wore rags for clothing and was filthy to the bone, he was the most wonderful man Joe had ever laid eyes on. "Thank you, Sir. I can't thank you enough." Joe collapsed on the ground once he was safely out of the muddy pit.

"You's welcome," the man gummed.

"May I ask how you knew my name? How did you find me? You can't imagine how relieved I am to see you. Thank you, God, and thank you, Sir!" Joe gasped, licking his cracked dry lips in desperation to keep them moist, his voice low and crackling.

"Wata?" the stranger passed his canteen to the dehydrated Joe.

"Yes, please," Joe gulped down half of a canteen of water, wiping his mouth with the back of his muddy hand.

"Uh, well, I was tole you went missin' off that there plantation. Cousin Samuel helps ya and he was a mighty worried 'bout where you been. So I tole him that I'd go a lookin' for ya. And here you is, all muddied up!" The man laughed and screwed the top back on his empty canteen.

"You can't know how grateful I am to you. I thought I was a goner for sure. I'm not sure I can walk just yet; I have no strength. Do you have anything to eat?" Joe looked at the man's pockets for any sign of sustenance.

"No, suh. I doesn't have any. How 'bout you wait here and I's be back?" And with that, the man left across the field and Joe fell to the ground in complete exhaustion and dehydration.

For hours, Joe laid on the hard soil, wanting to get up and run back to Laura. He crawled out of the forest and lay baking in the summer sun. He tried to keep his mind on the fact that the man would be there with Laura in a short time, but he couldn't stand it. He got up and began hobbling across the field. Within several minutes, he passed out on the fence, draped like a rag doll on a little girl's shoulder.

"Joe! Joe!" When his eyes were back open and into focus he saw her black hair hanging down over her face. It was his Laura.

"L...aura? Laura? Is that you, or am I dreaming?" Joe could barely speak as the water the toothless man gave him was the first he had drunk in three days. He was now ready for more, but was still limp and could not lift a finger.

"Don't try to get up. We brought the wagon. You are an awful mess!" Laura took her apron and wiped off his flaky muddied face, licking her apron as she worked. She hardly recognized him through the muck on his body.

"Just get him on the wagon carefully, please." She instructed the men to sit up front. She jumped in the back and cradled his head, lovingly holding it in her arms. She produced an apple from her apron pocket and immediately bit into the juicy fruit.

She gingerly pulled the small white flesh from her mouth and pressed it into his parched welcoming lips. The sweet liquid flowed down his cheeks as he eagerly devoured each bite. With each portion of the syrupy liquid Laura offered, he could feel the love that she had for her missing soldier. He felt as though he was in a dream. Even then, he could not have imagined how enchanting this moment was.

It was as if the fruit was pouring life back into his body. She seemed oblivious to the wet stream running down her arm as she clenched the fruit in her hands. He could feel the loving care with which she placed each morsel in his weakened mouth. Her eyes were watching his every movement as she fed him.

Joe gazed at the sky that passed above him, finally free from the five-day ordeal. "Thank you. Thank you for finding me," Joe strained to yell out to the others on the wagon.

"Well, it was Percy who found you." Isaiah continued looking ahead at the horses.

"Yes, if it weren't for Percy, I don't know what would have happened," Laura added, blinking back tears as she looked down at Joe.

"Well, Percy, you are a good man to have around," Joe spoke as loudly as he could. Percy turned back and smiled at Joe with his eyebrows arched.

Once back at the plantation, Joe recovered in his provisional guest room after a tub bath in the back yard. He felt embarrassed and exhausted from the whole event. Laura greeted him the next morning with a plate of eggs and bacon.

"Good morning, Joseph," she said as she walked in with her dress swaying from side to side like a church bell.

"Good morning and thank you. I have been worried to death about you." Joe sat up in the bed.

"Worried about me? Goodness, we have been beside ourselves with worry over you! You have been gone for days, you know!" Laura passed the plate to Joe. He quickly gulped the entire meal down before continuing his conversation.

"I am sorry to have worried you. There is no excuse for what happened." Joe licked the fork before setting it on his now-empty plate and passing it back to Laura.

"What do you mean? You could not have helped what happened. You just stepped in the wrong place." Laura sat the plate on the side table and rinsed a rag out of the bowl sitting on the same table. She dabbed at a large gash on his shoulder that began to bleed a little.

"I don't deserve your care. You have mended enough men for a lifetime." Joe grabbed her hand and gently pulled it to his cheek. "I'm truly sorry if I worried you in any way. It was my prayer that you did not believe me to have abandoned you."

Laura closed her eyes and breathed deeply. She made her other hand into a tight fist as if her emotions were taking control of her. It was unclear to Joe what she was feeling at this moment, but he didn't care. As long as she was not going to sock him in the eye, he wanted her gentle touch.

He had his thumb pressed against her wrist so that he could feel her pulse, feeling her heartbeat. He could sense those small delicate hands moving along his cheek so lovingly, so tenderly.

"I never thought that for a second. We combed every inch of our land looking for you. It was terrifying, but truthfully we began to think that maybe you had been taken by the Yankees and were in a prison camp. When Percy came and offered to continue looking for you, we were obliged. We had exhausted every place we knew to look."

Laura continued rubbing his cheek ever so gently and Joe's heart pumped more quickly, in unison with her accelerated beats. "Percy came running back after being gone for only half a day. He said he found you in a hole, of all things, and that he needed rope. We followed him, grabbed the wagon and headed to pick you up." Laura stopped and carefully delivered her next thought.

"When I saw you, I almost died. You were lying with your back against the fence, completely drooped over like a wounded scarecrow. You looked..." she dropped her hands into her lap as she spoke.

"I looked dead? Like one of those soldiers we carried into the house, didn't I?" Joe was sick with thoughts that he had worried her, wishing she had not taken her hand from his face.

"Yes. And I was ready to pierce myself on the fence with you. You can't know the worry I have been through while you have been gone. I...I don't think I could live without you." Laura squeezed the rag in the water and dabbed his wound again.

"I'm sorry, Laura. I would never have wanted to cause you pain. It was my only thought while I was down there in that muddied pit. I have to be thankful that I did not break any bones or worse. And I am so thankful that Percy found me. I hope you paid him well." Joe winced with the pressure Laura applied to stop the now-steady flow of blood from a cut on his shoulder he got while being pulled out of the hole.

"I paid him with a chicken and a basket of eggs! He was pleased, I must say. But I would have paid him with whatever he asked. I would have paid any price to have you back to me. I could never lose you; you must surely know that by now." Laura again tried to prompt Joe to return her affectionate words.

Joe laid there looking at her, his head a hot mixture of emotions. He could not quiet the conflict in his mind. He knew that it would be so easy to let his heart go and tell Laura exactly how he felt about her. But he was also well aware that no matter what brief love they could share, it would only end in everyone getting hurt. He had to return to his own time, and it would be sooner than later.

Joe slid back down into the covers, telling Laura he would need some rest to recuperate fully, but that he would be back to farming the moment his legs would allow. Once again, she accepted his lack of response, and did not press him. She wrapped his arm with gauze and quietly left the room.

He knew full well that it hurt her to not have him return her love. But he couldn't, no matter how painful it was for both of them. It would only be a few months now, and he would be on his way.

Chapter Thirty

June 6, 1865

Talley checked on Joe the next day and to his relief, Joe looked the best he had in months. "Boy, we was sure worried about you. I thought them nasty vultures got you!" Joe laughed and told Talley all about what happened. He told him all he could think of was that he needed to get back and see fit to harvest the last of the crops.

"We harvested some while you was away. The corn finally made ready to have us pick it. Boy, you would have thought that Miss Laura had found gold the way she went on and on with that corn. She canned for days when she wasn't lookin' for you. She shucked and cleaned every single cob to the bone! It was like God opened the sky and shined down on us." Talley continued smiling as he spoke.

"I would liked to have been here for that. We have filled her pantry for the winter, and that was all I prayed for. Lucas surely will be home soon. And then it will be my time to move on." Joe compressed his arm wrap, feeling the sharp pain of the wound.

"I was hopin' that I could speak to you about that. Kin we do that now?" Talley put his elbows on his knees and drew closer to Joe, his voice dropping much lower.

"Yes, of course. What's on your mind?" Joe worried that Talley was sick again. Of all the soldiers left on the plantation, Talley was the one who Joe wanted to stay and continue on with the farm.

"I don't rightly know how this happened, but while I have been here recuperatin' at Miss Chestnut's house, well, Joseph..." Talley sat back up and rubbed his head. He looked at Joe and then got up and paced a few steps back and forth.

"What is it? Are you sick again?"

"No, no, I am fit as a fiddle. I've never felt better in my life. And I don't know how to repay what you and Miss Chestnut have done for me. It was just a blessin'." Joe sat up in the bed in order to fully concentrate on Talley's concern. He continued to watch Talley pace up and down the room.

"What is it? Just go ahead and spit it out." Joe sat up in the bed a little more.

Talley plopped back down on the bed and rubbed his face with both hands. "That is just it, Joseph, I can't hardly spit it out. I don't want to offend you. With all you done and all, I just can't think of hurtin' you. It ain't right, but I can't help how I feel." Talley scratched nervously at his head again and then looked at Joe with his soft blue eyes.

"You know, whatever it is, it can't be all this bad." Joe pushed himself straight up in the bed and waited for Talley to find the words.

"Well, the truth of the matter is, I have some feelings that I maybe shouldn't expect you to understand, but they are my feelings," Talley said, his whisper almost inaudible. "My feelings for Miss Chestnut."

"You have fallen in love with Laura...uh, Miss Chestnut?" Joe had thought it several times before, but wasn't sure. He wanted Laura to be happy and to leave knowing she would have someone in her life to build a family with.

Talley Harrison was a good man. He nearly died of pneumonia in the Battle of Bentonville, but he had the heart of an ox. He was strong and clear-minded about life. He wanted all the same things that Joe could only hope for Laura. They had spent many a night talking, and Joe learned that Talley had no family to go home to. His parents and siblings all got measles and died before he went off to war. Talley wanted to die when he enlisted. He didn't feel like he had a life worth living. And he was the right kind of man. Joe knew it.

"Talley, I'm not upset." Joe looked directly at Talley's sweaty face.

"You, you ain't? You mean you ain't mad?" Talley blinked with each word that came out of his mouth, his face devoted to hearing the answer.

"I'm not mad. I think you are a good man. Of course, I am not the man of the house, so the final decision would be up to Laura's mother and, I suppose, Laura herself." Joe stared at Talley.

Deep inside, he was crushed. He didn't want her to be with anyone, but that would be selfish and unfair. He wanted her so badly for himself; it was a horrible pain that he wasn't sure he would ever recover from. How could he give up the only woman he ever loved?

But right now, he had to support Talley and his feelings. It would be up to Laura, Lucas and their mother to decide how this story played out. All Joe could hope for was that it would happen after he left. He could not stand to watch her with someone else. That pain would be truly unbearable.

"I hope you will forgive me for saying so, but I thought maybe you had taken a likin' to her, that maybe you hoped for Miss Chestnut's favors. That maybe you saved her for yourself." Talley wiped his sweaty hands on his pants as if he was trying to wipe off his handprint.

"No, I have a home. And I will return to it soon. I made a promise that I would come here and help, and I have. I have done the good that I planned to do and now we wait for Lucas to come home. I would recommend that you wait on sharing your feelings until Laura has received her brother and things have gotten back to something close to normal." The wind finally gifted the two with a welcoming breeze wafting through the room, relieving the heat from the intense conversation.

"I appreciate your advice, I really do," Talley told Joe. "I'm relieved to have talked with you about this. I didn't know what I was going to do. I'll let you rest now. Do you need anything more?"

Joe shook his head. Talley stood up and pushed the wooden ladder-back chair back to the corner. "Do you think she likes a man with chin whiskers?"

"I don't know Talley. I guess that is up to you to discover."

The minute Talley left the room, Joe sank into the pillow and felt sick. The conflict no longer raged in his mind over telling Laura how he really felt or not. Now, he had to decide how to turn all her affections off himself and onto Talley, whom he was very sure she had not taken note of for a second. Dealing with his pain was another thing altogether.

Chapter Thirty-One

June 9, 1865

On the third day back from his earthly prison, Joe was able to handle almost all of his original chores. He was working on pulling potatoes in the field when he saw a thin man coming up the driveway on foot. He was tall and lanky, but had earmarks of a strong build. His hat was glued to his head and a small sack on his back that appeared almost empty. As he came closer, Joe walked to the driveway with his bushel of potatoes.

"Can I help ya?" Joe sat the bushel on the ground in front of the soldier, still in uniform.

"I made it. I actually made it home. Oh, thank God." The leggy man exhausted himself with his words.

"You looking for the hospital?" Joe clasped his hands together rubbing them loosely to release the dirt.

"No, I *am* the owner of this land, Lucas Chestnut. I *am* Lucas Chestnut. This is my home." With that said, he stared at the house with glassy eyes.

He *was finally* home. Joe could not take his eyes off Lucas. It was if a dream had come true. He was so happy to finally see him there. He shook off his thoughts and extended his hand. "Boy, this is a pleasure to finally meet you! You can't imagine how happy I am that you are here!" Joe shook his hand and patted Lucas on the back.

"As thankful as I am to be home, and I don't mean to be impolite, but *who are you?*"

"Oh, yes, I'm sorry, I'm Joseph Cain. Formerly Corporal Cain. I've been here helping your mother and sister get the farm back into repair. I met someone in an infantry hospital who knew you, knew of this place and asked me to come tell your family that you were alive and well. And that is just what I did."

Joe hoped Lucas would buy his story. "And so I arrived in the middle of the Battle of Bentonville while this land and home was used for a hospital. Miss Laura, uh, your sister, could not handle all the men being delivered. I guess we had about five hundred in all. Once they were gone, we got creative with the available funds and now we're getting things back in order." Joe spoke quickly, again worried that Lucas would disapprove.

"You did all that for...?" Lucas paused.

"For a good family. I did it to help you and your family. And we have been anxiously awaiting your arrival. I've just been a ramblin' on here. Let's get you home. Come on!" Joe escorted Lucas to the front porch and waited for him to open the front door. He stood there, almost afraid to open it.

"You'd think I would just go running inside. I guess I can't believe I'm home. It isn't anything that I can come to grips with. I've been gone so long. I don't rightly know how to act, if you know what I mean?" Lucas turned to Joe.

"How about this? Why don't you wait on the swing and I will go get your mother and sister. Let me take your backpack. I think that might work better, don't you agree?" Joe was not sure how he felt. He could only imagine his shock of finally being home after so many years.

Lucas moved over and sat on the swing, with a stream of steady tears running down his face. "I'm home, I can't believe it. And my home is still standing. It wasn't burned to the ground, and there's green out there in the field. You can't know the worry I've had. Knowing I couldn't be here, worried about what was happening at home and, worst of all, knowing my poor mother and sister were all alone. I'm finally home!"

Joe stood by Lucas and allowed him to gently sob for what seemed like an eternity. The oak tree beside the house rustled its leaves and Joe came to the realization that Luke *was* home.

"I reckon I am a sight for sore eyes, just a blubbering here on this porch. Guess you don't think I am much of a man right now." Lucas wiped his face with his sleeve.

"Lucas, you only need to worry about one thing right now. How happy you will be when you see your family." Joe smiled at him, trying to formulate the right words to comfort him at this time of great homecoming.

"You think they still believe me to be alive?"

"I know they do. Your mother especially has been beside herself praying, waiting for this day. Can I get them for you?" Joe felt that Lucas would have to handle the flood of emotions sooner than later. No time like the present.

"Yes, if you don't mind, Sir. I know I got a rough appearance right now; in fact, they may have trouble recognizing me. But I'm back and here to stay. I wish I never left. I've seen enough death for a lifetime." Lucas stood up from the swing and thrust his chest out like a proud man.

"They would not care what you looked like right now. Shoot, they rescued me from a mud hole a few weeks back. I looked a fright! Let's get on with business now. I'll be right back," Joe spoke as he opened the front door and went into the kitchen.

"That was fast; you already pulled all those potatoes out of the ground?" Laura turned around and grinned.

"I have something better for you. You won't believe what I found. Where is Mother Chestnut? She has to see this too." Joe popped around like a clown in a jack-in-the-box.

"Oh, alright, settle down. I'll go get her. Where will we be able to view this treasure, my dear Joseph?" Joe's heart dropped...dear Joseph. I can't be dear. *She has to stop thinking about me that way.* Lucas is back. My days are numbered now.

"Go out the front door. I'll meet you there." Joe walked ahead and met Lucas back on the white slab porch.

Lucas looked more confident now, more excited that he was home. He seemed relieved and eager to see his family. He was patting his hair down and smoothing his beard around his face. "Mister Cain, I'm sure I'll learn more about you and what you have done for our family, but I have to tell you how grateful I am already. I never expected to see my home still here, standing, and definitely not in this good a condition. I almost thought I had the wrong place."

"No, this is your home sure enough. It's all going to be okay now, Lucas. God has brought you back to your family's loving arms." And with that, the doorknob turned and the black cotton dress that belonged to Laura moved out from behind the open door. She pulled her mother out into the sunlight and they both stood there on the porch with their backs to the two men, looking for their surprise.

"Mother! Laura!" Lucas firmly called out to them.

Laura slowly turned around and her eyes met Lucas' eyes. She ran to him and hugged him with such liberation from worry. "Lucas! Oh, my God! Thank you, Lord, he is home! He is alive!" she screamed.

Emotions pouring from her heart, Laura held Lucas tightly, patting his back as she held him close. After several moments she looked back at her mother. "Mother, he is home. Our Lucas is home!"

Mrs. Chestnut had slowly walked over and looked at Lucas and then back at Joe. "Lucas? My son? My boy? Is that you?" She looked confused. She was comforted that Joe was her son all these months, and now like a flood of water at the opening of a dam, she was remembering her real son. She was overcome with emotion. "*It is you, my Lucas!* You have come home! Oh my goodness, you are home! Wait until your father finds out. Oh, glorious day!"

Joe felt a little awkward watching the trio. He realized that Laura's mother was still not well. It seemed like such an intimate moment for the family; one that should not be witnessed by others. Silently thought, Joe knew it was gratifying that Lucas was back home to the place he could have only dreamed it would be.

June 9, 1865

Joe left the group on the porch and walked out to the field to continue his work of digging up potatoes. Now the countdown had started. It was only a matter of time before he would be on his way, but how long? He had already been gone so long now, he almost felt as though this was home. He felt such a strong sense of ownership to the land and to the house. It felt criminal to leave now when Chestnut Plantation would require winter tending.

After some time, Talley and the other remaining soldiers met Lucas and heard his tales of the last four years. He analyzed every battle and every outcome, telling of many instances when there were near-fatal consequences. Laura and Mrs. Chestnut were hanging on every word. It was a narrative that took the entire afternoon to unfold, with many continuing evening conversations to follow.

Joe was busy assisting with the farm and tending to every detail while the family spent time together. Lucas listened anxiously as Laura unraveled the years of toil. She carefully focused on the good things and skimmed over any losses as quickly as possible. It was clear that she did not want to burden him with things that he could not go back and change.

She told him of how the house turned into a hospital the year during the Battle of Bentonville. She could never have imagined herself to be a nurse, but she did it, she explained. She told of how Joseph came along and how he bought what was needed to get the farm back in working order, how he provided what was necessary to get crops planted, how he kept their spirits high. Even Samuel and Isaiah added their stories of coming along at the stockyard and seeing Joe looking like a fish out of water.

It was an often humorous recollection of the last few months, as the tension and stress of war had been released and the hard work of getting the farm back together was a happy, hopeful time. It seemed like such a strange group of people but it seemed like a family who cared about the success of the farm. Everyone contributed for the greater good of the plantation.

At bedtime that first night, Joe happily offered up his temporary room to Lucas and slept in the spare room with the other soldiers and Talley. "It is sure a relief to have Lucas home. I know it

was an answer to God's prayers," Joe spoke as he rolled his blanket out on the oak floor.

"Amen. We know it's a blessing," Talley agreed.

Chapter Thirty-Two

September 7, 1865

The end of summer quickly invited autumn to the plantation. Most of the crops had been harvested and the morning air changed into a crisp coolness that transformed to an even heat by noontime. The leaves were turning and Mother Nature was seasoning the earth for colder temperatures. Fall was on its way.

Joe did all he could over the next couple of weeks to avoid being alone with Laura. He went from ardent protector to unassuming guest in a short period of time. Lucas was firmly attached to his family, thankful for each moment. He was at peace and so proud of what was accomplished while he was away.

He spent many hours with Joe talking through what plans he had for the farm, and how he hoped to restore the plantation to its once self-sufficient and prominent glory. This made Joe's heart full.

Joe knew his days were closing in, his mission complete. Truth be told, he could have left months ago. But he was young and new at this time-travel business. He didn't want to be hasty on leaving his calling. He wanted to make sure all his work had been done, the way

God would have wished for it to happen. In all truth, he really still wanted to be near Laura.

Talley made no attempt to reveal his feelings to Laura, and with Lucas' return, Laura devoted all her precious love and attention on her brother. It was as if she was whole again, and could be stronger than she had ever imagined herself to be.

Joe felt that his work was complete. It was time to go. He made a plan that he would say good-bye when he had one last chance to give thanks. On this day, it was clear to him as to the date he would leave.

Lucas was a strapping man again, full of health and vigor. Laura was well and wholesome in her virtue. Mother Chestnut was again a woman of some standing in the community, her sanity well intact. They attended church and worked with others in the community to rebuild their farms. They were luckier than many others. "The good Lord certainly blessed us," Mother Chestnut would happily announce.

The neighbors' tongues were quickly put to rest when Joseph divulged that he was a wealthy man from Raleigh who insisted on helping those in need. He had only enlisted in the army on principle, to do the right thing. He'd believed in the Cause.

When questioned, he was only too happy to give out a cured ham or a sack of flour to anyone. Although the prices of food were completely excessive, buying the neighbors' affection seemed necessary to keep the gossip down.

The South was rebuilding, and although President Lincoln had been assassinated, the country was uniting and becoming whole again. There was hope in the air, as thick as pea soup. People joined together to rebuild their communities as a whole. And new faces – like northern carpetbaggers – crawled through the South, taking advantage of the forced reconciliation between the North and the South.

Chapter Thirty-Three

Thanksgiving, December 7, 1865

Joe woke up this early December day and knew it was time. He had been there almost a year, and he could, at last, think of no reason to put it off any further. He needed to go home. Joe knew it was a matter of time before Talley would make his claim on Laura's heart, and he could not be there to witness it. Albeit a real outcome of Talley's affection, Joe did not have the strength to watch Laura chose between someone she could have and someone she could not.

All he could think of that day was how satisfied he was with his accomplishment. He succeeded as he had planned. All the wrong had been turned into right. The family would go on, and be as God intended.

Now all that was left was the farewell.

That morning Laura was happily working in the kitchen preparing her first true Thanksgiving feast. She had respectfully requested that her mother leave her charged with the details of the cooking. She awoke early that day and began preparing immediately.

Joe walked into the kitchen and saw her merrily moving through preparations. "Joseph, are you ready for our wonderful supper today? I feel so thankful, you just can't imagine!"

"I'm also very thankful." Joe walked over to the blue glazed coffee pot and poured his morning brew. After several large gulps, he began, "I need to tell you something, Laura. Can I speak with you for a moment?" Joe said, inviting her to join him at the table.

"I know we have not had much time to have a conversation since Lucas has been back, but the time has come, and I need to tell you something." Laura must have known exactly what he was going to say. She quickly dropped her face into her hands.

"No, you don't need to tell me. *I know*, I know it is time," Laura spoke so quietly.

"I do need to tell you. I owe you that." Joe pulled her "L" handkerchief out of his pocket and gently wiped the back of one of her hands. It was all the strength he had to hold back his own tears. He loved her. Even distancing himself over the last couple of months did nothing to help him in this moment of great distress.

Laura peeled her hands off her face. "Please keep this for me. I want you to always remember me." Laura motioned for Joe to put the handkerchief in his pocket. He needed to say so much. But what could comfort her now? "Will you at least stay through dinner?" She breathed deeply and unsteadily as she tried to stop her sobbing.

"Laura, please allow me to say something," Joe pressed, his heart an open wound of pressure and pain. It was unbearable to see her like this. There was so much he needed to say.

"Please don't. We *have* to leave it all unsaid. You are leaving me and nothing you could say right now could lessen the pain. I knew this day would come. I just hoped it would not come so quickly. Please just stay with me today, and I will accept what is God's will." Laura stopped crying and straightened her hair back. She got up and turned to the cabinet.

Joe could not believe he would not be able to release all his heart had to say. He would never get to tell her how much he loved the way she nervously picked at her skirt when she talked or how he loved the way she bit her lip when she was thinking. He would never be able to tell her about the fact that she added the most wonderful sweetness to his life; he had never known love this way. And that even though they were never were to hold each other in their arms which he longed every moment to do so.

More than anything, he wanted to thank her for trusting him, without which, he could never have completed his mission. He could never have saved her. But the truth was, she saved him too. He went from being a young adult to a man. He learned what back-breaking hard work was all about. He learned about giving unselfishly to people in great need, and about doing something for someone without expecting anything in return.

His eyes were clearer now. He had to respect her wishes, the wishes of that sweet vision standing in front of him. Surely, only pain would come with all the things he wanted to say. It was the way things must end between them, each left alone to deal with all the passion and frustration, each in their own time.

How could he walk away though? Could he ever believe that he had done the right thing? He remembered the old adage, "It is better to have loved and lost than to have never loved at all." Keep reminding yourself of that, he thought. He had loved her and would always love her. And he was a better man for the love that they shared.

Even so, his heart yearned to love her more completely, and never leave her side for a moment. He was so frustrated with the nauseating dilemma, he had to do something.

He could not leave without one final touch of love for her. Joe walked up and tenderly kissed her on her cheek. "*I will never forget you,*" he quietly whispered in her ear. She touched her cheek with her small hand and stood there motionless.

He left the kitchen and walked out to the barn to collect what was left of his hidden items, tears slowing moving down his cheeks.

Once in the loft, he rolled up the remaining bank notes and other personal items that he brought. Walking back to the front door, he looked around the yard one last time. He left his backpack on the porch, full of only the things he arrived with. He re-entered the house through the front door, as he had done so many times before.

Lucas was agitating the logs in the fireplace that was nestled inside the family room. "Lucas, a moment with you please, if I might?" Joe moved into the room and stood beside Lucas.

"Happy Thanksgiving, Joseph, my friend. Lots of blessings to be thankful for this year, wouldn't you say?" Lucas patted Joe on his back as he happily agreed. "It's simply hard to believe that this time last year I was eating bugs and crackers for supper. Things sure have changed. What is on your mind, Sir?" Lucas put his hand on his hip inquisitively.

"It is time. I have to go home now, back to my home, Raleigh. I'm leaving tonight. All I needed is to say good-bye. It wouldn't be proper not to say good-bye," Joe pouted. "I have done all the good I possibly can do here, and now I must return to my family and carry on my life, as it was before the war."

Lucas dropped his head and began to pace the floor a moment before speaking. "Frankly, Joseph, I can't believe how much you have done for us. I owe you a debt of gratitude. I am forever obliged to you." The fire threw shadows around as if it wanted to agree with Lucas.

Lucas' body had become strong over the last couple of months, building to this moment where the man stood tall and healthy. His dark green eyes pierced through Joseph with tenderness like no other. His heart was full of genuine thankfulness.

"Lucas, you do not *owe me* one single thing. It was my calling to be here. God chose me to come here and help your family. It was my service to those who needed it." Joe looked at Lucas. "But I would like to ask for something as a personal favor, if you wouldn't mind."

"I would be honored to do anything that you ask." Lucas's eyes pleaded with Joseph's.

"As abrupt as this may seem, it needs to be revealed that Talley Harrison is in love with your sister. Now I am sure that will be brought to light as soon as he musters up the courage. The reason that I tell you this is that I want to give you the remainder of my savings to help Laura with her new life, if she should accept him as a partner, or any other man. I know it is not for me to decide. But the money should be used for her and Talley, or whomever she chooses to build a life with." Joe paused to hear Lucas' reply.

"I think I have already picked up on the affection that Talley has for Laura, I must admit. I don't rightly think he can hold it in, as he is bustling around trying to assist her constantly." Lucas laughed and then paused in his musings. *"But she loves you.* And surely you must know, I can't accept any more charity. I am here now, the man of the house, and I need to make my own way. It wouldn't be right." Lucas sat back down on the hearth, picked up the poker again and chopped at the fire. The logs were burning with an orange-red glow.

Joseph immediately felt that Lucas was embarrassed and that this was an awkward moment for him. What words to use to convince him?

"Lucas, it is something that I must do. It is my last gift for Laura. She can't know I left it for her. It is the one request that I ask of you." Lucas stood up and looked at Joseph again, pausing before answering.

"If that is what you ask of me, then how can I refuse? It will be done. Sir, I cannot extend to you the fullness in my heart for all you have done for my family. I know that God will follow you wherever you may go. And it is my hope that you will forevermore know that our lives were changed the moment you set foot on my land. May you and your family live in peace and harmony."

Joe nodded and smiled, leaving the money in Lucas' hands and quietly turned his back to walk out of the room. Lucas clutched the money and then carefully placed it in a small box that held pinecones on the mantle. Joe turned and smiled once more.

Supper was one of the most memorable meals of Joe's life. Although a simple meal, it was more than anyone could ever have expected. Percy, Isaiah, Samuel, the three remaining soldiers, Talley, Lucas, Laura, Joe and Mother Chestnut, all at the same table. It was a rare moment that in this cultural climate, no race or sex was distinguished. It was a family, a family of friends.

Everyone was thankful and pleased with the outcome of this year. Though it started out as the worst year of their lives, it would end as one of their best times.

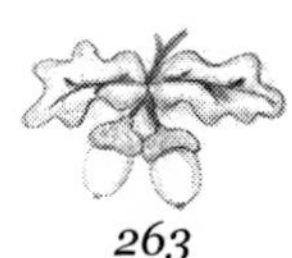

As Joe surveyed the table, he disappeared into his thoughts. There was one thing to look forward to. Once he got home, he could read about how the Chestnut family lived a full life. He wanted nothing more than to know they continued on and flourished. He wanted to know that they continued to rebuild the plantation and that crops were plenty and children abounded.

He could not think of a single thing that he would have done differently. Everything had been done; he had to go home. Almost a year had passed in his own time, and he was anxious to know what was going on in his world, in the future of this world. At this point, that was simply everything that he had to focus on.

After supper, Joe quietly walked out the front door. He picked up the backpack that he walked in with so many months ago.

At the end of the winding drive, tears streamed from his eyes as he looked back. The house, so simple, with the beautiful glow of the fireplace warming the window panes, stood tall as Joe gazed upon it.

"*Good night, Chestnut Plantation. Good-bye, my dear Laura. I will never forget you.*" Joe closed his eyes, said a little thankful prayer, and moved on. On opening his eyes, he sees the front door open and the warm light pouring out onto the porch.

In an instant he knew it was his beloved Laura, the woman to whom no other could compare. He could see her large bell-shaped dress moving back and forth as she made heavy strides towards him. He stood there frozen, not sure how to handle this moment.

He watched as she moved closer and closer, her long black hair trailing behind her until she finally met him and threw her arms out, flinging her body into his. His backpack fell to the ground and he enveloped her into his warm, welcome arms. They held each other for only seconds before their lips hungrily met. Joe could not stop the easy kisses that he delivered over and over to her. He took his arms and moved them to shoulders length and ran his hands through her hair, holding her head firmly against his.

All the passion and quiet obsession came pouring out of him. It was such an unexpected outburst of affection, he did not know how to control it. He wanted to hold her in his arms every moment that he had been with her, from that first evening at the pond when he did not know who she was.

"I do love you. You must know that. I do love you," Joe said in a low strangled tone, and then continued to kiss her. He could see the plea in her eyes; to stay, not to leave her, to love her. "I do love you! I will always love you! But I have no choice, please, I have to leave. I'm sorry that I don't have a better explanation."

The strong and heated affection that was pouring out between the two in the dim moonlight was enough for a lifetime. Neither one knew how to end the embrace.

Joe finally pulled back and looked at Laura, with only an inch between their faces. Tears were streaming down both of their cheeks. Their impassioned breathe was the only sound they heard until Laura spoke, "I love you too. I can't believe that you are leaving. I can't bear this. I do not want you to go. No matter how strong I have tried to be today, I do not want to lose you." Laura was sobbing, her head firmly attached to his shoulder now.

Joe hesitated. He wanted to let the flood of emotions overwhelm him and tell her everything. Tell her that he was a time traveler and that was why they could never be together. Tell her that he found her, in his own time, that she was going to be killed and he had to save her. But it would ruin what they had. She could never understand.

Joe smoothed her hair down as she rested on his shoulder. "I love you too, sweet darling. With all my heart, I will love you until the day I die," Joe whispered, continuing to cry. Their emotions were so overwhelming. How could he leave her now?

But he knew he must. Could he stay a month longer, a week longer, would that help lessen the pain? No, nothing would. They shared an unfulfilled love, a forbidden love. It was a love that would stay with him for the rest of his life.

"Could we go sit by the pond for a moment? Just another minute together?" Laura begged.

"Yes, I would love that." Joe led his love to the pond and they sat for hours looking out at the glass-like water. He recalled how he felt so long ago, watching her glide over the cool pond.

After what seemed like only moments, he walked his precious Laura back to the house and kissed her good-night forever, his mission fulfilled but his heart a mass of emotions.

He turned back one last time. "I promise you, somewhere in time, we will meet again," Joe assured Laura as he turned and walked down the path.

Days later, after Joe had made the journey back to Wilmington through the still war-torn countryside, he slipped into the large oak in the shadow of Holly's presence, and sat on the simple seat within.

I woke suddenly.

"*Joe!*" I yelled as I sat up straight in my grandmother's bed.

Acknowledgements

First, I would like to thank my Heavenly Father for giving me the blessing to be a writer. When people have asked me how I created the ideas for the book, my simple and truthful answer has always been "through daily prayer". He leads me and gives me direction each day.

Next, I'd like to thank you, the reader, for selecting this book and taking a chance on an unknown writer. As the sequels move along, I will continue to thank you for your support and readership. I appreciate your faith in my storytelling and I hope to always rise to your expectations.

I'd like to thank my daughter, Rachael, for being such an inspiration to me. She is such a joy in my life and gives me a direction to write the kind of books that I believe young adults will enjoy reading. She has been patient with me while writing and editing this book.

I appreciate the support of my husband, Larry. Most of all he helped with his understanding, when I had to lock myself away to make sure I was giving the book all the attention that it needed. Being a sci-fi lover, he and I share a love of time travel.

My parents, Curt and Sally Phipps, have been my greatest supporters and I appreciate them being there for me. Their guidance has been a blessing in my life. They have always believed that I could do it and I hope this book makes them proud.

I appreciate the fact that my cousin, Molly Harrison, took time out of her busy writing schedule to be my very first reader and guide me along. Her book, *It Happened on the Outer Banks*, inspired me with "if she could do it, so could I."

Thank you to my Aunt Lois, who gave me my first manual typewriter when I was thirteen years old. I spent many a happy day punching that old thing, one short story after another. Her love for reading and learning has been an inspiration to me to this day.

I want to thank my early readers, Beth Charles, Emily Sebastian, Erika Moore, Mike Barnett, Angie Robinson, Maryn O'Neill, Margaret Byrd, Kim Hatcher, Tyler Taube, Kate Stanford, and Erin Padgett. Without their positive direction and guidance, I don't know where this book would be.

A very special thank you to Kristen Sigler, my muse. I can't imagine this book without her. She has added excitement to my writing and I appreciate her encouragement more than words could ever say. I'll always remember us on the back of my boat in hot July 2009, yelling ideas back and forth to each other, as my husband flung us all over Lake Norman on a tube.

Thanks to my publisher, David R. Haslam and the rest of the team at HMSI Publishing. My project manager Jennelle Jones, designer Elena Covalciuc and the editors Monica Tombers and Kay LeMon. They believed in this project from day one and that has kept me focused and believing in the best. Thanks to my early editor, Amanda Clark for getting this project on its way.

I would like to acknowledge two special families in my life, the Cain's and Johnson's. First, thanks to Bill and Ericka Cain for providing me an opportunity that opened so many doors for me and to Bo and Christi Johnson, for showing me how important life really is. Even though Bo's life was cut short, he left a legacy of followers that will never forget him. He is still with us each and every day.

Thanks to Greg Dragos, my high school social studies teacher, for instilling a love for history that I will never lose. He made history

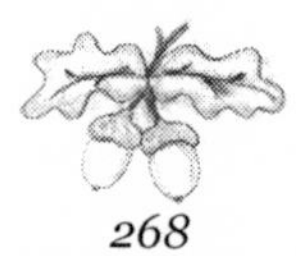

come alive and it was such a privilege to learn from such an exciting person. Too bad all of high school wasn't as exciting as his class was!

Thanks to Michael J. Fox. Through my love of your movies, you made me believe that "time travel is possible."

I want to thank Rachel Faunce for the photography on the jacket. And special thanks to Nick Newsom for my website, which exceeded my expectations! I hope to have tons of visitors to www.kimreynoldsonline.com .

I appreciate Kim Herrick, Jen Pace, and Jane Freeman for being my first "fans" to sign up on the Alex Charles Fan Page on Facebook. (There is plenty of space on the page for more fans! Hint! Hint!) Their encouragement makes me believe that I can accomplish anything that I put my mind to!

Kim Reynolds
Charlotte, North Carolina,
April 2010

LaVergne, TN USA
28 May 2010
184370LV00006B/6/P